HAT ARE THE CHANCES?

S
CO

First published 2022

Published under licence by Brown Dog Books and The Self-Publishing Partnership Ltd, 10b Greenway Farm, Bath Rd, Wick, nr. Bath BS30 5RL

www.selfpublishingpartnership.co.uk

ISBN printed book: 978-1-83952-540-7
ISBN e-book: 978-1-83952-541-4

Cover design based on Rochel Lucy Czerwinski's idea and visualised by Kevin Rylands

Internal design by Andrew Easton

Printed and bound in the UK

This book is printed on FSC certified paper

JANUSZ ROBERTSON

WHAT ARE THE CHANCES?

BROWN
DOG
BOOKS

I would like to thank my daughter Rochel Lucy for her
help with my book and for the front cover design.
Good Luck for the future.
Love
Dad.

I would also like to thank my wife Jesusa for her patience and
inhuman tolerance while I was writing this book.
Thank you and Love you Always.

Janusz
XXX

Life is Hard and Cruel, but what's important is what you make of it.

GLOSSARY

Cities of Arka – Ark (capital), Leso, Mera, Della

Little girl/queen's daughter – Beautiful, Olnia

Queen – Vianna

Queen's friend/seer – Sania

Queen's dad – Herc

Queen's mum – Yagi

Baron Rak & Baroness Mima Vos – Jihon's parents

People – Arkans

Capital – Ark (royal family surname)

Best character – Jihon

Linguist/translator – Professor Nata

Alphians are red

Morrins are yellow

Zolgs are dark blue

Queen's bitchboy – Gah

Kura Nectar – type of fruit juice

Garuga – Giant man-looking beast

Kani is like mythical harpies back on Earth

Beasts: Slinks, Meguns, Basins, Dags, Zarks, Fagans, Sarks

Man Eating Plant – Arkan Death

General Mass

High Prefect Baka

Seline –Baka's wife

What are the Chances?

General Akda the incompetent
Sergeant Tus
Chamberlain Vern
Beast that first attacked James – Sarks

Arkan Year – 13 months
Arkan months – 36 days
Arkan week – 9 days
PVA – personal virtual assistant (on his sleeve)
Mappen – beast usually found near a beach
Slinks – beast
Poto – local alcoholic drink
Lugii – Part plant, part animal beast … Tears flesh off of its
victims while they are still alive (Horrible way to die)

* * *

Monday – Magra
Tuesday – Tagra
Wednesday – Wera
Thursday – Tura
Friday – Fara
Day 8 of the week – Sura
Day 9 of the week – Hava
Saturday – Agra
Sunday – Sara
Weekend – Ferga

PROLOGUE

The US had won the race in space travel and their closest allies were left behind. Britain had to come up with something else, something new that no other nation could be working on. However, that was easier said than done. But every good idea starts with someone. The man for the job? Sir Lieutenant General Andrew Warburton. Or as James would call him, Andy. Everyone else would know him as the head of the new project. Since he was the start of the operation, he had no insight for what he had to do – not even how to go about such. But if the way the world flows is how it was meant to be, it will find a way. And by sheer accident, he met Professor Mia Eddings, desperate for help, though, she was not searching simply for any help; she needed the entire arm of the military to help her.

After she found out who exactly Sir Lieutenant General Andrew Warburton was, she told him the problem she had and after giving him a demonstration, the general finally found his project.

The project involved was not that of space travel, as the Americans are working to pursue, but time travel. But only into the past. The professor reiterated the mass destruction that could become of the Earth had the future been altered even minimally. The movies were true. Eddings continued to explain that time travel to the future wasn't possible even if they wanted to do so as the future had not happened yet. This meant there was nothing to anchor to if one tried to travel into the future. But the past? That has already happened and is well documented. Alongside him, Professor Eddings mentioned she had another partner who aided in the development of time travel, but he wanted to alter things, suspectedly within his own self-interest, while she insisted on keeping things as they were. Eddings was an intelligent woman, having an eye for spotting suspicious ulterior motives. Her now ex-colleague fell in contact with some disreputable characters. Subsequently, after much effort of investigation, she discovered how the past had already been changed several times to profit in their favour. Science should be beneficial, not for profit.

Naturally, the general was sceptical until Professor Mia showed him her detailed recordings of what had changed. Alongside this, she highlighted her 'secret' meeting with her ex-colleague, who warned her that things would get worse for everyone if these disreputable characters were not stopped. Needless to say, there was deep regret buried in the words of her colleague.

But what Professor Mia needed was military help and the general needed a project. So after careful consideration, the general decided to start his project and keep those who were profiting from damaging the timeline of the universe at bay, and hopefully, someday, eliminate them. By stopping them, they needed men and women who he could trust, and the first name on his lips was Major James Duncan.

Right now, Major Duncan was not a happy man, as he wasn't just famous among the populous of Great Britain, he was the war hero everyone wanted to meet and that reason made his life a misery. He had no private life of his own and he wanted out. When his friend, General Warburton, approached him about joining his project, James was on the verge of tearing his arm off to get into it from overwhelming desperation.

Although the way it was explained to James was that he, in effect, would have to die. And for that, James was willing to die.

Professor Mia had carefully chosen her staff to make sure that no one would leak any information about the project. She had also developed a nanochip that would be attached to the operatives who would time travel, so if any changes happened during the travel they would be aware of them and would be able to analyse the change's impact and hopefully solve it. Unfortunately, this is where many soldiers' surface-life deaths became their actuality. If not deaths, major damage to the brain. The nanochip had to be carefully implanted into the brain, meaning a very articulate and hazardous brain surgery with high risks of injury. When the general told her that there would be six time travellers, she immediately told him about the nanochip, and that she would make six more, but the general advised her that he would also be chipped, meaning seven more had to be produced alongside her own. She was also told that from now on, she and every member of her staff would be guarded 24/7 by men and women of the SAS. Additionally, he made a point of interest that the SAS could not know anything about the project, but would protect her and her staff with their lives.

They made their base in an abandoned World War Two facility, known only to the general and his great grandfather, who was in charge of this facility during the war. Keeping the public's nose out of such places really did come into hand after all these years.

Construction and renovation was swift as the base was set up and ready. The walls were reinforced and every inch of glass was bulletproof. This was merely a precaution against the obvious threat of human enemy. Majority of the institute was underground, where any crucial evidence of such a project would always remain out of anyone's eye bar those granted access. Even some of those in the institute did not understand the true purpose of such a facility.

After some time, eight of them were now chipped. The next step? Discussing security. That is, when James Duncan came up with the perfect name for the six operatives. From now on, they'd be known as 'Sliptimers'.

The six Sliptimers no longer had a name, but were known around the base solely as commanders. If any of the support staff needed them, they would address each operative as Commander, nothing else. Only the general and the professor would call them Sliptimers, and of course, the Sliptimers themselves too.

Each of the Sliptimers had no identities in surface-level society. To this populus, they had all mysteriously died in some horrific accidents. James even got a state funeral. If only he could be there to celebrate it. Only Professor Mia, the general and his best friend, King George, knew the truth that James wasn't dead. Although, despite knowing James' status of living, King George definitely did not know what James was doing. As far as he was aware, James was desperate for a change in career paths and to avoid any unnecessary attention, he 'died' and became a commodity broker in the city.

What are the Chances?

When the Sliptimers left the base to do some R&R, they all sported faux beards and wore contact lenses to change their eye colours. James' eyes were covered with brown contacts, concealing any sight of deep blue.

Unfortunately, as far as his family went, he was dead. Died in a terrible incident. Just like the other five Sliptimers. Although his family's grief was disheartening for him, as a soldier he had learned to contain his emotions and knew his further purpose would be for the greater good for humanity.

The project was ready to go, but with one exception. Since the powers wanted something to compensate for the money they used for the project, it was decided that every Sliptimer would always bring back some sort of artefact that could be sold to further fund the project and keep the powers happy, although extensive research would have to be conducted to assure no major alterations would be made to the timeline. In other words, no major artefacts were to be taken.

The first outing was to year 1908. The Hyenas, what the Sliptimers decided to call the profiteers, travelled back in time making frequent visits to that year. As Professor Mia was the main inventor of time travel, she also knew how to track the Hyenas every time they travelled back in time. This is the pertinent advantage they had over the Hyenas. The Sliptimers followed the information gathered from tracking, taking action when it was needed. And, of course, they did not serve years in the military to fail. Eliminating the Hyenas tracked was the swiftest way to decrease their numbers. And as expected from reputable heroes, they successfully brought back an artefact to be auctioned.

WHAT ARE THE CHANCES?

During one of the trips, one Sliptimer eliminated a Hyena team threatening a high impact on the timeline, changing the future for the worse. If it wasn't for the bravery of the Sliptimer, Britain would be ruled by a new king or queen. The Sliptimers were the barrier between humanity and complete destruction.

Over the years, all of the Sliptimers made hundreds, maybe even thousands of trips back in time, but not all of them successful. It was decided that they needed to find out where the Hyenas had their base of operations, so the gadgets that all the Sliptimers were given were called 'travellers'. Travellers were modified by Professor Mia, easing the capture of Hyenas' residue as they travelled back into our time.

'Time', the name of the project, was generally successful as the Sliptimers managed to thwart the Hyenas over and over again. As each Sliptimer always brought a very valuable item back with them, making sure it wasn't a crucial piece to the timeline, the project became self-sufficient. But alas, it had been two years since project 'Time' had started when the first disaster happened. Suddenly, one of the Sliptimers had vanished, and not just him, but all of his family in the present and in the past. Professor Mia, using the nanochip trackers implemented in each of their brains, concluded that somehow the Hyenas found out the Sliptimer's identity, travelling back in time to eliminate his ancestors, ensuring he was never born. But since the general, Professor Mia, and five other Sliptimers had the nanochip, they were also the only seven with knowledge that one of their own had fallen; only seven of them to mourn his death.

What are the Chances?

After this, they were always wary of who might've leaked the identity of their friend and colleague. Because of what had happened, all the Sliptimers went on the offensive and many of the Hyenas perished. As far as they were concerned, the fallen Sliptimer deserved justice, he was still family. However, because of the Sliptimers' vengeful rampage, they became very successful in stopping the Hyenas' plans. Unfortunately, the vengeful spirit grew stronger in the third year as two more Sliptimers had fallen. The grief pummelled the team like a boulder crashing down a cliff. Their grief prompted them to take extra measures; all the support staff were now under 24/7 surveillance and guard, and as a result, they had no private life.

Although the Sliptimers were reduced in numbers to three, they didn't ease up on the Hyenas, in fact they aimed to slaughter them with relentless force. The last three thwarted the Hyenas at every incursion into the past.

In fact, one of the Sliptimers had set the new record, travelling back in time by 322 years. The relics brought back were priceless and to boot, he also eliminated a four-man Hyena clan. That was a 100% success and they all had to celebrate.

On one trip back to the Victorian era, one of the Sliptimers had gotten lucky and somehow managed to collect a Hyena's travelling residue leading to their base of operations. This meant project 'Time' could move towards infiltrating their operations and taking down the Hyenas from inside their base. Unfortunately, when the SAS teams attacked the base of the Hyena's operations, three of them had managed to escape by travelling back in time. Retrieving the residue, Professor Mia was able to track to which timeline they were hiding. At this moment, project 'Time' began to worry. The Hyenas travelled back to the precise location where Professor Mia's ancestors resided. They had no choice but to send out their most accomplished Sliptimer to pursue the Hyenas. It was the first time that any Sliptimer would be travelling as far back as over 800 years. Now it was all up to James Duncan.

CHAPTER 1

I pulled tightly on the edge of my heavy navy tailcoat, tweaking my top hat, as I watched the workers, dressed in rags, build one of Britain's famous personal landmarks – London Tower Bridge. As I swung my cane, I watched every intricate move of each worker, alternating between who caught my suspicion. Speaking of which, there was this one 'chap' who kept dropping the hammer; it was almost as if he'd never worked a day of manual labour in his life. The leader of the construction dismissed him, provoking a smirk on his face, followed by a forced visage of disappointment to conceal his realisation. Slyly, he slipped away from the building operation, down an alleyway. Perhaps his business was not the matter of a weak wrist.

'There's our guy,' I sighed and smirked, unravelling my arms from their fold and walking in his direction.

Languidly, I strode down the same alleyway to reveal the sight of a man attempting to pull himself over a brick wall. He glared at me with panicked eyes, as the realisation of my identity pummelled him. I threw my cane to one side, along with this stupid top hat. Without hesitation, I ran down the dark alleyway with the intention of catching him. By the time I reached the wall, he'd already thrown himself over and ran off. I flexed my arms and cracked my knuckles and ran towards the wall, pulling myself over easily through the momentum. The Hyena entered the carriage, which shortly began riding off. Not today.

'Pardon me, ever so sorry, I just need this,' I say in a sickly posh voice as I push the coachman off and grab the reigns of the horse.

I sped the carriage towards the Hyena's, catching his coachman up swiftly. After shortening the distance between us, his coachman began to slow down. So I sped up. Fear enveloped the horses as their hesitation grew the closer I got to the carriage. The back window of the carriage slid open to reveal the alarmed state of the Hyena. For someone working for the Hyenas, he sure is cowardly.

'GO FASTER!' the Hyena desperately shouted at his coachman.

The coachmen turned around to make stern eye contact with me. 'What on Earth are you doing?!' he yelled.

One of the legs of the horses scraped a back wheel of the carriage, causing it to waver from side to side. The coachman pulled his reins as far to the right as possible, causing his carriage to swerve towards me and topple over and stop my carriage from moving. I jumped down and approached the carriage door. Assertively, I swung open the door, making direct eye contact with the Hyena. He was trembling in fear at the sight of me hovering over him, blocking his only route of escape. He reached into his pocket to pull out a device that looked similar to one that I owned; if it works similarly to my device then...

The Hyena's thumb pressed the button, a cloak of light enveloped his body, swiftly consuming him till he disappeared. Out of instinct, I grabbed my device out, opened its small compartment and caught the residue left from the Hyena before it disappeared.

'Catch him!' A cacophony of screaming women and yelling men resided behind me, looking all rather furious.

I should probably go.

I pushed the button of my traveller and braced myself to be sent back to the present.

Blurry vision. Nausea. And that damn four second headache. Man do I love time-travel sickness. Viciously, I freed myself from this idiotic and uncomfortable jacket and tore off my shirt along with the cravat. Normally, I would clean myself up and do my hair, but this time I simply cannot wait.

I began making my way to the general's office; if this residue is still active, this could change everything. Violently, I knocked against the general's office door repetitively.

'What on Earth are you doing, James?' General Warburton swung open his office door, furrowing his brows and frowning, clearly unimpressed by my intrusive knocking.

I smirked to myself, my heart bouncing up and down like a little school girl, as I held up my device containing the residue before his eyes. He glanced at me with fearful yet curious eyes, and then held the door open for me to enter.

'So did you complete your mission, James?'

'Well … not exactly. But I have something even better Andy—'

'Don't call me that, you know it's Andrew,' he stared at me sternly.

'Sorry, Andy. Now look,' I cautiously opened up the compartment to reveal a pale, glowing, blue-ish substance coated in a thin film. 'This is not my residue …'

WHAT ARE THE CHANCES?

'You're telling me you managed to successfully collect and contain a Hyena's residue?' Andrew glared at me with disbelief. But being his best friend of ten or so years, I could see a glint of hope lurking in his blue eyes.

'General Andy Warburton, do you doubt your best mate?' I press my hand against my heart, pretending to seem deeply offended by Andrew's doubt.

He merely sighs at my sarcasm, clearly fed up. 'I'll take your traveller to the lab to run tests on it, in the meantime, get changed for Pete's sake and get your backside to Buckingham Palace, King George is expecting you.'

'Sorry, King Geor—' I blurt out.

'Now!' Andy interrupts and walks out of his office with the residue.

I swear this man can be so difficult sometimes. However, he has a very good point; I should change out of these hideous and uncomfortable Victorian pants. As I make my way back to my quarters, I can't help but let curiosity encumber my mind. What could King George, of all people, possibly want from me? I'm sure I didn't alter anything in the past, although I should check in with the auditors later. Better to be safe than sorry.

My quarters aren't much of a home, but it's a home. I stepped into my shower, cleansing myself of the Victorian dirt. Hot water trickled down my face, and my back. Inhaling the hot air, my lungs were filled with settling warmth. The rarity that I am here, because I'm always on missions, being one of the few members left of the Sliptimer team, it's always refreshing to be sleeping in my own bed. After all, not many Sliptimers are still alive to experience the comfort of their own home. Since one of the most essential requirements is that our identities are not to be known to anyone that doesn't need to know, this means we are practically non-existent to our families now as well. Unfortunately, there are the few that slip. Like Mark Fraser. Great guy. Well was. Somehow let his name slip, so the Hyena's travelled back in time and slaughtered all of his ancestors, thus the Fraser bloodline doesn't exist anymore. Despite this alteration, as a fellow Sliptimer, we remember those who we have lost, always. A chip was wired to our brain that helps us store memories, regardless of the science of time; it's a hazardous process, but one worth it at that. Being a Sliptimer is a lonely life for the most part. I do miss my parents. But as a soldier, you learn to adapt and embrace your new family – but not everyone should be trusted.

After leaving my shower, I walked towards my wardrobe. Now that the king believes that I'm out of the military and working in the city and my staged death was only a ruse so I can have a peaceful life, what do I wear? I glanced over to my right to see my kilt. Naturally, as a proud Highlander, I have to represent my ancestry.

My heart jolted slightly at the sudden sound of someone furiously banging on my door. I approached the door and opened it to reveal a very upset Steve, the auditor. Here we go again.

Someone saw their arse and didn't like the colour of it. 'Who rattled your cage?'

'You know exactly what I mean, Commander.'

'Oh really? I have no idea,' I lied.

WHAT ARE THE CHANCES?

'It is strict protocol to go through the cleansing procedure on your return, Commander. And you keep ignoring this.'

'Oh I'm ever so sorry, Steve, must be the old age.' Steve exchanged a spiteful glance with me. 'Oh come on, I just got changed, had a shower even.'

'I don't care, Commander. It is protocol.'

If there is anything that I hate more than time-travel sickness, it is the cleansing process. I heavily exhaled and closed the door to my quarters, reluctantly following a clearly unimpressed Steve to the cleansing room. After stripping down butt-naked, I stepped into a large glass box and closed the door. Firstly, the idea of displaying my family jewels wasn't very appealing to say the least. And secondly, the gas. A gas was released into the container, surrounding my body. It was cold, and made me feel extremely nauseous every time – not that I'd ever thrown up from it, but it was a sickly feeling that would linger in the back of your head and throat for a few hours. The final step of the cleansing process was the scanning. The lights of the room shut off. So there I was, standing naked in complete darkness. The scanner was green, analysing me 360 degrees starting from my feet. As long as the scanner remained green, then we were all good. The scanner ran past my neck, past my chin. It was almost finished. The first breath of fresh air outside of this container was basically calling my name. The sudden change of the scanner's colour cut through my thoughts; the once mellow green became a vivid crimson blinding me.

'Sorry, Commander. Scanner says you're unclean. We'll have to start the process again,' Steve yells.

WHAT ARE THE CHANCES?

'Are you f—' my speech was cut off by the loud sound of gas being released into the container once again.

The nauseous feeling returned to me a second time. I closed my eyes, clenched my fists, and held my breath as I let the time pass by. Eventually, the gas subsided and the lights shut off once more. The scanner began travelling up my body. As it approached my face, I began profusely sweating out of nervousness. The light remained green as it ran all the way to the top of my body. Thank God. The lights turned back on signalling that the process was complete. Desperately, I pushed opened the door of the container and bolted out of there, faster than a car on the German autobahn. I rested my hands on my knees as I leant forward slightly, gasping for air, saliva drooling from my mouth. Squinting my eyes, I turned to face Steve.

'Why did the scanner go red? It's never done that before,' I manage to articulate through deep breaths.

'Oh I'm ever so sorry, Commander, I have no idea what you are talking about.' Steve smirked. That little rat.

Shaking my head, I brushed Steve's idiocy off and grabbed my clothes to get changed again. Never mind that imbecile, the low anxiety about meeting with King George began residing with me. What could he possibly want? Have I done anything wrong recently? Apart from that time I hid his three prized corgis in one of his many unnecessary guest bedrooms to spark a fright – which was very much hilarious. Yet in all seriousness, to request my presence so unexpectedly was nerve-wracking. Sure we were close, surprisingly, but that still doesn't alter the fact that he is royalty and I'm … well … a common soldier.

WHAT ARE THE CHANCES?

I made my way towards the main exit of the facility. After signing out, I used my fingerprint and glared into the eye retina scanner to open the door. The first breath of 2050's fresh air filled my lungs so pleasantly. Time travelling really does alter the way you remember experiences as simple as inhaling. Although we only sliptime for limited periods of time, you do start to feel a form of 'home-sickness'. I guess I'd call it time-sickness. The sudden change of environment and people all around you, never mind the immense multitude of risks of altering history, all accumulates to one vast cluster of constant pressure that a regular soldier could never withstand. Although it's not every day that you get to time travel, with exciting privilege comes a mandatory requirement for responsibility. This technology couldn't be shared with just anyone. But some cretin decided to leak this technology to some very bad people we call Hyenas. It is still unknown as to who exactly betrayed us, but what is known is that this traitor is still working in our facility somewhere. The general and I have sworn that one day, we and the security guards, aka Andy's Rottweilers, will kill that son of a bitch.

'Are you getting in the damn car, James, or are you going to keep me waiting?' my security guard, who is also my personal driver, asked, interrupting my thoughts.

'Hmmm, keep you waiting I guess.' I smirk, my arms folded, glaring at my driver.

'Just get in,' my driver laughs.

*   *   *

What are the Chances?

I enter through the palace door, seeing King George sitting on his throne at first sight, his facial expression stern, eyes displaying utmost seriousness. I approach his throne at an appropriate distance and stood formally straight. George stands up from his throne, a ceremonial sword in his hand.

'Kneel down,' he sternly ordered, while motioning towards a red stool – a knighting stool.

My eyebrows rose up in shock and confusion. After George noticed that I finally realised what was going on, his eyes lit up and a smirk adorned his face. I'm about to get knighted, and it's all out of spite. George knows how I feel about people that get knighted. And personally, I'm not for the snobby title.

'You can't knight me George,' I whisper. 'I'm a scoundrel, an absolute delinquent.'

'Well I'm going to,' he laughs and murmurs back.

'Don't make me hide your corgis again. I promise you won't find them this time.'

'Even more reason to knight you. Be thou a knight in the name of God,' his mumbles become loud bellowing words. 'Arise, knight.' He rests the sword on each shoulder, 'Rise up, Sir Major James Duncan.'

'I can't believe you,' I sigh.

'Well you better, I just did.'

'For someone that's supposed to be a king, you're so childish.'

'Not childish, in fact it makes sense that you are knighted. You earned two Victoria Crosses and this has never been done before, and more to the point you are still alive and kicking, James, that's grounds for knighthood.'

What are the Chances?

'That's Sir Major James Duncan to you now,' I cheekily snap, extra emphasis on the 'Sir'.

'And that's King "I-can-strip-your-knighthood-off-of-you" to you,' he chuckled.

'Go on then.'

'Oh no, you're not getting away that easily.'

There's something so pleasant about being buddies with all of the important people, like George and Andrew. Although I'm not just mates with them for their status, we go way back; met Andy back in the Middle East during a mission as a common soldier. And as for George, I knew him since he was still a prince, during the Malaysian uprising – I guarded him as security.

'I've got some snacks ready for us,' George trails off.

'Alright, but I need to get back to work soon.' We're close but he can't know about what my actual job is; for both his safety and the facility's.

'I'm sure that all the millions you are making can take a break, right?'

'Bollocks, I'm greedy,' I say both completely serious and completely sarcastically – if that's even possible.

We glanced at each other with serious eyes, before we both burst into hysterical laughter. George raised his left hand and motioned for me to follow. He guided me into the palace dining room, to reveal masses and masses of food on the table.

'George!' I exclaim. 'I thought you said snacks, not every restaurant menu in London.'

'I know you well, you always forget to eat. You've always got that head of yours permanently buried in your work. I get you're out there saving lives and all, but it's consuming your life.'

George, you don't even know a half of it. He clapped his hands, signalling a servant to come in and serve us more food. The servant placed the dish in front of me. The delicious aroma of a steaming hot pot of Ghurkha curry seeped through my nostrils, making my eyes smile and my mouth salivate uncontrollably – George really knows what I like.

'You know what, George,' I attempt to change the subject. 'You need to get married, matey.'

'Yeah … that's not going to happen,' he sighs. He sat down to start eating, to cope with the stress of the topic of marriage.

'You do realise that you're the king, don't you? There's got be an heir to the throne after you check out,' I attempt to reason.

'Well then, I'll adopt.'

'So you're telling me you're not the least bit interested in the Spanish king's niece, Isabella. I can tell she's got an eye on you.'

'And that's why I'm staying well away from her.' I swear George is the most awkward person ever.

Isabella was basically a royal supermodel. 'If I had a woman like that, she'd have twenty kids by now.'

'And that is precisely why I stay away from women that look like Isabella.'

'Let's make a deal, if you end up marrying Isabella, and have a kid with her, then you have to make me the godfather.'

'And when I don't?' he fires back.

'If you don't, then I'm taking you back to the Highlands out for a few drinks – just a few. And you remember what happened last time.'

'Don't remind me,' George snaps and rolls his eyes, setting down his spoon down to bury his face in his hands out of embarrassment.

Suddenly, I broke out into laughter as I recalled George's pitifully drunken state. It took him three whole weeks just to remember his name, or what country he was in. Scary at the time, hilarious now. I still haven't told him about the priceless skinny-dipping fiasco he did in the North Sea either.

Unfortunately, all good things come to an end as the sound of my phone ringing cut through my laughter. Andy sent me message, informing me it was a code blue, which isn't as serious as code red, but meant I'd have to go into immediate lockdown – despite its rarity, it's worrying. As much as I do invest a lot of time into my work, I do miss moments like these where I could just sit down and freely enjoy a peaceful meal.

'George, I need to get back. The office needs me urgently,' I explain.

The King's face fell slightly. 'I understand, go for it, mate.'

Before making my way out of the palace, I say a last farewell to George. 'And seriously, just ask Isabella on a date,' I pry.

'Fine, I will. But leave my corgis alone,' he reasons with a smile.

'Can't promise anything,' I slip in before I dashed away from the door to ensure I got the last word in.

As I walked away further from the palace doors, I sped up swiftly, my smile dissipating into a stern frown. Code blue is serious, very serious. And I think it has something to do with the residue I managed to preserve. And if so, pray for us all.

CHAPTER 2

As I neared the facility, I planned out every single situation that could possibly happen; whether it was out of anxiety or exponential mental preparation for code blue – I'm not sure. A call from my phone cut through my deep thoughts, almost jerking me out of my abyss of dwell back to the soldier's composure I should have. 'Professor Eddings' flashed across my screen. She was one of two scientists that invented the time travelling system. She's also one of the only two people that have direct numbers to Andy and the last three remaining Sliptimers, and that includes me. Naturally, communication is strictly kept to the minimum, only permitted if contact is unequivocally vital to prevent any breach of security. So for Professor Eddings to contact me is extremely concerning. I answer the phone with my fingers crossed, hoping the call was purely accidental.

'I need to see you urgently,' Eddings yells down the phone, a slight wave of shakiness in her tone.

Not right now, the facility needs me. 'I can't, it's code blue.'

'If that's code blue, then this is code red,' Eddings shouts.

You know when you hear that one sentence in your life that you've never wanted to hear? Well this is one of those moments. My eyebrows furrowed out of frustration and utter dread. I've got no choice, red takes priority over blue.

What are the Chances?

'Driver, we're taking a detour, Professor Eddings,' I authoritatively demanded, making my tone absolutely adamant that I didn't want to be argued with.

After notifying Eddings I'd be there soon, I ended the call and prepared myself for the worse.

*   *   *

I arrived at Eddings' gated facility. She was waiting outside for me in her lab coat, all dolled up as if she were going out on a date. I think she's taken that one night stand a bit too seriously, but I must admit, she does look good. Eddings approached me, giving me a peck on the cheek as a greeting.

'Follow me,' she orders.

'Well hello to you too,' I reply.

Instead of taking me to her house, she guided me to her underground lab.

'Now if you don't already love me now,' she begins. 'Then you'll definitely love me after this.' She winks.

She asked me to roll up my sleeve, which I did without a moment's thought. Eddings injected my right forearm with what looked like, an anaesthetic. I winced slightly at the unexpected pain, and looked at her inquiringly.

'I want you safe and protected,' she exclaims.

'You could've just given me condom.' I smirk.

A crimson blush adorned her cheeks across her pale skin as she lightly hit me on my shoulder. 'I'm joking, I'm joking.' I hold my arms up in surrender. My right arm started to feel a lot heavier than the left. Definitely was an anaesthetic.

'You know I still think about that evening,' she trails off.

'Mia, you're a very beautiful woman, and it was great, but you've got to stop being a groupie.'

She immediately frowns a little. 'Oh honey, don't call me that.'

'If I hadn't won the two Victoria Crosses, would you be interested in me? Would you even give me a second glance, Mia?' I ask.

As lovely as she is, she deserves better than me, which, unfortunately, is hard as her movements are restricted. She hesitates before answering, 'Probably not.'

'You know one of these days, I might not come back from a mission,' I remind her.

'And that is why what I'm giving you now will ensure that you will always come back,' Mia glares at me straight in the eyes.

'Interesting, would you care to explain?'

'I will once I've fitted it,' she weakly replies. Now I'm really curious. Mia begins prodding my forearm. 'Is it numb yet?'

'Well I can't feel you viciously attacking my arm so yes,' she glances up at me and pouts at my sarcasm.

She whips out a scalpel from God knows where and attempts to jab my arm. I back away from her a little bit in shock. 'Whoa Mia, what're you doing with that? I was joking.'

'Oh no, really?' she fires back sarcastically. 'But I still need to make an incision so you better hold still.'

Mia makes a cut and folds the skin and flesh away to reveal

the nerves in my forearm. She takes an odd-looking half-moon-shaped plate with things that look like wires, and starts connecting them to the nerves in my forearm. Momentarily, she proceeds to put everything back together, stitching up the incision after.

'This device will be part of you forever, don't mess with it, don't touch it, leave it like it is,' she bluntly instructs. 'Come back in three days, the code blue should be over by then. Then you get your explanation.'

Three whole days with this undying curiosity; no soldier's training could compare to this beefy exercise. Mia escorted me to my car, giving me a peck on the cheek again as a farewell.

'You do know that you were the first man, and the only man, to ever give me flowers.' She shyly smiles.

I looked at her and kissed her on the cheek, 'See you in three days' time.'

During my drive to the facility, I thought about Mia. I had to admit, I did like the nerdy professor. And if the circumstances were altogether different there could've been something more meaningful between us. I didn't care that she was over ten years older than I. But unfortunately, that's not the case. I pondered on our relationship for a 'short' while before realising I had already arrived at the facility.

As I entered the facility, Andy greeted me. 'What took you so long?'

'Mia called me,' I simply say.

Andy's eyes lit up mischievously at the sound of her name, a large grin overtaking his face. 'Oh your love interest?'

I brushed this fool's teasing off. 'I've got to go back in three days.'

'Then make sure you bring her some flowers.' He winks.

'Anyway, what was the code blue for?' I inquire. The facility seems to be rather calm in this section.

'The special unit is raiding the Hyena's stronghold,' Andy heavily sighs, 'but I haven't had any intel yet. So just go and rest for now.'

I nod my head in obligation, today really has been eventful, too eventful. Suddenly, the knighthood felt so insignificant in comparison to everything else. And a raid on the Hyena's stronghold? Not good. As I began making my way to my quarters, I hear Andy shout down the corridor. 'Sleep well, Sir Commander,' Andy laughs.

'Very funny,' I sarcastically spit. That toffee-nosed git knew about this damn knighthood.

* * *

Three days had passed and it was finely time to find out what this damn metal plate was in my arm. After the anaesthetic hard worn off, the pain was unbelievable. Eventually, the agony subsided after about twenty-four hours, but my arm has been twitching every now and then – probably something to do with it being connected to my nerves. I don't really understand the science behind it though, whether that's because I'm ignorant or an idiot, that's for Mia to decide. I leave the car, white carnations in my hand, approaching Mia once again to hand her the flowers. Her eyes light up, like a child looking at a second plate of dessert, as she gave me a small kiss on the cheek and thanked me. I paid her a compliment on her efforts to doll up, once again, as she took me into her underground lab.

'How's your arm?' she asks, prodding around my forearm gently.

'Alright, just been twitching a lot.'

'That's normal, it should stop in the next week or so,' she reassures me.

She doesn't seem at all concerned so that's quite reassuring at least. I begin to inquire about the device, completely unable to contain my curiosity for any longer.

'Well that depends, how much time do you have for me to explain?' she says, pushing a strand of her hair behind her ear and suggestively biting her lip in anticipation.

Truthfully, I wasn't too sure. Sure code blue was over, but the mission isn't exactly complete. Three Hyenas managed to escape, but to what time period, your guess is as good as mine; that's why we have the auditors attempting to trace them down. But that could take basically forever. Plus I don't mind where this is going.

'I'm free until Pandy calls me back,' I chuckle.

She lets out a light laugh. 'Stop calling him that, he's your friend, your general. Now wait here while I go get something.'

She leaves me in her underground lab alone so I decided to take a look around. I approach her desk, looking at the paperwork scattered everywhere. A blueprint with a diagram drawn caught my eye, the design rather similar to the plate she put in my arm. There were several, of what looked like prototypes of the device lined up on her shelves, some in the bin even. Whatever this thing is, she spent a lot of time perfecting it.

I quickly dropped the paperwork back on her desk as the sound of her high heels became louder; I'm not so sure she'd appreciate me rummaging through her work. In a slightly panicked state, I spun around swiftly only to her see her, with her perfectly-curled long blonde hair let down. She seemed to have reapplied her red lipstick, as the shine was fresh, and honestly she'd never looked so good. Gradually, she began approaching me. Her hands undoing each button of her lab coat until they were all undone. Mia let the lab coat slip onto the floor to reveal her mesmerising bare body. For a woman that was twelve years older than me, she looked twelve years younger.

I do not need a second invitation.

I lifted her up, kissing her as I carried her next door to her bed, telepathically praying to Andy to not call me for a while. Like a year or so.

Another three days had passed, and I was still with Mia. After we had finished enjoying ourselves, Mia got up from the bed. 'Come on, get dressed. It's time to try out your armour.'

'My what now?' I exclaim, desperately trying to pull my pants up.

She puts on her lab coat and waits for me in the lab as I dress. Once I was fully clothed, I made my way into Professor Mia's Lab. The first thing I saw flying at me was a pointy dagger coming my way. Mia had thrown a dagger at me, and not even my reflexes could block it. I held my arms up in front of my face by instinct, closing my eyes, bracing myself for the pain. Several seconds had passed, and there was utter silence. I felt nothing. Cautiously, I opened my eyes. As I looked around the room, there were small diagrams in front of my vision, like a heart rate metre, and what was labelled a '360 degree awareness level'.

'So it works.' I look at a largely grinning Mia.

I glance up to my right arm, holding up the dagger by its blade, caught in my palm. I clenched my fist a little, completely crushing the dagger into pieces effortlessly.

'When I thought you said armour, I thought you meant a condom, not this,' I say confused.

'Like I said, I want you safe. This armour will protect you against everything; you are the only one that has it – because I want you to come back to me, safe and sound.'

'Oh so you do have a soft spot for me?' I smirk.

'What do you think the last few days were about, James?' she lightly retorts back.

I look around at myself. It was like a whole suit of high-tech armour surrounding my whole body. My left hand even turned into a weapon. It was very cool, I must admit – something straight out of a movie.

'As amazing as this is though Mia, how do I ... well, put it away?'

'Just think happy thoughts,' she says with a small smile.

Vindaloo curry. Vindaloo curry. Vindaloo curry. I chant the dish's name in my head, thinking of its sweet spicy aroma. As I do, the armour begins to recede itself back into the plate on my arm, and I was free of it once again. Mia starts asking me questions in relation to the quality of comfort of the device. Surprisingly, it was super comfortable, I mean, as comfortable as a metal plate in your arm can get.

'Honestly, Mia, I have no idea how to thank you,' I begin.

She winks. 'Oh I know exactly how you can thank me …'

*   *   *

Two days had passed and I'd returned to the facility; the last three Hyenas still hadn't been tracked. Currently, all that I could do is prepare to time travel again. Andy advised me to start packing things away for possibly one of the most important missions that I will ever do. If we put an end to the Hyenas, we put an end to all of this, and I can finally have a life. As selfish as that sounds, I want a life, a future, with my own family, and Mia features prominently in it. Although, right now, packing is far too difficult – I don't even know what timeline I should prepare for. Until the Auditors find out, there's little I can do. For now, I'll embrace the comfort of my own bed in my own quarters. As I lay on my bed, I closed my eyes, surrendering to the fatigue.

'Sleep is so, so good,' I murmur to myself as I finally begin drifting off.

Bang bang bang. The loud sound of persistent knocking against my door caused my heart to rise out of my chest suddenly.

'Are you kidding me? Can a man not get some sleep?' I cursed at myself.

Frustrated and angry, I swung open the door to my quarters to see Andy. I look at him, dark circles underneath my eyes, my bed hair sticking up, my gaze half-dead and completely unenthusiastic.

'Get ready, we know the timeline now. You're going back to 1203,' Andy informs me.

'What?' I say, confused and still half asleep. Wait. 1203. Medieval times? I hate the damn medieval times, everyone always wants to kill everyone – they're all so aggressive.

'Go on, gather your things. You're leaving tomorrow,' the general says as he takes his leave. I guess the sleep is going to have to wait another day.

*　　*　　*

Personalised weapons, ammunition, camouflage nets, three replicators, a solar power generator, home comforts, a DNA kit, and a tank. And I think I'm set to go. Before I take my leave, Andy enters the specially designed room, probably to give me a dumb pep talk.

'Listen, James, stay safe, and finish it. No hesitation, alright,' he begins.

'Have you ever known me to fail?' He laughs light-heartedly at my comment. But deep down, we were both as nervous as a soldier could be.

'I still think you're going a bit overboard with the tank. But if that's what you want, then that's what you take,' Andy says.

'You're joking, right? Every tree is going to have a longbow pointing at me. Before I forget though, if George asks, I'm on holiday, a long one.'

What are the Chances?

'I know he's your friend, but call him the king, for my own sake.' We slightly chuckle. 'At least his corgis will be safe.' Both of us burst into hysterical laughter, trying our best to calm down.

'I hate to intrude, General, but we must go through the briefing with the Commander,' an Auditor says, as they walk in.

This is the last time I could see Andy. It'd be a lie to say I wasn't a little upset. 'See you when the job's done,' he speaks up, leaning in for brotherly hug. 'And stay safe, yeah.'

'Will do. You know me, I'll be back, making your life miserable again in no time.' I weakly smile.

We both exchange our last farewells, before waving each other off as he leaves the room. The auditor begins conducting the briefing.

'As you know, you're going back 1203, the medieval times. But unfortunately for you, it's not only the three Hyenas that you should be wary of. We've identified that Professor Eddings' direct ancestors are living in this timeline. It is pertinent that absolutely nothing happens to them.'

Way to drop a bombshell. Not on my watch, that's not happening. If there wasn't enough pressure then, there certainly is now. The auditor hands me another DNA kit, informing me it had Mia's DNA in. But that means, she's here. I look at all the observance windows, then to the viewing room and see she's standing there behind the glass, looking rather teary-eyed. The auditor leaves the room, notifying me I have two minutes. I approached Mia, her hand pressing against the glass as a tear rolled down her cheek. Raising my hand, I pressed it against the window, aligning it with her hand. I mouthed 'I love you' to her before I backed away to prepare. I stood in the centre of the room; the glossy white walls' deflective ability ensured that nothing else outside of this room would get transported with me. The countdown started, as the sky blue light surrounded me and all of my gear. Before closing my eyes to brace myself, I quickly observed all of the faces looking at me through the glass, but my gaze was always drawn back to Mia. This is it. Let's finish it.

CHAPTER 3

Before I could open my eyes, the strongest feeling of nausea overcame my body. I keeled over, clutching my chest as my body convulsed, wanting to throw up badly – time-travel sickness has never been this severe. As I tried to steady my vision and calm down, my armour activated independently and covered me. What from? I look around me to see hoards of flying creatures with sharp claws circling around me. I get the feeling that they're not very friendly. Come at me you medieval scumbags. After grabbing my katana, given to me personally by the reigning emperor of Japan, I began fighting the creatures. Easily, the blade cut through their bodies. Despite the ease, they were relentless. They just kept coming, but from where? The nausea was still ripe in my body, but I'd have no chance to throw up my, potentially, last meal of 2050.

Eventually, their numbers began swiftly depleting. Thank God. As I severed the torso of, hopefully, the last creature, I glanced around me to see a full courtyard of their dead bodies. With caution, I approached one and hovered above its corpse, analysing its obscure features. They look like … harpies. Like from Greek mythology. But they're not real. Or maybe they were, and history now is a complete lie. Although if I remember correctly, they're vulnerable to higher frequencies, beyond the human hearing, which causes their nervous systems to shut down, thus they fall to their deaths from the impact. I grab a couple of sonic pulses from one of my bags and place them at strategic points on the courtyard. Hopefully, this'll keep me safe from them. I definitely wouldn't like to wake up next to one of them, no amount of alcohol will ever.

Funnily enough, I don't remember this from the medieval era at all. Then again, I've never been this far back in time either. If harpies exist, who else knows what else is going to try and kill me next. I'll take care of this in the morning. It's too dark to see much now, all I can make out some sort of castle but I'm not so sure. For now, I best retreat to my tank – where it's safe, probably. After closing the lid of my tank, I wrapped myself up warm as I slept off the sickness.

Surprisingly, I slept quite well – not comfortably, but well, considering I slept in a stuffy tank. As I climbed out, I took a deep breath of fresh air. Today was going to be a long day of cleaning up those harpie-looking things. Don't need anyone unnecessary to know I'm here. I explored the courtyard a little, finding an odd-looking wheelbarrow that could help me transport the bodies. As I piled the bodies onto it, I looked at, what I thought was a castle initially, but turned out to be one hell of a palace. The design of the palace was nothing like I'd ever seen, and it looked totally unconventional of your average medieval architecture. Something tells me I should check it out soon.

Once the wheelbarrow was filled with the first batch, I ventured out to find a better place to burn them. I came to find a drawbridge that had two paths. The smell of brine was rich in the air; the left path seemed to lead to an isolated beach. Perfect. There was a high sand dune, high enough to mask the smoke from burning the harpies. Taking out a flare, I lit up the bodies after tipping them out of the wheelbarrow. I watched as the carnage burnt, the flames rising high, and the smoke disappearing into the mesmerising sky. I've never seen such a clear beautiful sky, the perfect blend of blues and yellows. I spun around, just to admire the sky from all angles but stopped midway. That sun moved fast. I look behind me and saw the sun; I looked in front of me and saw the sun again. Either I've taken hard-core drugs, or there are two suns. Why are there two suns? I squinted my eyes and look for more unusual inflections in the sky. There's the moon, in front of a massive planet.

Why can I see another planet?

Immediately, I buried my face in my hands, walking towards my tank and got in it, leaving my wheelbarrow on the beach. After closing the lid, I crawled into a ball. I must be going crazy. Desperately, I rummaged through my bag to find my traveller. The first thing I noticed was the absence of the pulsating light of my device. Through sheer panic, I flipped the safety catch, on the top of the traveller, and pressed the button to go back to present day; quite frankly I've had enough. This is not funny anymore. The button didn't work. Repeatedly, I smashed the button a hundred more times again, hoping to God it would work. The more I did, the more desperate I became, and the more hopeless I grew. I knew I had to accept it, but I didn't want to. There really is no going back. But there is no possible way that I could have space-travelled. What happened? What went wrong? Think James. I closed my eyes, attempting to remember something, anything. All I could remember was seeing Mia's tearful face, and Steve behind her.

Steve behind her?!

That wide grin plastered across his face as he waved me off. Now that I think about, his eyes were filled with malicious intent, as if he knew this was going to happen. And as an auditor, no doubt would he have such knowledge on how to do such a thing. Steve was the traitor of the facility all along. He was the branch connecting us and the Hyenas. But now I'm stuck here, which means I'm going to have to fortify this place. I won't be leaving for a while – and quite possibly, never.

Firstly, I finished clearing up the courtyard, throwing all the rest of the harpies into the fire. I had to block the entrance to the palace courtyard in order to separate me from everything outside. So I set up a force shield on the gate after the drawbridge. Unless I invite them, no one's coming in. But that palace is still a problem, who knows what or who is in there. It wouldn't be so nerve-wracking if I knew I wasn't on a completely different planet.

I gathered some resources and grabbed my katana, as well as a sidearm. The palace door was made of heavy metal; some sort of emblem engraved either side of each door. It was also slightly ajar, a sign that the place was desolate. Carefully, I pulled the door open, its creeks echoing loudly throughout hallway, and invited myself in. As I entered, it slammed itself shut behind me, causing me to jump a little. This world's unfamiliarity was getting to me. I still had the soldier's training, yet my soldier's composure wasn't active right now. I analysed my surroundings. There was one large hallway, the walls were beige, and inscriptions adorned the walls in some foreign language, like alien hieroglyphics. Upon reaching the end, I noticed a throne placed in the centre of the audience room the hallway expanded into. A thick layer of dust coated the throne; clearly this place has been abandoned. I wonder why – although it did look rather impressive. It seemed to be carved out of bone, given the way the bone was chipped. The design was so intricate; some kind of royalty probably lived here before. Even though this place is most likely abandoned, I'll keep my guard up just in case.

To my left were another set of double doors. It led to a massive dining room, large enough for balls and all that stuff that royalty do. The whole place was dusty, even the plates of food and cutlery had been left on the table. Whoever used to live here left in a hurry. They'd taken no time put anything away. The repulsive stench of rotting food seeped through my nostrils – I've had enough of this room for today. I approached the large glass windows of the dining room, they showed a beautiful view of the garden – pity all vegetation was rotting and withered. As I leaned on the glass, the windows split in half and I almost tripped over and fell through. Looks like the windows also double up as doors. After pulling myself back up, I walked through the garden. From here, I could see a few dead harpies on the ground. Thankfully the sonic pulses are working. When I reached the end of the garden, I could see what looked like the ocean. The crystal clear reflection of the two suns, moon, and planet waded within the deep blue water. Despite my bleak surroundings, I felt some unusual form of peace for the first time on this planet. But I knew that could never be forever, not anymore.

I made my way back into the palace, there was a staircase leading up to the second floor leading to a master bedroom. This was extremely different from my quarters; the bed actually looked comfortable. That's my bedroom then, if no one else is going to claim it. I opened what looked like a fancy closet. There were still clothes in there. Although both the design and fabric were unlike anything I've ever seen before, I knew this room belong to a royal persons now, just by its enforced intricacy.

After exploring all the bedrooms, and I swear there were about fifty, I think it's safe to say this place is unequivocally empty. Also known as, mine for the taking. Might as well move all my stuff in and make this place my own. I never thought I'd say this but this obnoxiously large palace is going to the best camouflage for me now.

*   *   *

It's been almost a week, I think; I'm not so sure what day it really is anymore, but I think my renovations are satisfactory to my tastes. I set up the replicators in the kitchen to help me gather ingredients. It's one of the best inventions in the entire world, ask for any ingredient and it gives it to you. Seems impossible, and don't get me wrong, I'm still astounded by the science – not that it makes any logical sense to me. I also rearranged the audience room into a sitting room, with my television, powered by my solar power generator, propped up against the wall. It was a delight to be able to watch Earthly shows again, and thank goodness for this godly USB that lets me watch anything. (USB, my life on a portable stick) It took me a few days to clean out the hefty dining hall, but needless to say, it doesn't smell like rotten meat anymore. Unfortunately, the original garden hasn't changed much. I watered the plants but they don't seem to react to water – damn aliens. Luckily I cleared half of the garden out, replacing the completely dead plants with four fresh raspberry bushes and strawberry plants that I brought with me; at least they react with water. I don't even know why I have brought them with me. Home comforts I suppose.

Needless to say, I think I've done a pretty good job. However, I'd be lying if I said I wasn't rather lonely. Besides, I think it's time for me to do some exploring, outside of palace grounds. It is absolutely crucial that I'm properly equipped and have a plan for every scenario. Who knows what's out there and what kind of danger the locals pose.

CHAPTER 3.5

'King Herc would have wanted it done this way,' the overseers exclaim.

'Don't you dare tell me what my father would have wanted!' I threw my glass onto the floor in anger, the kura nectar leaking onto the floor through shattered glass.

Everyone's heads turned towards the chamberlain as he announced Seer Sania was here to see me.

I glared back to the overseers. 'Out, now!' I spat. Hurriedly, the overseers scurried off. I slumped back into my chair, covering my teary eyes with my hand.

She softly spoke up. 'We need to talk, privately.' I nodded at her and we went to my bed chamber, where no one would dare to disturb us. 'Are you alright, Vianna?'

Of course I wasn't. All those scumbag overseers want is to exert more power, Gah gave them more power than he should have. I didn't have the willpower to lie about how I felt right now, so I remained silent. It seemed Sania got the notion that I wasn't in a talkative mood right now. My pensive mood made it difficult to remain collected and civil right now. Call me sensitive, but I had no emotional resilience when it came to my parents, no tolerance for those who degraded their memory. King Herc was a great man, and so was Queen Yagi – they were the best parents. The flyer crashing wasn't my fault. The saddest part is that there is only one coffin in the mausoleum, King Herc's, my father's. My mother's body was never found, just a lot of blood. A lot of it. Everyone loved their queen, yet no one has anything to grieve to.

But I don't miss that good-for-nothing I married half a year later. King Gah. He didn't care about me, he didn't care about anyone. The only interaction I had from him was on our wedding night. He wouldn't even touch, or even look at our child. All that moron cared about was the title of 'King'. That power-hungry arsewipe deserved to die, should have been sooner than three years ago. Arka is not on friendly terms with the Zolg at this moment, but I have to thank them for Gah's death. I was seriously considering having him killed.

'Vianna?' Sania calls out to me, clicking her fingers in front of my face to catch my attention. 'Finally. You weren't responding again.'

'Sorry, Sania. I've had a rough day,' I trail off.

'Sorry, Vianna, but I'm going to have to make it worse. I had another vision, and this time it involves you directly,' Sania explains quite apologetically. I nod in response, sitting properly on my chair and perking up my posture in intrigue.

Suddenly, Sania's eyes transform from a deep brown to a blazing topaz blue. She began reciting her vision, speaking like a recording.

'A warrior, from the stars, will come. From tragedy, there will come happiness. What once was lost will be found. The warrior from the stars will end the war, and send the occupying force home. He will take a queen and her child as his own. And the people will love and call him "The White Arkan King".'

Sania's eyes revert back to their deep brown colour as her vision recollection ended. The White Arkan King? Does that mean he has white skin? But there is no one in our galaxy that has white skin: the Alphians are red, Morrins are yellow, and Zolgs are dark-blue skinned. He couldn't be from our galaxy. The thing about Sania's visions is that they always came true, so I would never ignore any of her visions.

'I wonder which galaxy he's from!' Sania exclaims.

'Me too! I wonder if he's tall and handsome!' I squeal back.

'Or what he looks like. What if he looks like a slink alien?'

Well he is from another galaxy. All right then, 'White Arkan King', give me all you've got and bring me and my daughter happiness.

CHAPTER 4

It was about time that I started exploring the east side. It's taken me a whole month just to basically navigate the west properly; it's safe to say I know 50 miles of it inside and out now. Cataloguing the endless varieties of species that I've discovered was a very good idea. I've concocted a personal encyclopaedia, including their danger levels, and their weaknesses and features and so on. Although, I haven't found the weakness for these stupid snake-like creatures. They coil and pounce at you; they don't seem harmful at all though, just petty little things. But I don't doubt for a second that there's thousands left for me to discover, and this research book of mine is already big enough. Thankfully, I got a body camera with me, so I'm able to document each one, along with images.

Even after hours of exploring the east side, I haven't discovered anything quite notable yet. Not to mention I'm running out of food for this trip. Better to start setting off again, this break has been long enough. I gathered my things, my backpack and my weapons among other stuff. Just a few more hours.

* * *

WHAT ARE THE CHANCES?

This trip is beginning to feel pointless; no structures, no people, nothing. The most interesting thing I've found is this wall of tall reed-like greenery. Don't get me wrong, it's cool, but feels quite ominous. What's a chunk of greenery suddenly doing in the middle of a vast field of pure isolation? Or maybe I'm too highly strung. The heat must be getting to me. I sigh but can't resist the temptation to inspect it. As I reach my hand out to it, I hear sudden screams from a distance. They sound like people, like children. Suddenly, I couldn't care less about the reeds, and automatically run towards the screams. I don't know whether my curiosity fuelled my impulsiveness, or the rare sound of another person's voice other than my own did, but right now I really didn't care. The cries became increasingly louder as I got closer.

Those screams were, in fact, children. A child was being attacked by a large beast. A beast none like I've ever seen before, not in the west side at least. By impulse, I grabbed my katana and charged towards the beast that was about to attack the child. Nothing else mattered in this moment. My mission was to save this child. Since none of the three beasts were aware of my presence yet, that gave me a clean angle to kill the first one. Holding the hilt with both hands, with the right angle and force I swung the blade unto its neck, slicing between its head and body. As its head rolled onto the ground, the little child backed away as the other two beasts charged at me simultaneously. I stood in front of them in a protective manner, holding out my katana in front me. Just as the second beast pounced at me, I positioned my blade to aim for its eye. It pierced the large creature's eye, pushing through the eye socket deep enough into the brain. How lucky. Swiftly, I pulled the katana out to prepare for the final beast already coming for my arse. Unfortunately, this one was feistier and much faster. I didn't have enough time or room to kill it quickly. I pushed the kid gently away behind me. There wasn't enough time to move to the side and dodge. So the only way there was under. As the beast jumped to attack me, I slid under it, holding my blade upright to slice through its stomach. Its flesh folded out, guts pouring from its torso. The creature fell, its lifeless body surrounded by a pool of crimson blood. I wiped the sweat off of my forehead. It'd be a complete lie to say I wasn't a nervous wreck on the inside throughout that whole fight.

I took a moment to stabilise my breathing. As I do, I walk over to the child, making sure they were still alive. It's seems she was a girl. Most of her clothes were completely saturated in blood. She had deep gashes adorning her arm and leg and cheek. With injuries like those, she'll die. Not on my watch.

'Let me look at them,' I gently speak, pointing towards her profusely bleeding cuts.

I took out my healing spray, specially developed to heal severe injuries with special nanites that miraculously mend the skin and organs, and spray it over her leg and arm. I looked at her and tried to tell her to shut her eyes. She glared at me clueless. The little girl muttered something in some strange language. Of course. Couldn't be that easy, could it? I emphasise the squinting of my eyes, motioning for her to imitate me.

She weakly chuckles and shuts her eyes tightly. I hovered my hand over her eyes and spray her cheek. It takes time to work, and most essentially, you shouldn't be moving while it's doing its magic. But I'm not sure how to translate that to her.

I open my palm and hold it in front of her face. 'Stay.'

Slowly, I back away from her and cautiously approach the bodies on the ground. I check one woman's pulse. Nothing.

'I hope she wasn't her mother, or that'd be really shitty,' I said to no one in particular.

All the others seem extremely dead to me. As much as I'd like to give them a nicer burial, I can't stick around. By now, it's clear that there are another people, another race out here. God forbid they ever found me. I'd be the first to be blamed for the deaths of their people. That means a target on my arse. I turn back to the girl. Now what am I going to do with her?

I knelt down in front of her. 'So what's your name?'

She gives me a blank stare and replies in the same language. Hanging my head low, I sigh. This is a lot harder than being a foreign tourist in another country. Actually it's quite much like that. Except, instead of being a mere tourist, I'm the only person of an entirely different race and on ANOTHER PLANET.

'Okay. Me,' I say pointing at myself, 'James.' I point at her and wait for her to reply.

No response, just another blank stare.

I sigh. 'You're very beautiful. So I'll call you Beautiful, okay.'

She gives me a cute smile, and starts pointing to another direction. She grabs one of my hands and starts pulling me towards that way. I frown, not knowing whether I can trust her or not, but she was so adamant to go. And for some idiotic reason, my gut was telling me to comply.

I shook my head, as sudden confusion overthrew all my thoughts. Swiftly, I spun back around to look at the little girl.

Her skin was sky blue.

Looking back at myself for reference, to make sure that I'm not the alien here, I glanced back at her. So I am on another planet, definitely. And it's not totally compiled of a heck ton of monsters that want to eat my heart for dinner. That's both relieving and extremely concerning.

Beautiful dragged me by the hand, running into this direction. Can't believe I'm practically trusting a little girl with my life right now. As we rounded the corner of the reeds, I immediately pulled her behind me quickly as I saw two more of those creatures. Before they noticed me, I killed one off with ease. However, this caught the attention of the other one. It charged at me with force; I pulled Beautiful towards me and rolled to the side with her. As I do, I hold out my katana, slicing the back of the beast. He turned his body towards our direction, his bright red eyes clouded with a visage of malevolent intent, saliva dripping down its jaw with an overpowering thirst for our lives. I backed up as much as possible, shielding Beautiful, until we couldn't anymore; a large structure obstructed us. Think, James, think. I couldn't move to the side, my only choice was head on. If I time it just right, I could immobilise it. The beast reaches one of its arms out to claw me. My blade severed straight through it, a bit too easily. It collapsed onto the ground, whimpering in agony, unable to get up.

What are the Chances?

I rested my boot on top of its head, pushing down to secure the beast, before thrusting my katana straight through its leather-like skin. After pulling my weapon out, I glanced back to Beautiful, checking if she was okay. Apart from a subtle tremble of fear, she seemed content and safe now. I looked behind her, observing the large structure. It looked like a huge bus but with no wheels. It was shiny white, with a black stripe across it. Didn't look old at all, but appears abandoned. Walking around it, I tried to find a door, but there seemed to be no entrance. Beautiful tugged on my clothes gently to get my attention. She pointed to something upwards, trying to reach for it but obviously not being tall enough.

Gently, I lifted her up. Beautiful put her hand on the side of this panel. Although it was chest-high, I wouldn't have known to do that. As she did, a loud ensemble of clicks and swishes rose up. A massive flap folded out of the structure, revealing the entrance to the space-like thing. Beautiful pushes me, insisting I go in, so I do. Looks like some form of transport, like a flyer or something like that, considering the high-tech engine things attached to the back that I saw beforehand.

The interior looks like a school environment.

Quickly, I put two and two together. That wasn't her mother dead back there. That was her teacher. And the other children were Beautiful's classmates. Poor girl.

Speaking of Beautiful, she started pressing a bunch of buttons, one in particular that sends a transmission from the cab. Once she finishing talking to whomever, I realise that other people are coming. This is bad for me. Hurriedly, I construct a plan to remain hidden. Crouching down to Beautiful's height, I hold the sides of her arms in a reassuring manner.

Signing my words with my hands in attempt to be understood I tell her, 'Beautiful, I'm going to wait there, you stay here.' I point at her then to the floor. 'Anyone asks about me, shhh,' I place a finger over my lips and whisper, 'Secret.'

Hopefully that did the job. Hastily, I run and hide near the reeds, concealing most of my body within the greenery and wait for the people. I have to make sure Beautiful is safe.

CHAPTER 4.5

Chamberlain Vern notified me about a transmission coming from the flyer that my daughter was in. Arriving at the flyer, I saw Olnia, standing inside covered in blood. Concerned, I ran up to her, pulling her into a hug.

'My baby, are you okay?' I ask, tearful but glad she was alive.

Her garments were stained with blood head to toe; she might be injured under it all. I order a doctor to examine her. Dear I hope Olnia's okay. It can't be all of her blood, lose that much and you're very much dead. So it must be someone else's, and I pray it's not what I think it is.

'Your Majesty, you need to see this,' General Mass exclaims.

He leads me to an area of bloody carnage, Olnia's teachers and class mattes all ripped to complete shreds. There were two beasts near the flyer, and three more here. Sarks. Powerful creatures. I don't understand what they are doing here. This area is supposed to be completely safe.

'General Mass, I want this investigated. Something doesn't add up,' I instruct and watch as they walk away. 'Commander, I want both of the recording devices of the teacher's, now.'

From the slaughtering of the five sarks, to Olnia being the only one alive, there's something big we're missing. As I head back towards the flyer, the doctor approaches me, her facial expression eager to tell me something.

'Your Majesty, your daughter has wounds inflicted by the sarks, however, she is making a miraculous recovery at an impossible rate. Whatever medicine was used on her is definitely not from this planet, we do not have such medical advancement to do this sort of thing. You should also be aware, your Majesty, that whoever saved your daughter from the sarks has saved her life twice.'

I confront Olnia, both of my hands on her shoulders in a reassuring manner, crouching down to her level in hopes she'll feel comfortable being totally honest with me. 'Olnia, who saved you?'

'My hero.' She smiles.

'Who, Olnia, who?'

'Shh,' she places a finger over her lips, 'secret.'

I hugged her, thankful to Olnia's hero, whoever he may be, that she was still alive.

After arriving back to the palace, in the capital, I put Olnia to rest. Poor girl must be exhausted from her ordeal. And as tired as I am, I have some very intriguing recordings waiting for me to listen to.

I retreat to my quarters for privacy. I brace myself as I play the audio from the first recording device. All I could hear was a cacophony of the screaming of children and growling of the sarks. As a queen, I should be resilient, but as a mother, I am not. It was upsetting and I don't want to have to listen to it again. As disheartened and disturbed as I was, I had to muster up the courage to listen to the second device. Shakily, I pressed play. I heard the man's voice, speaking a language I am not familiar with. I stopped the recording, keeping the device with me, and headed to the throne room.

'Please contact the linguist, Professor Nata, at the Academy; I need to see him urgently,' I ask Chamberlain Vern.

Out of all of the palace staff, Vern is one of the best, if not the best. When my parents died, he was there for me, so sincere and so supportive; he took care of me like no one else could. He has my greatest respects.

I couldn't get that voice out of my head. Is this the 'White Arkan King' that Sania had told me about? I won't lie, part of me was excited, but I was mostly afraid due to my unfamiliarity. It's extremely difficult to kill one sark, never mind five. What kind of skill does my daughter's hero wield? More importantly, should I be afraid? I don't want another Gah in my life, no one does.

My musing was cut off shortly by the quick arrival of Professor Nata.

'Thank you ever so much for coming so quickly, Professor, please follow me,' I thank him and lead him to the my private audience room, shutting the door behind me.

'What I am about to play to you stays between us, do you understand?' I firmly instruct, my deep stern facial expression making it clear that I was serious. He nods in obligation.

I played the recording back to him, watching as his eyes widen as the recording went on. He smiles, his hands nearing the recording device. 'May I?' Nata asks, excitedly but politely. I comply and allow him to replay the recording countless times again. If there is anyone that can decipher this language, it will be him, who's solely responsible for deciphering Alphian, Morrin, and Zolg in the entirety of the galaxy.

'I've never come across a language such as this before,' he says eagerly. 'Is there any possibility, Your Majesty, that I could take this with me?'

'Well of course, how long?'

'Around seven to ten days,' he estimates. Then so be it.

I returned to the throne room, instructing Chamberlain Vern to contact General Mass.

'I need an officer who thinks fast on his feet, and who's intelligent, and can work independently. The second they are detailed, they will be under royal command.'

The following morning, Captain Jihon arrived, presenting himself as my new personal officer. I have ultimate faith that he will conduct my investigation quickly, and thoroughly but discreetly. I know I can trust him, his parents, Baron and Baroness Vos, are very loyal subjects.

'Captain Jihon, be ready for an extensive field trip in about a week's time.'

*   *   *

'I've done it, Your Majesty,' Professor Nata exclaims, quite obviously over-excited. As eccentric as he was though, it'd be a lie to say I was not desperately excited myself. 'Now now, I'm gravely sorry, Queen Vianna, but whoever this man is, has said a rude word.'

'It's all right, Professor Nata. I'm not that delicate,' I inform him, weirdly flattered.

He plays me the recording, but this time translated into Arkan.

'I hope she wasn't her mother, or that'd be really shitty.'

Interesting.

I thank Nata one more time. 'But remember, Professor, this stays between us,' I say calmly with a slight undertone of threat. He glances at me, clearly understanding the message, gulping in fright.

Shortly after Nata's departure, I had contacted Captain Jihon, instructing him to come to the palace immediately. Like the punctual officer he is, he got here in no time. The chamberlain had escorted him to a private audience chamber.

'Understand this, Captain, you are under my command, whatever you hear and whatever the investigation will bring stays between you and I only. Do I make myself clear?' He nods for validation. 'I am going to play you a recording.'

He listens intently.

'Go to the place where the school children were mauled by the sarks, and that will be your starting point. Your mission is to find the person that this voice belongs to. You are to make contact and establish dialogue between him and I. But under no circumstances kill him. You've been allocated a flyer at your disposal. I have two bracelets, one for you, and one for our mystery man. Yours has the authority of a royal command, so you are able to communicate with him. Good luck, Captain.'

CHAPTER 5

Taking a clean towel, I wiped away the dirt and dried blood from my hand. It wasn't a major cut, just a slight scrape from tripping over as I slipped away behind the reeds when I knew Beautiful was safe. I didn't even see that brown and black ball thing sticking out of the ground. But I wonder what it was, maybe some sort of a plant. Either way, I've got to be more careful. Especially now since I might have a whole regiment after me; who knows whether Beautiful kept me a secret or not. She couldn't even understand me; guess I'll just have to put my faith in a little alien girl. Still, that must've been traumatising for her to see her teachers and classmates ripped to complete shreds by those big beasts. What even were they? They're probably the most vicious creatures I have fought so far. With skin like thick leather, and a large jaw with countless sharp teeth. Surely, my katana shouldn't have seared through them that easily. That katana should be long gone by now. I grab it, unsheathing it, and closely analysing the blade. Barely any nicks, still as sharp as ever. I pinch myself, checking I was still awake. That fight was far too easy to be real. I've either been working out in my sleep, or I've suddenly gotten stronger without realising.

I can't believe I'm saying this, but it looks like I'm the alien on this planet. My white skin in comparison to their sky blue hue certainly proves that. While it is surreal, in a cool way of course, I wouldn't opt to be living on another planet right now. I should be on my planet, eight-hundred years back in the past, hunting down the Hyenas, saving Mia. I don't even want to think about what's happening on Earth. Can't say I don't miss Andy, and George. I miss Earth. Something tells me that mission was unsuccessful. Somehow science spat me out here, time travel turned into space travel. I suppose I have to make the most out of it. As a soldier, I should be able to withstand isolation, but due to slightly inconvenient circumstances, I'm not sure I can endure a lack of socialisation for very much longer. It's only a matter of time before I become a senile old man. But for the time being, I'll have to lay low.

Speaking of staying put, my PVA, on my sleeve, lit up like the fifth of November; that means someone tripped the silent alarm. I'd set up cameras monitoring the outside of the palace for good measure, and monitors in the throne room. I best check them. As I did, I could've sworn I'd seen a man. A lone man. A soldier. I have to be very careful now. How did he manage to find me so quickly? Looks like that little girl talked, but why is he alone?

It's been around three days, and I don't believe that man has left. He seems to monitoring me, while hiding in the bushes. The poor guy, whoever he is, must've run out of food and water. I've got to hand it to him, that's dedication. I've got to take a leap of faith here. I'm sure if he had malicious intent, he would've tried to cross navigate the ravine and surpass my barrier by now. I grabbed a couple of energy drinks out of the fridge and went outside. After lowering the drawbridge, I took a deep breath; I trusted my gut that I wasn't about to die.

WHAT ARE THE CHANCES?

While still on guard, I approached the place where the soldier was still hiding, opening the bottled energy drink with a hiss as I prepared to offer it to him. He slightly flinched at the motion, but shortly composed himself as his eyes widened at my peaceful gesture. Gradually, he came out of the reeds, his shaky hands reaching for the drink. He pursed his cracked lips in preparation to take a sip. Swiftly, he chugged the fluid down, the sky blue colour returning back to his face as he hydrated himself. With his hand, he wiped his mouth of the excess fluid dripping, and said something to me that I obviously couldn't understand. He took out, what looked like a bracelet and held it out to me. I took it from him as he pointed to his own bracelet. Out of politeness, I didn't want to insult him so I put the bracelet on.

'Can you understand me?' the man says.

Wait, whoa. I can understand him. 'Can you understand me?' I repeat back.

'Yes I can,' he replies.

'Wow, you could make billions on my planet with this!' I explain, looking at my bracelet in utter fascination. The language barrier broken down with such ease, I am impressed.

'Billions of what?' he enquires, to which I, naturally, say money. He glares at me totally clueless, questioningly. Briefly, I explain to him what Earth money is. 'Oh, on Arka we call those credits.'

Now what the hell is Arka? This place is called Arka apparently. Good to know. 'I take it you were told to find me. Did the little girl talk?'

'No, she didn't. This little girl you speak of happens to be the queen's daughter. As far as I know, she never told the queen about you. We know about you because of the recording device, belonging to one of the dead teacher, that we retrieved.' My bad, I remembered what I said.

'I see. I understand it's a bit late, but what's your name?'

'Jihon.'

'I'm James. Are you hungry, Jihon?' Without hesitation, he nods strongly. I guess it's about time he has a decent meal. I could learn a lot from a native of Arka. I lead him towards the barrier to the courtyard of the palace, and ask him to place his thumb on my PVU to record his thumbprint and allow him past the barrier.

We both sat at my dining table. I served him an Earthly meal with a glass of orange juice. As I place the glass down, he inspected its strange orangey-look, inquiring what it was. I explained what it was. He seemed so fascinated by it I guess they don't have it here.

'So what spaceship brought you here?' he asks.

'It's not a spaceship that brought me here. Science spat me out on your planet,' I say. I shared my experience with him about my Earth life. From the time travelling to the Hyenas to my soldier life. 'You see, space travel wasn't very advanced, but time travelling is something we can do very very well.' I even told Jihon about my theory on how I ended up here, about Mia's work, and Mia.

'Well I'm only a captain, that would make you my superior, Commander. But what does "Sir" mean?'

So I'm guessing 'Sir' doesn't have meaning on Arka. I explain to him it's like a lord, but his facial expression remained utterly perplexed. What's the closest thing to a lord? I tell him it's like a baron, hoping he'd finally understand. His eyes lit up in familiarity. Excitedly, Jihon explains that it's a noble title on Arka as well; his parents are barons.

'So what's life like on Arka?' I'm curious. I've been here for over a month, and I still feel like I know nothing.

'Well we have four main cities: Ark –the capital – Leso, Mera, and Della. There's various beasts across the planet—'

I politely interrupt him, 'What are those beasts that I killed when I saved the little girl?'

'Sarks. But there are bigger threats. You should be more worried about Arkan Deaths. We lose many people to them each year, we keep burning them down but they keep growing back. They have tentacles that are dormant till you stand on them, then it pulls you by your feet and drag you in, enclosing your body in its petals. And the next time it opens up, it's just to spit your skeleton out. They are the biggest threat.' Noted. 'There are about 62 million people living on Arka,' he continues.

'Only sixty-two million. And how many nations are there on Arka?'

'One. We are the only nation, ruled by Queen Vianna.'

'One? There's billions of people living in nearly two hundred nations on Earth.'

'Billions?! Two hundred?! How do you all live?' Jihon asks surprised.

'With great caution,' I say. He asks me why there are so many people on Earth. And honestly, I have an idea. 'My friend, that is because it is free for all. Everybody has sex with everybody, we breed like rabbits.'

'What's a rabbit?' Never mind, I give up, you Arkan. I tell him it doesn't matter. 'James, you cannot have unmarried sex on our planet. If you have sex outside marriage, it's a death penalty.'

'You're joking?' Jihon frowns at me, deadly serious. Well isn't that unfortunate. 'I have no intention of getting close to any Arkan female on this planet. I'm just going to isolate myself till I check out.' He looks at me, confused once again. 'Check out means death.'

'Please don't do that.'

'You can only be alone for so long before doing something stupid.' Jihon tells me he'll come visit me often, which I doubt.

Jihon takes out a tablet-looking object from his bag and shows me something called the Arkan charts. It represents all of the known galaxies, but the Milky Way was not there; there's no chance they'll know what Earth is then. For all I know, Earth is a trillion light years away. Looks like my plan to hijack a spaceship and fly back is out of the window then.

Jihon began telling me about a five-year-long war between Arka and a nation called the Zolgs living on a not so distant planet. Apparently, some Arkans are still in disbelief that the once friendly nation had turned hostile since five years ago. One of Zolg's strongest defences is the large force-field surrounding the well-protected and impenetrable fortress they built themselves. So far, over 100,000 Arkan soldiers have died in attempt to storm it. This is just like the Hyena Institution back at home – except we were successful, sort of. I explained that, back on Earth, the generals would have stopped the attack after losing 200 soldiers.

WHAT ARE THE CHANCES?

'Looks like Arkan generals are incompetent butchers that need shooting.' I made Jihon an offer to hunt them down and kill them; that's what I would've done on Earth – sacrifice one life for many.

Jihon chuckles at my statement. 'Didn't you say you were going to keep a low profile?' Good point.

Jihon informed me that they don't attack the Zolg fortress anymore; they haven't for the last two years. Alternatively, they've co-operated with their allies, the Alphians and Morrins, who volunteered to help, to put up a barrier around Arka so no Zolg ship can land or even get within a 30,000 mile radius. If they tried to, their ships would be instantly destroyed. We continued comparing differences between Arka and Earth till a late hour drinking beer; it's amazing how our planets have minimal similarity but still a lot in common. Jihon sipped the beer from the bottle. 'This is nice. It's my first beer,' he says proudly.

'Haha, yeah, mine too,' I say sarcastically.

After another hour of drinking, and as much I'd love to learn more, I think it's safe to call it a night. Jihon already fell asleep on the sofa, hugging the now empty beer bottle in front of the television. I just leave him there.

The next morning, I made him a bacon and egg butty. When I handed it to him, there seemed to be some confusion with the translation. 'Pig' on Arka meant 'rodent', now I don't know about you but I don't enjoy rat in my butty. I showed him a picture of a pig back on Earth.

'It's got funky tail,' he laughed as he took a bite of his breakfast. 'Wow this is amazing. So exotic. Can I take one back with me?'

WHAT ARE THE CHANCES?

Looks like I'm making another one.

After breakfast, I escorted him back to the flyer left at the carnage site of the school children and teachers. I want to make sure he gets back safely; I don't want any misunderstandings with the queen if something were to happen to him. Without a doubt, I had to admit I really enjoyed Jihon's company. Didn't realise how refreshing it would be to talk to someone other than myself again.

'Well, Captain, it was fun while it lasted,' I smile.

'Thank you, I thoroughly enjoyed our discussions.' Jihon made his way onto the flyer and waved his wrapped butty in the air. 'And thanks for the "butty", Sir Commander!' he exclaims, trying way too hard to pronounce the English word. I waved him off as he flew back. If we meet again, Jihon.

CHAPTER 6

My foot kept tapping the floor uncontrollably as I buried my face in my hands. As a queen, I had to put ultimate faith in Jihon's confrontation with the white hero. But I still couldn't help but nervously anticipate for his return. I want to know everything about the white hero: where he came from, how, why, when? I have so many questions. The sound of a knock on my door and the familiar sound of Jihon's voice asking for permission to enter made me think my questions would not be left unanswered for not much longer. I've never been so exhilarated to see Jihon in my life.

I greeted him, glad he came back very safe and very much alive. 'Did you find him?' I eagerly blurt out. I was so curious.

'Yes, Your Majesty. I found him. And you'll never believe where he's staying,' I stared at him with a burning curiosity in his eyes, waiting for his answer. 'At the Kani palace.'

'My parents' holiday palace? How?' That's impossible, it's plagued with kanies. Why does it have to be that place, of all places?

'I quote him, "Science spat him out". And he had no choice but to fight for his life. Actually, he holds the rank of a commander in the military, holding a noble title equivalent to a baron on our planet.'

WHAT ARE THE CHANCES?

Jihon went through everything he had gathered from the white hero. Fortunately, he was very open about his life and what he did and was very friendly towards Jihon. It was relieving to hear such news. Couldn't say I wasn't impressed. The captain informed me that our white hero's name is James. What a unique name, I love it. Apparently, James had no intentions of interacting with other locals, he aimed to keep himself isolated until it was time to check out.

'What's "che—'

'And before you ask what "check out" is, it means to die,' Jihon further explains.

Instantaneously, a firm frown dominated my face. 'Now that is not happening. Captain Jihon, I want you to escort me on my visit to James, tomorrow at the Kani palace.'

Jihon seemed rather taken aback by my sternness, but I had to see this James. There's no way he's going to live on my planet without interaction. My unequivocal curiosity aside, I just wanted to personally thank James for saving Olnia's life. Twice. 'Report to the palace at ten-hundred hours,' I order Jihon. Now all I can do is ponder for hours over this so-called James.

After arriving near the Kani palace, Jihon escorted me towards the palace courtyard. It appears the drawbridge was down, but our white hero was not there. Jihon assures me that James definitely does live here, but we can't seem to find him. After a short while of searching, I was ready to give up, I was already exhausted from the travel that all of this was too much effort.

'Hello, what can I do for you?' he says just from behind. His sudden voice surprised me, that damn hero snuck up on us. Jihon spins around in utter delight at the familiar sound of the man's voice and greets him.

Once I got a good look at him, I could feel my cheeks burning up, my face turning a bright red colour in embarrassment – which is certainly hard to do since I have sky blue skin. So this is our future White Arkan King. I am meeting him, in this moment. A tall man holding a fish in each hand, his pale white skin slightly covered in a thin layer of sand from the beach, approaches us. The man looks straight at Jihon, seemingly quite delighted but confused to see him again. He then glances at me, quite amused that I couldn't get past this damn barrier in the way. Jihon can, but I cannot. The white man comes closer to us both. Instinctively, my body tenses up on its out. I was very nervous.

'Sir Commander James, I have brought Queen Vianna to see you, by her request,' Jihon introduces me. I have no idea what Jihon just said, who is 'Sir', I thought his name was James. Is the translation bracelet not working? Unless Jihon pronounces 'seer' strangely.

'May I greet you, Your Majesty, the way I would greet a queen on my planet?' he asks me. What a peculiar request, yet I'm intrigued, so I nod.

Gently, he takes my right hand in his and kisses the top briefly. I've never experienced this before, it's so strange, and in fact so strange I couldn't help but blush even more. I cough, and quickly shake it off in attempt to compose myself. 'So you must be James?' I begin.

'That I am, Your Majesty. I'd be more than content to invite you in, but you see the barrier is there to keep all uninvited guests out; only those I invite can pass through. Wouldn't want to be breaking into my home, would you Queen Vianna?' He smiles and winks. Preposterous!

He grabs my hand gently once again, and motions for me to place my thumb on this strange monitor he has on his arm. It scans my thumbprint, which seemed to allow me past the barrier finally. So this is how he's survived for so long. With great intelligence and other-worldly technology beyond our knowledge – how incredible!

As the three of us cross the drawbridge, Jihon speaks up. 'Sir Commander, I thought you should know that one of the fish you're carrying can cause a severe stomach ache and vomiting.'

Promptly, James squeals a bit and throws the fish down the ravine below, stretching across the drawbridge, his facial expression representing disgust and alarm. I smirked a little, and chuckled. Well he is a funny character, I'll give him that. James took us inside the palace. As soon as I entered, I immediately got shivers down my spine. The whole thought of just being here, and my parents. It felt almost unbearable, but I could not falter.

'Are you hungry?' James asks. I was rather peckish. Actually scrap that, I was starving, but do I want to risk eating food from a man who was about to eat a bad fish? Jihon leaned in and smiled, whispering to me to say yes. So I did. 'Great, then come to the kitchen.'

'It's all right, we can wait for you,' I say.

'No no, you're going to want to watch. To make sure I don't poison you of course,' he said, brightly smiling and casually walking off as if he didn't just insinuate our murders.

WHAT ARE THE CHANCES?

He started fumbling around in the kitchen, taking a large pot and throwing random things together. Most of the ingredients I didn't even know of, but I had to admit that the aroma was clearly out of this world. I inquired on what the strange dish was, apparently on his planet, humans call it 'chowder'. When I asked him about his origins, he told me the exact same thing that Jihon told me. It still all seems very surreal, almost impossible that science had spat him out. After the dish was cooked, he led us to the dining room to eat. It's been many years since I've been in here. James has taken good care of this place; since its abandonment, it should look incredibly worn down and dusty. But that's not the case. Even though there are a few intricacies that have been altered, all in all, it has not changed from what I remember. Nervously, I held the spoon of chowder in my hand and brought it up to my lips. How can I be sure this won't make me sick? I'm the queen, I have important duties I have to be alive for. But I'm so hungry. I procrastinate for a short moment, balancing out the pros and cons. Hunger overwhelms me. Chowder over queen. The second the chowder touched my tongue, it was an explosion of flavour I have never experienced before; James' cooking was tremendous. After devouring more of my plate, I decided to stimulate conversation again, since there was ultimate silence.

'So, Seer Commander James, I wanted to thank you for saving my daughter, Olnia.'

'Olnia?' he says perplexed. 'Ah your daughter, I just call her Beautiful.' What a strange man. I do love the nickname though. 'It's no problem, but she's very lucky.' Yes she is.

What are the Chances?

'So, Seer Commander James, you should know that as a queen, I am not naïve. I'll be honest, I find it rather difficult to believe that "science just spat you out" onto Arka.'

'I assure you, Your Majesty, that is the truth. Follow me.' he finished his chowder and stood up, motioning for me to follow. He took us to the master bed chambers, where my parents used to sleep. The desk was full of clutter, as he rummaged through it, he pulled out a strange looking device with a button on top. 'This is the device I would've normally used to get back to my time, but there's a comforting blue light that always shines in the traveller that is there no more. So I'm stuck.' His usual smirk-ridden face fell as he finished his explanation. He must be so scared, soldier or not. I can't help but feel great pity for him. But I will not let him breathe in isolation. 'Please listen here, Queen Vianna, believe me or not, I'm not here to cause problems; just to basically co-exist with the situation I've been thrown in.'

Throughout the whole conversation, I kept staring intently at James, attempting to depict any furtive inflections in his voice, but there is nothing. But I was still curious. Though I had to return back to the capital, I really didn't want to.

'Thank you for your visit, Queen Vianna. Nice to see you again, Captain Jihon.'

'As you too, Seer Commander James,' I say. He chuckles at my words, so I give him a light frown.

'Haha, and it's not pronounced "seer", Your Majesty. It's pronounced "Sir", Captain Jihon told me it's like an equivalent to that of a baron on our planet. "I am definitely no seer, although it'd be great if those actually existed," James chuckled.

Actually existed? What's he talking about, they do exist. Sania is one. But now I just felt stupid, I guess even with a translator bracelet, there's still a slight language barrier. After we bid our farewells and prepared for our departure, I couldn't help but submit to this gut feeling that I should go back. I told Jihon I wanted to back and see James tomorrow, the same time as today. Well, Sir Commander James better get used to me.

*　　*　　*

For the past two months, I've visited James almost every day. And during these last couple of weeks, I learned a lot about him. Although, at my most recent visit today, James requested I pass on a message from him to Beautiful. Since this morning, I had a good feeling that it was time to tell Olnia about James. I think now was a good time. I looked at her in the eyes and tell her I knew who her saviour and hero was. She cutely pouted in disbelief. I told her he had white skin, and was from another planet.

Her brown orbs glowed up. 'Don't do anything bad to him!' she pleads. I assured her I would never.

'Of course not. I've been visiting him for the last two months, with Captain Jihon. His name is James, and he calls you Beautiful. I actually have a message from him for you.' She eagerly waits for it. 'Stay strong, Beautiful,' I repeat and kiss her on the cheek gently, as James requested, as I tuck her into bed.

She squeals and holds her cheek where I kissed her. 'When I

grow up I'm going to marry James!' I choked at her statement. Not on my watch, missy, he's mine.

'But Olnia, he's old enough to be your father,' I try to reason with the six-and-a-half year old.

'Then mummy has to marry him so he can be my real father!' She smiles in delight and incredible happiness. Maybe one day, Olnia.

She continued interrogating me about James, relentlessly throwing questions about him. After all her spam, I made it adamant that she had to keep James a complete secret from every one, no matter what. She agreed and placed an index finger over her lips and hushed.

'Now go so I can dream about James being my loving father!'

I laughed and kissed her goodnight.

As I made my way to my chambers, I felt the blush rise back to my cheeks as I recall the moment James kissed me on the cheek earlier today. The entire journey on the flyer back to the capital I was flustered, holding my cheek where he kissed me. Even if the kiss was for Olnia and not me, it was incredible. The way he greeted me every time, taking my hand in his and kissing it. It was perfect! I felt like a giddy teenage girl again. I think Jihon noticed my flustered state as he mischievously smirks every time I bring up James. That damn captain better keep this to himself. I guess I never really got to be a giddy crushing teenage girl anyway, since I was too focused on the death of my parents. Although, I know for a fact James is better than Gah. Anyone is better than Gah. What am I doing right now. I'm already thinking about marrying him? I huff and turn to lie on the other side of the bed, hugging a pillow out of frustration. Tomorrow I'm going back, but this time, I'm going alone.

With all of this excitement, I couldn't sleep, not right now anyway. As if on cue, someone knocked on my door. The soft voice of what sounded like Sania asked for permission to come in, to which I agreed. Sania entered and closed the door behind her, and then told me she sensed that I was thinking about something deeply. I don't blame her for feeling worried; it was true that I had a lot on my mind right now. In a few days, it'll be the anniversary of my parents' death.

'What you need is some good old-fashioned cheering up!' Sania proposed, cheekily holding up a bottle of Poto, a local Arkan alcoholic drink. Like the good old times, Sania invited herself to stay the night so we could get drunk together as friends. But I most definitely did not need a second invitation to drink with her. Being queen certainly is exhausting, but it's moments like these where I can truly feel Arkan again.

After a couple of utterly drunken hours, I had the strong urge to tell Sania about James. It was probably a bad, well not bad but not good, idea to tell her, since the fewer people that know the better, but after all, she is the one that brought this white man to my attention.

'Sania, this is going to sound c-crazy,' I say, feeling awfully light-headed from the alcohol. 'I've met that White Arkan King from your vision.' My words stutter as I struggle to explain.

Suddenly, she jolted her body up and widened her eyes in surprise. 'You what?! Vianna, explain!' Sania exclaimed as she grabbed both of my arms a shook me in desperate curiosity.

My explanation turned into more of an investigation, no, interrogation from Sania; she wanted to know anything and everything about him. We talked until very early hours into the morning, hours of her practically begging to meet him. Eventually, being the great amazing spectacular friend I am, I agreed. But on a certain condition.

'You can meet him, but NOT tomorrow, or in this case today as it is early hours,' I declare. She pouts at my condition. 'Because I want him to myself,' I giggle. Her frown quickly sprouts into a smirk as she winks at me.

'Alright alright, fine. I can wait,' she laughs. 'But you know what I want more than to meet your man right now … to sleep.'

Good idea, Sania. Promptly, she fell into a deep slumber, which left me with my thoughts. Later, it's going to be me and James, with no damn Jihon around. Amazing as a captain, but I can't do anything with him around. What I really want to do, I can't with Jihon around. I just want some sort of relationship, or contact with James at least. But I might have to sleep on it. It'll come naturally, but I'm so impatient.

The next day, after taking Olnia to school, I had taken the flyer to go see James. As soon as I stepped out, I rubbed my head to ease the headache from the hangover, I probably shouldn't have stayed up so late drinking, but it won't stop me from doing it again. I looked around me and caught sight of James coming across the drawbridge. Somehow, my headache seemed to dissipate as my heart fluttered when I saw him. It's only been two months, but I felt like deep down inside he was my destiny. Never mind Sania's vision, since day one I've known he was special. And this exact moment has just confirmed it. But I know nothing about humans, or what a human man wants or needs, I need a way to let him know I'm interested without coming across as a desperate pathetic fool. Don't mess this up, Vianna. You got this!

Now if that was not the most amazing day of my life then I don't know what is. It felt so much like a date, the fantastic meal he cooked was a delight as usual, and we talked endlessly for hours. Even better, he looked so handsome today. Every time I visit him, he just looks better and better. In all honesty, I was disappointed that I had to go back. Going to my parents' holiday palace was not much of an issue anymore, because for the first time in my life, something actually good has happened. Sometimes, even I forget that I'm queen, I just feel so normal around James. The way he walked me back to my flyer, I offered him my hand. But he didn't kiss my hand this time; instead he pulled me in and kissed me so passionately that my left leg rose up. I was so surprised, so caught off guard. But it was magical. Call me corny but this queen likes a bit of cheese. A battle of thoughts were rushing through my mind. I want more. I got what I wanted but that kiss made me want even more. So much so I gave Captain Jihon the rest of the week off so I could see James alone again and again. I've never been kissed like that before. The only reason I had to leave was because James reminded me I actually had a daughter I had to pick up from school. As much as I do love James though, he was right, Olnia was very important to me. As fatigued as I am from drinking the night before, and my travels to see James, I don't think I'll be able to sleep tonight. If anything, I was thinking of bringing Olnia to see James on the ferga. I think it's time Beautiful is reunited with him.

Agra had come around finally. I had dressed Olnia very nicely, and myself, to see James. When he saw Beautiful, his blue orbs lit up and a smile spread across his face. He was very happy to finally see her again. Olnia ran up to him and gave him a great hug and kiss. Oddly, nearly all men that Olnia met would have never squatted down to embrace a child but James did not hesitate. He got down and gave me daughter a genuinely loving hug, something no one ever did, something Gah would refuse to do. James was more of a father to Olnia than Gah could ever be. Olnia was very delighted to be within James' presence once again, I've never seen her so delighted.

CHAPTER 6.5

It was great to finally see Vianna again after the two days I hadn't seen her since that kiss. Was beginning to think that this planet had weakened my charm and scared her off. In all honesty, I'm rather surprised myself that I pulled such a bold move on a queen, never mind on an alien queen. Grabbing her so abruptly and kissing her so passionately, it's just not done – but I did it. But now she is here and she has brought Beautiful with her. Since her daughter is here, I decided to take them both to the nearby beach. Vianna told me that this was actually Beautiful's first time on a beach because of the beasts that lurk on it. But there are no beasts this time, so Beautiful was loving it.

'Call me a terrible mother or whatever, but Beautiful actually has no idea how to swim,' Vianna says.

'Then get her ready for the water, I'll teach her the rudiments of how to swim,' I laugh. Vianna and Beautiful both got in the water with me. Gently, I grab both of Beautiful's arms and place one of each shoulder and tell her to hold on and start kicking her legs vertically. She giggled cutely as she was having fun learning to swim.

'Can you be my real father, James?' Beautiful blurts out.

Naturally, this left Vianna and I stunned, although she seemed more flustered by her daughter's question. Taking Beautiful with me, I swim to her mother's rescue.

'Haha, how about we go back to the palace and I'll cook you something delicious to eat?' Vianna eyes lit up at the sound of food. That woman really does love food, or maybe Earth food, or maybe because it's made by me; regardless, she truly enjoys it.

As we walked back into my palace, I asked Beautiful if she would like something nice to drink, like it was a trick question to a child. Of course, she nodded very excitedly. From the replicator, I obtained some hot chocolate powder and made a large hot chocolate with whipped cream and marshmallows. I explained, to Beautiful, that the trick to drinking hot chocolate is that, if you can comfortably hold the sides of the cup, then it is ready to drink. Beautiful just kept staring at it pouting in impatience. Vianna told me that hot chocolate doesn't exist on Arka. I picked up the hot chocolate and took it to the coffee table, and put on a kid's film for Beautiful as I really needed to talk with Vianna. To my amazement, they have no such thing as kid's films, or any films to be exact. Boring farts. I had to explain to Beautiful what a movie was, but ultimately left her super confused. I suppose it's a lot to take in for a six year old. Ultimately, I ended up telling her to just enjoy it as children on my planet enjoyed them. She sat down to watch it, eagerly eyeing the hot chocolate. Almost forgetting about Vianna, I offered her a drink. Shyly, she muttered that she would as like a hot chocolate as well. You know what? So do I.

I took Vianna to the kitchen and begun to cook. While I was gathering ingredients, I was intently thinking of a way to broach the matter of that kiss, but Vianna beat me to it.

'Are you angry, or upset about me kissing you? Before you answer though, you should know that I won't apologise for it. I wanted to do it and really enjoyed kissing you so …'

'In fact, you're lucky enough that I did enjoy it, James,' she declares with confidence. 'I hope we can have more in the future.'

I smiled at her response, I genuinely was not expecting such an answer but I am not complaining. I went up to her and kissed her again, keeping my dirty hands, from cooking, away from her. She embraced me and kissed me again and again and again – a little too much to be a friend at this point. Suddenly, our session was interrupted by Beautiful's scream. Immediately, we both ran to the throne room where she was. I was ready for a fight as kids don't just scream that way without reason. But as we arrived, we saw her fully engrossed in her film, and her upper lip was covered with whipped cream. We asked if she was all right, clearly concerned.

'This hot chocolate is amazing!' she squeals and promptly screams again with delight.

Vianna and I looked at each other, slightly annoyed for the disruption of our glorious moment, but we just chuckled and left her again to return to the kitchen. I was in deep thought, concentrating on cooking our delicious meal, until Vianna suddenly screamed, telling me that the hot chocolate really was amazing. What is with people on this planet and screaming over food and drink? I told her she could have all the hot chocolate she would want, but cheekily said it'd cost her a kiss every time. And with zero hesitation, she agreed.

WHAT ARE THE CHANCES?

As luck had it the film had finished just as the food was ready to eat. The three of us made our way to the dining hall, where I placed the food before Beautiful's food-thirsty eyes. This expression quickly fell from both of them, as they eyed the dish with suspicion. I explained to them what spaghetti actually was.

'I promise you that they are not worms or snakes. It's pasta made from flour, egg and water. And this is beef, from a type of farm animal on my planet. It's called Spaghetti Bolognese, just try it,' I reassure them.

To say that both Vianna and Beautiful enjoyed the food would have been a humungous understatement. They both requested an extra plate. Silently, I smiled to myself knowingly. After all, which child doesn't like Spaghetti Bolognese?

After dinner, I put a family movie on for all of us to watch. They practically begged me to make another hot chocolate for them each, and being the kind-hearted man that I am, I did. We had plenty of fun until later hours. Vianna had never stayed this late before, but since Beautiful is here, it's different. I was getting ready to walk them back to the flyer, but to my surprise, Vianna asked if they could both stay the night. So I had to very beautiful guests sleeping over tonight.

When Vianna put Beautiful to sleep, I opened a bottle of red wine for us, after explaining to her what it was. As the night went on, we had a nice time with a lot of kissing. Sadly, in the back of my mind, I remembered Jihon's warning about sex outside of marriage being forbidden for it meant a death sentence. With utmost of restraint and self-control, I told Vianna that we should call it a night. She frowned in sadness, but understood. Tiredly, she made her way to her bedroom and I went for a very cold shower to finish off today.

By the time the pair had to return to the palace, Beautiful could swim fairly well; not to say we could chuck her straight into open seas by herself, but enough to not drown in the shallow end of a pool. We had plenty of fun; Beautiful watched another kid's film after dinner, while Vianna and I went to the palace gardens to do a lot of kissing. I was very sad that they had to leave, since I really loved them being here. Strangely enough I find myself wanting them to come back. Back on Earth, there was no real time for family, since I had to hide everything from anyone I loved, and the one person who knew my true life that I did love, nothing could've ever happened between us, nothing more meaningful. But alas, I've had a taste of what having my own family feels like, and I could not say I did not like it. The highlight of their visit must've been the way Vianna pulled me in and kissed me right in front of Beautiful. I vividly remember looking at her, and luckily, she was very in favour of her mother and I getting together. Her last words before getting on the flyer were: 'James is my real father now!' If that's not convincing positive response, then I don't know what is.

The next couple of days were rather lonely, Vianna and Jihon hadn't visited, and I was starting to think I had to find another way to occupy myself. Solution: exploring. It was something I hadn't done for over two months now. By sheer coincidence though, as I was making preparations for my venture, Jihon and Vianna showed up, but this time they had brought a guest. It was lovely to finally see Vianna again, and Jihon. Jihon, over the past few months, has become like a brother to me, that's why I've started calling him 'baby brother'. When I first called him that, I can recall his exact shocked facial expression. He was so stunned, clearly flustered by the honour of being on nickname terms with each other. Eventually, Jihon mustered up enough courage to call me 'big brother'. He reminded me a lot of Andy, it was refreshing.

I steered my attention towards the guest that they had brought. She was really pretty, maybe the same as Vianna. Looks like on this planet there's only supermodels. I came across the drawbridge to greet them. Once I was introduced to Vianna's best friend, Sania, I invited them all in. We sat around my bar-like table and offered them beverages. Without hesitation, Vianna asked for a cup of hot chocolate. I swear I don't put nicotine in my hot chocolate. Sania and Jihon asked for the same out of curiosity, since they have no such drink on Arka. Actually, this is a very nice opportunity to try something out.

'So, since Vianna has already had hot chocolate before, Jihon and Sania, you have to perform a ritual as you are both hot chocolate virgins,' Vianna looked at me very confused, but I nodded and cheekily smirked, telling her to keep hush. I told Jihon he had to spin in one place twenty times, so he did.

'Yeah I'm not doing that,' Sania exclaims.

'Oh you don't, females must honour the holy beverage in a different way. You don't have to do it, but my people would certainly be offended by such refusal,' I explain. She frowns but gives in, asking me what she had to do. 'All right, pretend to say "uh, ah, uh, ahhh ah, oh my Lord," and slap both of your hands on the table top. But it must be said with a lot of passion and a lot of effort.'

Honestly, I was expecting her to not do it but she did it without complaint, probably not to upset Vianna. She sat up, repeating what I said, slamming the table with both open palms of her hand. She did it very very well. In fact, so well that all three of us were staring at her for some time. I was the first to recover from Sania's performance; I turned to Jihon and advised him to marry this girl and fast. Both Sania and Jihon blushed at my statement; Vianna leaned towards me and whispered in my ear that Sania liked Jihon. Oh, so that's how it is.

'Jihon, as I hold a higher rank than you, and I am your big brother, tonight you either take Sania on a date, or next time I see you, I will shoot you,' I say in a deadly serious tone. 'And I don't miss.'

He was so shocked by my blackmail that he agreed almost immediately. From Sania's reaction though, you could tell that she was very much in favour of this date. Being the kind-hearted human I am, I made everyone hot chocolates like they deserved. Looks like it's a running trend for Arkans to squeal over the taste of something good as Sania and Jihon did so in unison.

'This is amazing!' Sania exclaimed.

Knowingly, I smiled in accomplishment, recalling Sania's 'ritual' in my head, 'Yes, the hot chocolate gods of Earth would be very pleased with your efforts indeed.'

While we were chatting, collectively enjoying our drinks, Vianna announced that we were officially dating. She told them about last ferga, the equivalent to a weekend on Earth, what we did and how I taught Beautiful to swim. Sania reacted defensively about this, concerned about the unsafeness of the beach since it's polluted with mappens, a type of beast. I reassured her that the beach was very safe now, and promptly invited her and the others to see for themselves.

When we arrived at the beach, Sania couldn't believe it. She inquired on how I managed it, so I told her that I persuaded the mappens to leave, and they did. She still did not believe me, asking how. My reply was simple, I told her I killed lots of them for fun and they decided to go somewhere else. To say she was impressed was a massive understatement. Stripping down, I went into the water, motioning for them to do the same. I noticed Jihon was staying at the shallow end, so I came up to him and asked him why. He told me he couldn't swim. So naturally, I began teaching him, like I did with Beautiful, except with a man, who's like four times bigger. Sania even joked that I should open a swimming school.

'Not at all. Jihon is just saving his energy for their date that's happening tonight, right Jihon?' I stared at him directly into his soul slightly threateningly.

He nervously laughed. 'Yeah, what he said!' He then whispered to me, 'Hah, you're not going to actually shoot me, right?'

'No, baby brother. Maybe,' he yelped at my last word.

After we had fun and a refreshing swim together, we went back to the palace where I cooked everyone another meal from my planet – which of course they had enjoyed. I was sad to see them leave. Sorry, I will rephrase that: I was sorry to see Vianna leave, but I was happy that Jihon and Sania were leaving, since its date night for them. I even gave Jihon some tips as I was teaching him to swim. Apparently, he's likes Sania a lot, but has never been on a date before. On Arka, it's common for parents to pick who their child marries, and that I did not like. But I do wish them both good luck, and if Jihon listens to my advice, then he shall have a very successful date with Sania.

Vianna let Jihon and Sania aboard the flyer first so she could give me a long hug before she left, she even kissed me – she sure does like to kiss a lot. Maybe she thinks that I'm a frog, if she kisses me enough, I might turn into some handsome blue-skinned prince. It's always a shame that they have to go, but I have to face that this is my life now. If I tried to live alongside the Arkan civilisation, the colour of my skin would always bring attention; who knows what could happen to me.

CHAPTER 7

Over the next three months, Vianna and Beautiful spent every weekend at my place, after many cold showers, and inhuman restraint. But since Jihon and Sania are officially a couple now, they have stopped by almost as often as Vianna, always so thankful for my threatening order for them both to go on that date. My relationship with Vianna and Beautiful had most definitely strengthened. Honestly, they really did feel like family. We didn't have to hide our relationship from Jihon and Sania; they approved with no doubt. Beautiful had been calling me her 'real father' without raising an eyebrow, which was to say the least interesting. Odd, since I'm personally not used to it, but sweet nonetheless.

Everything was going great, however, I've noticed I'd become somewhat restless as I felt that I was losing my sharpness as a soldier. So after another amazing weekend, or ferga, I informed Vianna that I'll be away for about two to three weeks exploring the jungle. As you'd expect, she was not happy about that. Luckily, she understood but made me promise I would be very careful. I did promise her, but you never know, I can be a real idiot sometimes.

Trekking through the first part of the jungle was more or less uneventful. I'd encountered no beasts, but a vast amount of vines that belonged to that Arkan Death that Jihon told me about. When I first came across the vines, I ran a small, possible fatal experiment on them, just out of pure curiosity. I remember Mia was telling me about the properties of sulphuric acid one time; of course I blanked out at some point – that science stuff isn't mates with my brain. Briefly, I remembered something about it having a negative effect on the pH of some vegetation, causing death to the plant. And to my luck, I had a breakthrough. Once I poured a few drops of acid onto them, suddenly all of the vines retracted, and the plant shrivelled, almost like an animal dying. It happened so fast, I was petrified by its sudden movement. I didn't expect it to happen instantly, but alas, Arkan Deaths hate that stuff a lot. Of course, in order this to be a fair trial, I had to repeat this as many times as possible. Every time I came across an Arkan Death, I poured the acid onto it, and it had the same results. Looks like I've discovered an extremely effective way to get rid of Arka's biggest cause of death.

It took me two days to get to this river that seemed to divide the jungle. After a closer inspection of the water, I decided I wouldn't risk swimming across it; too many small bubbles were coming from underneath the water surface. Jihon did warn me about some aquatic beasts called zarks that inhabit jungle rivers. I assume they're like crocodiles, except far more vicious. At the time, I didn't have enough energy to explore, so I climbed a tree and slept up there, hopefully safely. I don't think people realise how noisy the jungle gets at night, I'm just glad I didn't sleep on the ground. The next day, with the aid of two well-thrown hand grenades, I was able to get across the river on the dead zark bodies. Then the next two days were just as uneventful as the first. But just as I was about to turn back to start making my way home, I came across something interesting. I won't hold my breath and assume anything, but I decided to leave majority of my refreshments behind.

At this point, I was running out of food and water, so I was forced to return back to civilisation. Even after re-tracing my footpaths throughout the jungle, it still took me an Arkan week, which was nine days, just to get out of the jungle, and then a further six days to get back to the palace. Over the last three days, during my return to the palace, I'd been thinking a great deal about Vianna and little Beautiful. In conclusion, if something serious became of this thing Vianna and I have, then I will just have to see where it goes. I really do like her, and I've never felt this way about a woman before. I cannot believe that I had to travel across the universe to finally find the women who I'd fall for.

Just as I was approaching the palace, a flyer was landing near the drawbridge. With caution, I neared it. I'd been away for around three weeks, I couldn't have any idea what has been going on. When the flyer door opened, it brought a great big grin to my face as Vianna and Beautiful stepped out of it. Now that's what I call a proper welcome back. For some idiotic reason, a very cheesy line popped into my head, 'Honey, I'm home'

It was a nice welcome back and you could definitely tell that both Vianna and Beautiful really missed me, but the warm welcome didn't last long as I was quickly told to go and shower, as after three weeks in the jungle I stank. What do they expect? We all went into the palace; I went straight into my quarters and showered. Once refreshed, I was properly welcomed back by mine two beautiful ladies. We had a really good weekend and after being away from them for so many weeks, I realised how much Vianna and Beautiful actually meant to me. But all good things must come to an end, as they did have to return back home. But before they boarded the flyer, I pulled Vianna to the side to ask her for a favour.

'I actually have to go back into the jungle, I left something extremely essential there. I have to get it no matter what. Can I borrow my baby brother, Jihon, to help me? It'll be quicker with the both of us,' I pleaded with her.

Quite obviously, Vianna was not happy that I had to go away again, but agreed since she knew I'm too stubborn to reason with. Passionately, I gave her a long kiss and told her to tell Jihon to be here first thing in the morning, fully armed, as we're going deep into the jungle to get my stuff. Inquisitively, Vianna asked what I left behind that was so important, but I was very evasive and insisted that she must go home and get some rest.

Next morning, at 0700 hours, Jihon had arrived exactly as instructed: fully armed to his teeth at that. I showed him where we needed to fly to, explaining how once we arrived; we'd be trekking across the jungle in order to retrieve my 'stuff'. It took me a week to walk from the palace to the edge of the jungle, but in the flyer it took less than an hour. We disembarked from the flyer. After Jihon closed the flyer door and made sure it was secure, we proceeded to walk towards the jungle. But just before we entered, I made it absolutely clear that Jihon had to walk in my footsteps, otherwise Mum and Dad would kill me if I let anything happen to him. He laughed because I didn't even know his mum or dad. After finding the marker that would guide us into the right direction into the jungle, we began making our way to retrieve my things.

The journey towards the river was unexciting; maybe because I was following a track already known to me; it only took us a day and a half to get to this river. Although we still had plenty of daylight to cross the river, I decided against crossing it. Instead, I set up a small camp for us and even found the tall tree where I slept up high in it last time. Once we had our food, Jihon climbed up the tree while I set up beast traps below to give us extra protection while we slept. I also climbed up the tree, and once I got to Jihon, I tied two ropes to him: one around him, the other end secured to a branch higher up, and the other around the tree and Jihon. I really wanted him safe. When I was positive that Jihon and our belongings were safe, I joined Jihon on the neighbourly branch, secured my ropes, and stuck one of my headphones in his ear, and told him that the music would help him fall asleep. And wow! It didn't take him long to fall asleep at all. Lucky him. Unfortunately, I had to sleep lightly, as I always do when I'm in a hostile environment.

It was a very late hour, or even very early hours of the morning for that matter, when I suddenly awoke after a horrifying screams. Trees were being ripped out with their roots as other beasts began fleeing in terror from what I can only describe as a massive giant, and he was vicious. He was killing every animal he could get his hands on, stuffing them in his mouth while they were still alive. I quickly looked at Jihon and I could not believe that he was fast asleep. All that noise and he sleeps like a baby. Quickly, but discreetly, I woke him up, looked him straight in the face, pointing my finger at the massive giant and said, 'What the fuck is that?!'

Half asleep he took one look at the giant and immediately became very afraid. It wasn't just any fear that I saw in his face but a panic fear. He was visibly shaking. He swallowed hard and in a low shaking voice he said: 'James, this is very bad. That giant is called Garuga. We all thought that they were extinct.'

Pointing my finger at the Garuga I said, 'Does that look like they are extinct?'

'We have to be very quiet. The last time a Garuga entered one of the cities, it killed thousands. The military took heavy losses that day. Eventually, after two days, they managed to kill him, but by then the Garuga had already killed and eaten thousands.'

'Jihon, I understand that you are scared, but I need to know if there are any weak points.'

My baby brother informed me that the only weak point on the Garuga is its eyes, but coming near that is next to impossible between the two of us. Ignoring the latter part of his statement, I quickly got my crossbow out of my bergen and cocked it. This crossbow bolt can penetrate a brick wall or sheets of steel, but this time it will have to kill a Garuga, or Jihon and I are dead meat. I told Jihon to calm down and gave him a loaded flare gun.

'Point the flare gun at the Garuga's head then raise it four more times above his head and on my command, shoot.' He must do it or we are both dead.

'James, are you crazy?! We will give our position away,' Jihon exclaims worriedly.

'Jihon, look! See what the Garuga is doing? He is sniffing the air around. He already has our scent. It is just a matter of time before he gets us. Just do what I have told you and leave the rest up to me.' He nodded his head and I carefully took aim with my cocked crossbow.

I put my night vision goggles on, slowed my breathing and closed my eyes once I was ready and commanded Jihon to shoot the flare. It was still dark and the flare had not only given our position away, but also illuminated the night sky. Although I had my eyes closed I could hear the Garuga roar with fury. I heard the three loud footsteps getting closer. My instinct told me it was all right to open my eyes, so I did, and it was dark again, but the Garuga's eyes were like a homing beacon for me. I readjusted my aim and gently squeezed the crossbow trigger. The Garuga was just around four steps away from our tree, then it stopped and toppled backwards onto the ground below us. Clearly, I could see the crossbow bolt feathers sticking out of the now dead Garuga's eye. I took my night vision goggles off, and as I was about to store them away, along with my crossbow, into my bergen, I saw Jihon's face. He was looking at me with total admiration.

'When I was little it took over ten thousand soldiers and two days to kill a Garuga and you just did it with that little weapon of yours and in only one shot! No one ever could have done something like what you just did. I thank you for my life and for being my friend and big brother,' he blurted out, amazed.

I looked at Jihon and smiled and told him that he has no need to worry, I am not that easy to kill and I definitely am not anyone's or anything's supper. 'Go back to sleep baby brother, I will too after I put my things away.'

WHAT ARE THE CHANCES?

Since all that excitement it wasn't easy to fall asleep but eventually we did it.

When we had awoken, I climbed down first to get rid of all the traps that I'd set the previous evening. After that I made us some breakfast. While I was finishing preparing our food, I began thinking about how much I really hoped that what I had left behind was still there, otherwise it'd be embarrassing to come all the way here.

Before crossing the river, Jihon and I went to inspect the body of the dead Garuga. I climbed onto its corpse and pulled my crossbow bolt out of its eye. A slimy liquid began gushing out from where I pulled my bolt out from. And it did not smell good at all. Because of this, Jihon and I decided to promptly leave and approach the river instead. Carefully, I studied the surface of the water, looking out for the tell-tale signs that showed me where the zarks were. After a good ten or so minutes, I found the bubbles coming from underneath the surface, I gave Jihon one of my grenades and after a brief explanation of what they were and what to do, we threw them into the river and waited for them to detonate. The bodies of the dead zarks started to float up and form a type of bridge – probably not the most secure one, but it shall do. As soon as all of bodies were in place, Jihon and I ran across our zark bridge.

Soon after we neared the boundary of the jungle, I spotted my markers to let me know where we needed to go. Not much had happened over the past few hours, but I did make it to where I wanted to go in a shorter time now than the first time. It always amazed me that, for some reason, it always takes less time to travel to somewhere that you had already been, although I suppose that makes sense. Jihon was a little surprised when I told him to climb the boulders near the greenery because we had to wait. I was hoping that what I had left behind would show up, despite the arduous journey here, there was no guarantee. The things that I did leave behind last time are gone though – this is a good sign.

When both of us were in our hiding place, I finally told Jihon about how, the last time I was here, I saw a woman that looked like she really needed help. When I attempted to approach her, she couldn't understand me so she ran off. As the provisions I did leave were all gone, I assumed that she'd come here for fresh water from the stream in front of us. All we had to do was wait until she came, then Jihon could go and converse with her and ask if she needed help. Either way, we'd help her. Jihon's imagination ran wild at this news. He began coming up with all types of bizarre scenarios, but all he got off of me was, 'Just wait and see!' After all, I am his big brother and must keep his feet rained in, or in the case, his brain firmly on the ground so to speak.

Alas we were in luck, the lady in question didn't make us wait long. She appeared from the same directions as last time and went directly to the fresh water stream. After she had a drink from the stream, I asked Jihon to get down there and talk to her. He jumped down and approached the lady, who was busy filling empty drink bottles. He came up to her and plainly greeted her, the lady turned and as soon she did, my baby brother suddenly went pale – which was not easy for someone who had blue skin. I heard him shout, 'Ohh my faith! Your, Your Ma- Majesty! You are alive!' Immediately, he bowed down in respect.

WHAT ARE THE CHANCES?

I looked at her closely, and although she was dirty and malnourished, I could clearly see the resemblance. This woman is Vianna's mother, who was thought to be dead. At once, a tsunami of questions flowed into my head, but that will have to wait for now. Jihon looked up towards me and asked me to join them. Vianna's mother smiled when she saw me again, a glimpse of pure shock in her eyes that I had returned after two weeks. After a brief conversation Jihon told me that she is very grateful for leaving her those provisions. Quite clearly, I could see that the queen had a lot of questions as well, but I wanted to be back across the river before dark.

'I apologise, but Jihon, cut this short, let's go back before the suns go down,' I instruct.

CHAPTER 8

On the way back I took the lead and Jihon was at the rear, so we could protect the queen as best we could. This was and is still an extreme hostile environment and it was no place to drop our guard. When we finally got to the river, I smiled as the queen was still holding the bottles I'd left her with a tight grip. Honestly, what are the chances that I come from another planet, and somehow discover the queen is alive? Even I'm amazed at myself, to be honest. Jihon saw that the zark bridge was still there and moved towards it. But I sensed that things were not right. This is a river and the bridge has not moved. I told Jihon to stay away from it and keep the queen away from it too. I then took my bergen off and told him to wait, with the queen, while I get something.

About twenty minutes later I returned with an innocuous-looking beast, but the reaction of the queen told me that there was nothing innocuous about it. Jihon shouted a warning but when I came closer, he saw that I'd cut off both of the beast's arms.

Dragging the beast towards the stationary zark bridge, I shoved the beast onto it. Within seconds, the zarks became alive and ripped the beast apart. Jihon was shaken as he was ready to cross it.

'So, you still want to cross the bridge Jihon?' He shivered at the thought of that beast being him. 'Thought so. Anyway, we have to go down the river to see if there are more zarks under the water,' I explained.

Briefly, I took a subtle glimpse at the queen. From the way she was intently staring at me, I believe it's safe to say that she was most definitely observing me. Whether that was because she was curious about me or fearful towards me, I do not know. Either way, I pray that Jihon hasn't let it slip that Vianna and I are dating – I mean, why would he? Speaking of Jihon, I inquired about that beast that I had captured.

'It's called a fagan. They are really poisonous; from one scratch of its three-fingered claw it would have killed you.'

On the bright side, to my possible near death experience, I was thankful that my survival instincts looked like they were still top notch. When I initially saw the fagan, my gut feeling told me that I had to chop off its arms with my katana, so I did. Thank God, that was a life-changing decision.

Approximately thirty minutes later, I'd spotted the bubbles rising up to the surface of that water, revealing the location of the zarks. My baby brother asked Queen 'Yagi', which I assumed was her name, to stay behind while we approached the river. Jihon and I repeated the grenade ritual we did last time. Vianna's mother jumped in fright when the two underwater explosions threw vast amounts of water upwards and unto us. A few minutes had passed by and Queen Yagi saw the result as newly dead bodies of zarks started floating upwards.

As Jihon attempted explaining to Queen Yagi that we would be using the zarks as a bridge to cross the river, I just grabbed her,

What are the Chances?

lifted her in my arms and ran across to save us the time. Stunned, Jihon immediately followed me, but as he was almost completely across he slipped. Quickly, I put the queen down, but gently, and ran to him to grab him and prevent him from failing into certain death. After saving his life, again, I scolded him. 'Do you want your mother and father to kill me? Because that's what they'd do if I let him get killed.' The boy had a sheepish expression adorned across his face as he apologised for his life-threatening clumsiness.

Night was fast approaching, so I had to hurry both of them up so we could get back to our tree for the night. It took us almost an hour to get back and dusk was ascending. While I made up some boil-in-the-bag meals, the queen and Jihon were inspecting the dead Garuga. One thing that struck me was that its dead body was here, a massive quantity of meat for any beast to survive on for weeks, or even months, but not even one animal was there to tuck in. I suppose, even after death, the Garuga still terrified the beasts.

After dinner, Jihon and I helped Queen Yagi unceremoniously climb up the tree where we'd slept the night before. Wow! I touched, accidentally of course, the queen's backside to help her climb up, I haven't even done this to Vianna. I just might get told off when we get to our branches, but I don't care. That was a hefty experience. But I still had to set the traps before I could even contemplate going to sleep. Once I finished, I climbed up to where Jihon and Queen Yagi were. They seemed to be deep in conversation, so I checked all the safety ropes that they were secure and then found myself a branch to sleep on. I told them to keep their voices down then I stuck my headphones in my ears and went to sleep.

WHAT ARE THE CHANCES?

It was very early next day when Jihon gently shook me awake. I woke up straight away expecting trouble, but Jihon asked me if I would go down and get rid of the traps as Queen Yagi needed to go to the toilet. After I did just that, I started the fire to make our breakfast, then shouted up to let Jihon know that it is now safe to climb down. We got our gear down while Queen Yagi was using the vast toilet facilities. For breakfast I made us all porridge and I melted some chocolate in the centre so we could be fully energised for the journey out of the jungle. The queen and Jihon were bit reserved when they looked at their breakfast, but once they have tasted it, the chocolate did its job and they ate it all.

While I was up and ready to leave, I had to admit that I was slightly annoyed with Jihon and Queen Yagi as they insisted to take some photos of themselves with the dead Garuga. What the heck is this, a tourist trip?! After what felt like hours, I came up to them and told them that we are leaving now. My baby brother pouted at me, but I told them that I wasn't about to argue about it, so Jihon picked up his gear, and we stuck the queen between us and started back out of the jungle and towards the awaiting flyer and civilisation.

On the way back, we had come across plenty of Arkan Deaths. And with my newfound discovery, I used the sulphuric acid on them to destroy them again. This left Queen Yagi impressed. But as we began nearing our stop-for-the-night tree, a wave of uneasiness flowed through my body. My instincts were telling me that something bad was coming. As I started to turn my head to the side, I saw from the corner of my eye that my baby brother was about to step on a vine of the Arkan Death. I reached over the queen and pushed him back and pointed to the vine that his foot was going to step on. I could see the clearest image of relief splattered across his pale face as I bent down and squeezed some drops of the acid onto it. To our surprise, a large host of vines instantaneously disappeared from all around us. Cautiously, but quickly, we moved towards our new tree that we used before on the way here. Because it was already dark, we had to have cold food high up in the tree.

Once again, I ended up accidentally putting my hand on Queen Yagi's backside to aid her up the tree. I think that I might just have to go into hiding once we get back to safety – don't want her to put a bounty on my head or my hand in this case, or something like that, because I 'tried' to violate her. Surprisingly, she didn't actually complain; she did look at me with a knowing smirk. Crap! I wonder if Jihon will help me steal one of their spaceships to get off the planet before Queen Yagi has my hand chopped off.

We went to sleep without any further incidents and I was glad to shut my eyes as I sensed that Queen Yagi was looking at me to intently. When I closed my eyes, I started to think about returning to Vianna. Of course, admittedly, I'll be thrilled to see her again, but how am I going to explain this? 'Hi darling, here is your mother, oh by the way: I grabbed your mother's arse on two occasions.' I really can't see that going down well. And believe it or not, I was still thinking about my hand being chopped off when I woke up. That woman, no matter how powerless she looks right now in her dirty clothes, strikes endless fear and nerve in me.

WHAT ARE THE CHANCES?

For breakfast I made porridge again, it was fast and simple to make and I really wanted to get out of this jungle now. I wouldn't be able to withstand this tension between Vianna's mother and I for very much longer. Although, to my glorious luck, Queen Yagi and Jihon did not complain this was a very peaceful change that I very much did appreciate. I think I speak for all when I say that I think we all just wanted to be back in civilisation. Being in the jungle for so long messes with your head in multiple ways. Honestly, I have no idea how she survived for so long out here, and to be able to still function as much as she does, it's too good to be true. Miracles do happen, I guess.

As we continued on with our trek out of the jungle, I was able to get the thought of Queen Yagi making my hand go 'poof' out of my head since I was more concentrated and concerned for our safety. After a few hours, coming to the near exist out of this damn place, we heard the dreaded clicking noise. We were being stalked by a swarm of slinks. Queen Yagi became afraid, and rightly so. Jihon reminded me to keep them away since a scratch from their claws could induce instant paralysis. The Arkan weapons are more of the laser-type fusion kind of weapon, so they are relatively quiet. This meant that Jihon and Queen Yagi were not prepared for the noise and the brass empty cartages flying from my weapon after being fired. It looked like my weapons were more effective than the weapon Jihon uses because as I shot the slink, it stayed down, while his were able to get up and he had to shoot at them again.

After about fifteen minutes, the slink losses were heavy but they were still relentless from all directions. But as I was just about to reload my weapon, two slinks appeared, but they were different from the others, more colourful and much bigger and their claws were within reach of me. As their claws extended, without a moment's thought, I reached for my 'final-solution' weapon – as I called it. But it is more commonly known on my planet as a double-barrelled shotgun. If this doesn't stop you, then nothing will. Quickly, I aimed at the first slink's head and pulled the trigger. Its head basically disintegrated, so I aimed my last shot at the other slink's head and pulled the second trigger. When I fired, the same thing happened to that slink. The minute I obliterated those slinks, the fierce slink attacks came to halt and so did the clicking.

Jihon looked at me, shocked, obviously startled by the loud noise and damage dealt. 'What is this weapon you used? The slinks stopped their attacks and ran away. I've never seen this done before!'

I pointed to the two headless slinks and said, 'Amazing what happens when you blow somebody's head off their shoulders.'

'Thanks again, big brother. For you now, saving my life ... multiple times,' he says sheepishly. We then look at each other and laughed. No doubt he would've been a goner had I not been there. Then again, I did drag him into such a situation. Queen Yagi suddenly embraced me and kissed me straight on the lips. Well, that was a bit of a turn up. Looks like my arse-grabbing hand is safe.

Once we made sure that it was safe to carry on, we moved towards the direction of the flyer and salvation. While I was busy protecting the front, Queen Yagi and Jihon were in deep conversation again; it wasn't long before I could see the vast field where the flyer was waiting for us through the trees. Never have I ever felt so exhilarated to finally see that darn flyer again. Once we came out of the trees, it was there waiting for us, but me being careful as I always am, I instructed Jihon to tell Queen Yagi to stop and wait. As we did Jihon informed me that every time he spoke to me, the queen understood what he was saying as he was speaking Arkan to me. And my bracelet made it possible to understand him in my language. I didn't even consider this, but we didn't say anything bad. Good job!

As I was analysed the area surrounding the parked flyer, I saw two mappens circling around. When I looked a bit further out, I saw that there was an entire herd of them. This wasn't the time for stealth or direct confrontation. I knew very well that they were not easy to kill. What can I say, I'm experienced but unfortunately, I did not have my tank with me this time. I turned to Jihon and told him to take the queen and run towards the flyer without stopping, no matter what. Swiftly, Jihon executed my instructions before they broke into a sprint. As fast as I could, I rummaged through my bergen to get two shuriken. In order to use these, I had to get the mappen facing me first. Looks like I didn't have to wait long as the second mappens saw us, they began charging towards us. Overtaking Jihon and Queen Yagi, when the mappen were close enough, I threw myself onto my knees while still sliding and leaned back, throwing the shuriken with full force at each mappen's head. To my delight, they both dropped dead in mid stride.

I went to retrieve my shuriken. meanwhile Jihon opened the flyer doors before himself and the queen entered. Soon afterwards,

WHAT ARE THE CHANCES?

I joined them right before other mappens started charging towards the flyer. We took off just in time for the attacks to be harmless to the flyer. We were seated comfortably and looking forward to a long refreshing shower. I closed my eyes for a second, finally letting our trek into the jungle and back settle in. And boy was I tired. But the exploration was certainly something I needed, as a soldier, the adrenaline was thrilling.

Once I'd mustered up enough energy to get back on my feet again, I opened my eyes and looked at Jihon piloting the flyer. I noticed he was going in the completely opposite direction to the palace.

'What the heck are you doing?' I say, grabbing Jihon's shoulder gently but firmly.

'I'm flying us back to the capital, Ark, and to Vianna,' he replied innocently.

'I'm sorry but you're going to have to change the direction. Take us to my place first.'

'Why?'

'Jihon, my friend, this is Queen Yagi, Vianna's mother, that she has not seen for over eight years, and you want to take her looking like this,' I say pointing to her, 'back to the capital? Are you nuts?! Take her back to my place where she can clean up, refresh, and eat a decent hot meal and put one of the hundreds of dresses that she left in the palace before she disappeared. Then tomorrow after a decent sleep and a filling breakfast, then she can go back looking all regal to the capital. All right, my baby brother?' Jihon nodded and quickly translated what I said to the queen. To Jihon's relief, she also agreed with me.

What are the Chances?

But if I'm being honest, yes I am doing this for Queen Yagi, and Vianna, and Jihon. But truthfully, I wasn't prepared with the idea of me, an alien, waltzing into a brand new civilisation just like that. Especially not after I'd just spent weeks in the jungle. All I needed was some decent shut eye, so that's what I was going to get.

CHAPTER 9

Jihon had landed the flyer, and I awoke from a short nap. Together, we exited the flyer and walked the queen towards my home ... well ... her home. She looked up and down the large white sheet that acted as a barrier for my home, perplexed.

'Place your thumb on this device,' I say to the queen, pointing to it, 'your thumbprint will allow you to pass through.'

After Jihon translated my instructions, the queen did just that, and with that, we were all able to enter the palace grounds. As we walked through the courtyard, the queen's eyes began welling up. I suppose returning back to your home, well one of your homes, has to be overwhelming. She probably missed this place a lot, missed the comfort of salvation. Poor woman must be somewhat traumatised. Queen Yagi covered her mouth with her hands in shock as she looked in the corner of the courtyard that my tank was parked in.

She pointed at it, exclaiming something that was most likely on the lines of 'what is that?!' I laughed a little bit at her reaction. Surprisingly, I still tend to forget that this isn't Earth and they are certainly not used to this Earth stuff. Jihon then explains that it's a type of weapon from my home planet. 'I don't know how it works, but James assures me that it is very powerful,' Jihon explains.

What are the Chances?

After the queen finally brushed off the surprise, we continued on inside the palace. I asked Jihon to give me his bracelet to hand it to the queen, I wanted to be able to talk to her directly. My baby brother took his off and lent it to her. She flinched slightly at first, not knowing what it was, but then again, that's understandable.

'I'm sorry, Your Majesty, the bedroom that was yours, I use it now. But not tonight. I'll sleep in the throne room, you sleep in your own bed, I'm sure you miss it. But if you want to use the shower, I only have toiletries from my planet. I hope you're all right to use them. The blue and white bottles are for your hair, and the black ones for your body. There's already a fresh towel in there.' I hope I didn't miss out anything.

Jihon glared at me dumbfounded. I suppose he hasn't heard me speak English for a very long time, it must be very strange.

'That is very gracious of you, thank you,' the queen thanked. 'I must admit I am very much looking forward to this shower, it's going to be the best shower in Arka. I have eight whole years' worth of dirt to wash off. It'll certainly be a delight.' For someone that has been lost in the jungle for many years, she still retains her regal mannerisms.

'Right I'll leave you to it. Jihon, you can have your bracelet back,' I say, implying that she should take it off and return it back to him. Although a minute glimpse in her eye told me that she was reluctant to do so.

The queen departed to have her shower, with Jihon, so I made my way to another one of the many showers in the palace. As the hot water trickled down my body, washing away two weeks' worth of sweat and dirt, I started thinking about those things we fought back there. I've never come across such creatures before – not that worked like that, no. Jihon is the closest to an Arkan encyclopaedia that I'll have right now, best off asking him later.

Once I wrapped my shower up, I made my way to the kitchen to make us a decent meal. Don't get me wrong, boil-in-the-bag meals aren't bad at all, but nothing beats a home-cooked meal. After plating up our steak and chips, I put each plate on the table and called for Jihon and the queen to come to the dining room. I was hoping they could hear me from the sitting room; sometimes living in a big palace is a huge disadvantage.

Momentarily, both of them walked into the dining room together. Their once tired, dark-circle ridden faces now glowed up at the impeccable aroma of piping hot steak and chips. They both hurried around to their plates and sat down. Without hesitation, the queen dug straight into her meal. Honestly, it was quite frightening to see how she ripped the steak apart and devoured it the way she did. Although, I guess this is officially her first real meal in eight years. Still wonder how she survived as long as she did. But right now, I'm more so surprised that she didn't double-take the foreign food in front of her. After chewing her food ravenously and swallowing, she slowly looked up to see our shocked expressions. Shortly, she raised an eyebrow before she looked down at herself and realised her stuffed mouth was incongruous to her regal status. She blushed a fair bit out of embarrassment and said something.

'She said she apologises for her non-ladylike behaviours. In the jungle, she had to eat all sorts of things, this felt no different.'

What are the Chances?

'Tell her it's all right, I hope she enjoys the meal,' I ask. Jihon did just that, and the queen shyly but gratefully smiled.

The queen started bombarding me with a tsunami of questions. 'I hope he doesn't feel I'm ungrateful, but what is he doing here, on Arka?'

'You know what I'm doing here, Jihon. Just tell her what I told you, science spat me out, that's the truth.' Jihon turned to the queen and answered all the questions that he could.

After her questions, I then raised some of mine, but directed to Jihon. 'You know those slinks we encountered as we were exiting the jungle, the two that I blew the heads off of, how come they looked different to the others?'

'Each swarm contains two alphas, you just happened to kill them both.'

'So what you're telling me is that, you kill the alphas, the rest stop attacking?'

Jihon looked like he's about to disagree but frowns before his eyes widen in realisation. 'You know what, you might just be right. But on a side note big brother—' Queen Yagi let out a surprised exclamation, with a gobsmacked face, interrupting Jihon. Jihon says something to her to make her calm down a little.

'Queen Yagi was confused about how I addressed you,' he laughs. 'But James, can I have one of those weapons?' He must mean the shotgun.

'Baby brother, if I had a spare one, I would give it to you. But I wouldn't even know where to start to make one of them,' I chuckle. His face falls slightly in childish disappointment. 'I know how to use them, but I definitely don't know how to make them.' I explained to Jihon that I called the shotgun the 'Final Solution', once you shoot that at someone in close range, there are no arguments. 'Right ... let's celebrate!'

I walked over to the drinks cabinet and pulled out a bottle of champagne. After I poured each of us a glass of champagne, Jihon asks me what it was. 'It's like a sparkling wine that we use to celebrate on my planet. And we definitely have to, for Vianna's mother's return.'

I made a toast, to the safe return of Vianna's mother. Simultaneously, they both took a big gulp of the champagne. Quite obviously, neither of them were used to the fizzy alcohol as the bubbles went into their nose right up to their eyes. They both gasped for air in fright, squinting their eyes. These two are like little kids; even have to show them how to drink. I'm not so sure I should be giving children alcohol.

To sum the evening up, Jihon got sloshed, and Queen Yagi fell asleep so I had to carry her to her bed for the night. I went back down the stairs, so put Jihon in another bedroom. As for myself, I crashed on one of the sofas. After a filling breakfast, Queen Yagi and Jihon left in the flyer heading for the capital Ark and Vianna. Honestly, I was a little disappointed that I couldn't be there to see everyone's faces when they saw Queen Yagi. On the other hand, I'd rather stay unobtrusive, but not just from Arka's people this time, Vianna too. Who knows what she'll do to me when she finds out that I made the last eight years of her grieving over her mother somewhat pointless.

CHAPTER 9.5

It had been a while since I boarded the flyer with Jihon. I have no idea how long we'd been flying in silence, or how much longer that would take honestly. I decided that since I was deprived of any social interaction for quite some time, I should make the most out of it.

'Who are you exactly?' I ask Jihon. Honestly, this isn't the most pressing question I wanted to ask, but I figured I should build up to it.

'I'm the son of the Baron and Baroness Rak. I'm under royal command, to Queen Vianna, your daughter,' he replies.

I can understand why she chose him; he is very concise and precise with his job. Good to know my daughter has an eye for competency, as a queen should. I really do wonder why James wouldn't come with us though. 'Well, Captain Jihon,' I say motioning towards his insignia, 'is there anything going on between Vianna and James?'

Jihon was rather taken aback by my question, which I understand, but leaves me even more curious as to the peculiar reaction. I could tell he didn't want to answer this question directly and instead answered proudly with, 'My apologies, Your Majesty, but it is not my story to tell.'

What are the Chances?

He should be relieved I didn't feel like pushing it with any further questions; I suppose it'd be easier to accept his avoidance of the topic as there seemed to be a good enough reason behind it. Although, I could tell Jihon could see I somehow figured something out through just the few broken conversations between James and himself, which is indeed correct. From the short period I was able to fluently communicate with James, I noticed that he talked about Vianna in a very endearing way, not to mention the complete elimination of the appropriate honorific. However, I think it's too early to assume anything. But for now, I asked him to fill me in on absolutely everything that has happened regarding Vianna and the capital.

It was late morning when Jihon had landed the flyer at the palace pad. The smell of the city air was so different to that of the humid jungle. But I did have to admit, the nerves were finally setting in. I'm not usually the type to get nerves, but I am now somehow. As I flicked my hair to the side, the strong fruity scent of James' shampoo I used calmed me down.

A tsunami of nostalgia washed over me as I took in my surroundings. How can things look so familiar but be so different? The capital has definitely changed, or well, evolved more like. Vianna has definitely kept this place in check. This was one of the busiest times for everyone at the palace; Vianna was holding audiences with various functionaries, the palace hallway throne room were full. Jihon had already decided to lead the way. Since he was under royal command, no petty functionary would even attempt to get in his way and he wanted to really surprise Vianna.

What are the Chances?

Queen Vianna, planet Arka's sole ruler, had a hefty schedule this morning. Oh, the wonders of being queen. I must admit I was quite the strange one; I actually loved the overwhelming number of duties I had to carry out as queen. I had to live up to the title after all; I am not one easy to crack under pressure. But I can only speak for myself, since I haven't been close by to see Vianna grow up sadly. Jihon told me that she was in fact married to a man called Gah, who was a terrible ruler and husband, Vianna even has a child – I have a granddaughter. Unfortunately, Gah was more interested in being a king rather than being a good husband and a father. He even turned against his own family. He's lucky he's dead, otherwise I would have killed him myself. And now, there's a war going on between the Zolgs and the Arkans. The Zolgs have an impenetrable fortress and the Morrins and Alphians are our allies providing protection in orbit and prevent any Zolg ships from landing. I remember Jihon's smirk as he told me that the whole of Arka actually celebrated when they found Gah dead.

As we entered the palace, I became increasingly nervous. I grabbed a strand of my hair, smelling the shampoo that calmed me down. Vianna was in deep conversation, dealing with the generals and the overseers who represent her government. As I neared the doorway to the throne room, more and more people started to recognise me. This concocted commotion, commotion disrupting enough to catch Vianna's attention. Since I couldn't see her because Jihon was stood in front of me, I heard her say, 'What's happening?' Those who recognised me immediately bowed down. Chamberlain Vern, who I remember very well, even began crying.

WHAT ARE THE CHANCES?

The entire throne room became silent. 'Captain Jihon, what's going on?' Vianna inquires. For a second, Jihon fidgets around a little, as if trying to contain himself of his excitement. After some time, he steps to the side to reveal me. I wasn't entirely sure what I should say, or whether I should say anything at all, so I just smiled and opened up my arms.

'Your Majesty, what was lost has been found!' Jihon exclaims. It looked as if she hesitated for a second before shaking it off and running straight into my arms. We both spun around in a deep hug, embracing each other closely. She really has grown up. It felt completely surreal to be in her embrace again. As the former queen, I had to persevere through the jungle, and quite honestly, I hadn't even realised a year had gone by, let alone eight – I certainly lost track of time. While I did not lose hope, I didn't expect to return to civilisation. Even I'm surprised I managed to survive the jungle and its dangers.. But now I was back here, safe, and with my daughter, in civilisation. Despite missing many significant events in her life, I hope that I can witness my daughter still reign as a remarkable ruler. In addition to all of this though, I cannot help but feel a greatly suppressed curiosity waiting to explode with questions about James – and his involvement with Vianna.

It seems I really was the life of the party; suddenly everyone was overjoyed by my return to life. Even High Prefect Baka, the second most influential person, after me of course, ran into the throne room in response to promptly hearing of my return and began crying in joy.

Eventually, Vianna pulled away her tear-smeared face to

thank Jihon aloud for bringing me back to my child. Although, Jihon was too busy recording the events so James could see how overwhelmed with happiness Vianna was.

While I did like Jihon, I had to step in and tell her whose doing this really was. Casually, I sauntered to her and whispered in her ear, 'It's your love, James, who found me.' Surprisingly, Vianna did not even cast a second thought to my remark about her and James' relationship. Her eyes just lit up, as if something finally made sense to her, but now didn't seem like the best time to pry.

'I'm glad you know, as I intend to marry James. He is more of a man than any other on this planet. He loves me and my daughter, your granddaughter, Olnia,' she says as if she was trying to convince me that he was worthy enough. I simply just smiled at her, implying that it's possibly better to talk about this later.

I then announced to everyone in the throne room that for his exceptional bravery and selfless duty Captain Jihon is therefore promoted to a rank of commander with immediate effect.

*   *   *

High Prefect Baka had escorted me to my Herc's grave. The room was circular, the walls made of stone, with a gap in the roof allowing sunlight to pass through. Like a mausoleum incorporated with nature. Moss and other greenery had grown on the walls and around his stone tomb. Next to his stone tomb was mine, although no body was clearly in it. Unlike a normal mausoleum, this space had a tranquil ambience, as if the walls enforced an impenetrable barrier to threat. This place really did remind me of Herc. Although he was dead for almost nine years, I still miss him dearly. He was a great ruler as king, nothing like this so-called King Gah Jihon had told me about. What this planet needs, what Arka really needs, is a worthy king, just like Herc. Baka and I stood there in silence; we didn't talk at all but still knew what each other was thinking. We were both reminiscing about the good old days before I decided to break the silence.

'What would you do if I told you that it wasn't Commander Jihon that found me, but rather an alien from a planet called Earth. His skin is white, unlike ours. But I assure you, Vianna and Olnia are in love with him?'

Baka was taken by surprise, which didn't shock me at all. Instead of losing his composure, he calmly asked to hear more about this white alien called James. We had been close friends for many many years, and nothing has changed now, I trust him. I told him everything that I knew, but shortly suggested that we should return to the palace as Vianna, being so close with him, would know far more about him than me.

CHAPTER 10

I really miss James. Honestly, I wished that he wouldn't just risk his life the way he did. He truly is a very gallant soul, in a way I do admire him. As queen I should be able to live independently, but for some reason, I feel quite dependent on James. Although the primary reason for this is unknown to me, it still does not change the fact that I do miss him. I spent all of last night thinking about him, not knowing whether he is safe and alive right now is driving me undeniably insane. Today I was going to officially announce that I was in a relationship, and also announce that he was from another planet. I have no idea how my people will react to being reigned by a foreign king. Gah's reign definitely has traumatised most of the civilians, so it's important I reassure them that James is nothing like Gah – I know for sure. He has potential, even if he says he wants to keep his presence completely secret from my people for the rest of his life. I can't let him do that. As selfish as that sounds, I do not want that at all.

To add to the anxiety of making such an announcement, I was delayed of making it, raising my anxiety through the roof. The overseers were trying to exert more power again.

'Unlucky Gah is dead,' I say bluntly as an attempt to leave the conversation. But obviously that did not work.

WHAT ARE THE CHANCES?

As I was in deep conversation with them, I heard several gasps and yells coming from the doorway to the throne room. Some people dropped straight to their knees, foreheads touching the ground as they bow, as whimpers of crying filled the room. Even Chamberlain Vern was doing the same. Naturally I was confused, bowing was only reserved for the queen and king, and I was standing here. Intently, I looked in the direction of the doorway about to say something about the commotion until Captain Jihon appeared. He was still dressed in his jungle fatigues and under arms. He seemed to be containing his excitement as he attempted to obviously fight back a smile. I was about to raise my voice demanding to know what he was doing until he gave me an odd look as he stepped aside. It felt as if time slowed down, like in one those movie-thingies James watches from Earth. Completely paralysed with shock, I stared straight at the reason why everyone was bowing. I could not believe my eyes, I just could not. Right in front of me was my mother, who I thought was dead for close to nine years now. She can't be real, but she is? Has missing James finally turned me mad? Am I seeing things?!

'Your Majesty, what was lost has been found!' Jihon exclaims. For a second, my heart skipped a beat. Why those words specifically? Sania vision, she was indeed correct. I didn't think I'd be this happy to have the lost returned back to me; I feel like I'm mentally underprepared for such a situation.

After taking a few moments for hesitation, I launched myself at my mother, swiftly embracing her and weeping from the floods of joy filling my body. Momentarily, we pulled away from each other.

What are the Chances?

I didn't want to but I wanted to see her face. With watery eyes, I stared right into hers, fully embracing her presence. Publicly, I announce my gratitude towards Jihon's accomplishment, but deep down, I felt like James was positively behind this. Not to mention the powerful smell of that fruity shampoo James lets me use sometimes. My mother came up to me to whisper into my ear, 'It's your love, James, who found me.'

My question is now answered then, it was as if she read my mind. To be honest, I'm not at all surprised she managed to figure out our relationship. From the stories I heard about her growing up, she was a very intelligent woman. But I do hope she approves of us, for all I know, she could detest him or want to steal him! 'I'm glad you know, as I intend to marry James. He is more of a man than any other on this planet and he loves me and my daughter, your granddaughter Olnia.'

I tried to convince her that he was a good man, but I feel as though the conversation needed to fully do that would have to be much longer and in private. She merely smiled at me, notifying me that we should indeed do it in private. 'So when can I meet my granddaughter?' I suggested that when it was time to pick Olnia from school, she should accompany me.

My mother simply nodded and turned to General Mass, 'From this moment on, as queen, Captain Jihon is now promoted to the rank of commander,' she commanded. The general responded immediately by announcing to everyone present that is was now the new appointed Commander Jihon under royal command. Jihon's eyes widened at his achievement, he should be proud, and I am certain James will be too – since he is the same rank.

Jihon's parents, Baron and Baroness Rak, had just arrived at the palace after hearing Queen Yagi was back, entering the throne room at the exact moment of Jihon's promotion to commander. I made my way to him and quietly asked him if James found whatever it was that he had left behind. 'Yes! It was your mother.' He smiled.

He went through all of that effort, risking his life, for some stranger that he didn't even know. What are the chances that he rescues my mother and a queen at that? He truly is a brave soul, a great man. I say without any hesitation, 'And that is why I love him so much!'

After all of the greetings and well-wishers were finished with my mother, I informed her that it was time to retrieve Olnia from school. I wonder how Olnia is going to react, or feel. She has never met her grandmother, I am her only family. Well I was, but she seems very keen on the idea of James being her father, and now she has a grandmother. I am positive that she'll be exhilarated to meet her.

When we arrived at her school, everyone waiting for their kids kept staring and bowing to us both, I assume mainly to my mother. We were both so lost in the commotion we had created, we didn't even notice Olnia running up to me. With rapid reflexes, I manage to catch her in my arms and spin her around. After engaging in a tight hug, I introduced her to her grandmother. To say the least, Olnia was indeed overjoyed. My mother picked her granddaughter up, calling her beautiful, and holding her firmly in her arms. Of course Olnia, being the curious little child she is, wanted to know anything and everything about why Yagi was away from us for so long. When it came to light that James had seen my mother in the jungle two weeks ago, Olnia exclaimed, 'That is why my real daddy, James, is so amazing!' She innocently smiled.

'Hah, what a delusional child ...' I nervously laugh, 'You see, Olnia is very over-imaginative,' I stutter. As much as I did try to hide it though, I do wish that would happen. I wouldn't mind getting married to that man. But I didn't need my daughter embarrassingly exposing my life like that, I can't control the flustered expression on my face. 'But yes, we both do love him very much. This is one of the several reasons.'

Olnia proceeded to whisper to her grandmother, telling her to keep her hero a secret as people might not like that he is white and not blue like them. My mother assured both of us, primarily me, that everything would be all right as her lips were sealed.

Later on that day, the evening was full of celebrations. So much for making my big announcement today about James, I suppose that is going to have to wait yet another day. I really do wish James could have been here. I'm relieved that he got home safely though, very few make it out of the jungle. Needless to say, I am impressed.

*   *   *

The celebrations yesterday left me very tired today, but I didn't want to miss the opportunity to talk with Sania again as I'd been busy lately with preparing for my announcement. We were having a quiet conversation as my mother entered the throne room. She whispered to me, informing me that she had told Baka and that we needed to talk privately. Obviously, I agreed immediately but told her that Sania does in fact know everything so she will also be joining us.

Before we entered the queen's private office, I informed Chamberlain Vern that everyone here will be indisposed until further notice and we are to not be disturbed under any circumstance. He simply nodded without any further questions.

Once we were comfortably seated, my mother was just about to speak before I held my hand out to interrupt her. 'Before we begin discussing anything, Sania had a vision I want her to recall for you,' I state, turning my head in Sania's direction.

Sania looked at me and nodded before she moved into her seer state. As usual, her eyes lit up like two blazing blue topazes as she recalled her vision. 'A warrior, from the stars, will come. From tragedy, there will come happiness. What once was lost will be found. The warrior from the stars will end the war, and send the occupying force home. He will take a queen and her child as his own. And the people will love and call him "The White Arkan King".'

Once she finished reciting the vision, High Prefect Baka was the one to speak first. 'Seer Sania's vision does not leave anything to misinterpretation.' I smiled as Uncle Baka asked when he could meet the future king of Arka.

With this, he definitely caught my mother off guard, but she had to admit that fate had taken hand in her being reunited back with me, and she was overwhelmed with happiness about it. I mean, James is very handsome – not that I'm biased or anything – even if he did grab her arse on a few occasions when they were climbing a tree in the jungle. Having my mum back is great and all, but there are just some things I don't want to know.

'What was lost will be found. That is me as I understand it,' my mother says.

We exchanged warm smiles and I embraced her lovingly. 'Yes, that was you, Mum. Now you understand why I momentarily hesitated when you came back. Jihon had used those exact words even though he has not heard Sania's vision.'

After a while of informing Baka about everything and forming a plan for the future, we decided that we all, including Commander Jihon, were going to pay a visit to see James tomorrow, after Olnia was taken to school.

The next day felt very unusual. This was the first time a high ranking officer of my own government would be meeting James. The only thing that gave me confidence was that my mother seemed to really like James, so it was next to perfect. The nerves still stirred up butterflies in my stomach, but I was still excited. And when I say I ran back to the palace, with my mother, after dropping Olnia off to school, it would not even be an exaggeration in the slightest. I really wanted nothing more than to see James and thank him properly for finding and returning my mother back to me where she belonged. And by the time we did arrive back to the palace, everyone was there and ready to go.

*   *   *

WHAT ARE THE CHANCES?

After the flyer had landed, we all rushed the leave the flyer in desperate eagerness. During the whole flight, it was like a competition to see who was more excited than the other. Other than that, I gave Uncle Baka and my mother their own bracelets and explained that this would help them communicate with James themselves. My mother already seemed quite familiar with the bracelet; she most likely had to borrow Jihon's at one point then. Once we eventually managed to exit the flyer, in a not-so-orderly fashion, Jihon, Sania, and I were puzzled as it didn't seem that James was at the palace. Jihon suggested that he may be at the beach so he ran off to try and retrieve James. I was about to walk into the palace courtyard until I remembered that James probably only have my mother a temporary pass through the barrier, and Uncle Baka definitely would not have one.

It was a little while before Jihon finally returned with James. Surprise surprise, of course he was fishing at the beach again. He had two ginormous fish in each hand; he does certainly have a talent for catching fish. Well, now that he's gotten out of the habit of catching poisonous fish. The general rule is, the pretty fish are most likely poisonous, and the ugliest ones are the tastiest.

I ran up to him to give him a hug, but the increasingly powerful stench of fish and sweat made me hesitate for a second. He laughed at my slightly grossed out facial expression and waved the fish in front of me, saying we can hug later. I pouted, but complied, I didn't want any fish slime on me. James then glanced over at the other guests that he had. He smiled at all of them until he saw Baka. He didn't exactly frown but he didn't exactly smile. Instead, he noticed Baka's insignia that told James that he was of a high rank of office. He peered at me a little worried, but I gave him a reassuring glance.

'Right, well, this way,' he says and casually uses the fish to point in the direction of the palace.

After going through the procedure with Baka and my mother to allow them to pass through the barrier permanently, we all entered the palace. James had asked Jihon and I to entertain everyone while he went to tend to his freshly-caught fish and get some food cooked for his unexpected guests. And Jihon and I did keep everyone occupied until James entered the throne room.

Suddenly, Sania blurted out the millisecond she had seen James, 'James! May I have a cup of hot chocolate?'

These darn fools. My mother and Baka gave out confused expressions, one of them inquiring about what such a thing was and if they could have some too. Once again, I repeat, these darn fools. James is going to make them sing and dance first before he'd even entertain making any cups of hot chocolate. As expected, he turned towards Baka and Yagi, explaining the 'ritualistic' motions they had to do in order to commence their initiation to consume such a drink. However, to our sweet surprise, without hesitation, my mother began dancing. I assume as a queen, she had to have done worse things than this, but this really does take a toll on the dignity when you know it's all a sham – of course, I'm not going to spoil James' little game, it is rather entertaining. Naturally, Baka did not want to be left out or considered disrespectful, so he too joined in and began singing, and he had a very pleasant voice.

What are the Chances?

As their initiation was complete, James made them a cup of hot chocolate, as well as the rest of us. Once my mother and Uncle Baka had their first sip of hot chocolate, we were met by their expression of a visual 'wow' moment as both of them made a joyful sound as their lips stuck to drinking the sweet beverage out of the cup.

As we all gathered and sat around the table, drinking our hot chocolate and eating the meal James had prepared for us all, Baka and Yagi bombarded James with questions of how he got here and so on. Baka was astonished when James filled him in on everything. I mean, I can't blame his shock and slight disbelief, it would've taken me a while to trust him too had it not been for Sania's vision providing me with advantageous insight. Baka sought for a better explanation from James, other than science spitting him out onto Arka, so James challenged him to come up with a better one. Though it had to have been difficult as there was no spaceship, and that simply was the truth. As expected, Baka, holding an extremely high rank of office, interrogated James with floods of questions, as if he were interviewing him for some sort of a position, or something like that.

Luckily, everyone enjoyed the Earth meal James had made for them. Baka and Yagi even had a second plate each. I'm not going to completely assume anything yet, but tonight has led me to believe that Uncle Baka and my mum do approve of James, and no thought makes me happier. Maybe soon, with any luck, I can introduce James to civilisation.

It was getting late so everyone decided that it was time to return back to the capital. I informed them that they'll be returning without me. I hadn't even gotten the chance to hug James and thank him and tell him how much I had missed him yet. Politely, I asked my mother to pick up Olnia from school so I could spend a little bit of time with my love.

Once everyone had left, I ran into James' arms and hugged him. 'I love you so so much, and I could never live without you, you know that right?' He nodded and smiled. 'And thank you ever so much for returning my mother back to me, how can I repay you?'

'I am very flattered, but I must admit, for the first time in my life, I am happy. I want to be with both you and Olnia forever, I'd do anything to protect you two. Just be there, that's how you can repay me.'

CHAPTER 11

During these past two months, Vianna and Olnia had been spending all their free time with me at my place. The circle of people who knew about me had increased by one, High Prefect Baka's wife, Seline. In fact, my friendships with everyone had grown so much that almost every ferga they would all come over and stay at my place.

Now I'm no sociologist, but from recent observations, Queen Yagi has already begun treating me like her son-in-law. But if I'm being honest, I actually don't have a problem with it; it's nice to have that essence of family again. I just love Vianna a lot and want her family to love me too.

Today was the first of September back on Earth, and in sixteen days, it'll be my thirty-fourth birthday. Luckily, it lands just nicely on a weekend where everyone would be coming over. Vianna, Beautiful, Yagi, Baka, Seline, Jihon and Sania were all going to come and stay at my place. After making a special meal for all of them, then I was going to announce that it was my birthday. This means I have to go all out to create delicious food from Earth in order to celebrate properly. I'm not quite sure what made me want to celebrate this much, I just wanted to. Maybe it's because it's the first time I've really felt like I had a life. I have friends, who I class almost like family, and a beautiful girlfriend with her amazing daughter. Back on Earth, I was not living, my identity was hidden, I had no life. But now I do. And that is something I need to celebrate.

Call me a child but I was extremely excited for this celebration. My last birthday, I vividly remember sitting in my quarters, a sad mini cupcake with a used limp candle struck through the centre on my desk, that I blew out wishing myself a happy birthday alone. I suppose I could have celebrated with friends, like Andy, or even George at that, but honestly, that would have made the whole celebration more depressing. I wish I could say that this only happened once, but countless birthdays were like this and some of them were even not in my timeline. I genuinely cannot recall what a proper celebration feels like. But now, I have everything I could possibly want. You're delusional if you think I don't want a big fat Victoria sponge completely smothered in diabetic buttercream for my birthday.

Ferga had finally come, but no one was here. It was already the afternoon of Agra, they usually come in the morning. As disheartened as I was, I'm sure they'd come. My birthday fell on the third day of ferga so I wasn't too disappointed. Luckily, Arka has a three-day long ferga – it is much better than Earth's two-day long weekend.

The evening of Sara had come around the next day, and there still wasn't anyone arriving. If they decided not to come over and stay this weekend, I am really damn unfortunate. I laughed at my supposed 'misfortunate' wryly but kept my chin up. It's a real shame I have no way of contacting anyone.

It was finally the night of Sura, the third and final day of ferga. Still no one. What a weekend to miss, trust my luck. I couldn't even lie, I was encumbered by an overwhelming feeling of sadness and bitter disappointment. It sounds immature and selfish, but I really did miss them all, and I was really looking forward to today. In such instances, I would usually do something that would relax me, my favourite hobby, cooking. I took a brief moment to decide what I wanted for my birthday dinner. Never mind, skip the dinner; I want a big fat Victoria sponge completely smothered in diabetic buttercream.

Two days had passed and Tagra had now come around. Worry began to settle in as I had heard from no one for over a week now. A time like this has made me realise how inconvenient it is to be living so far away from civilisation. At the very least, there has to be some way we can communicate. For all I know, they could be dead, or just too busy, or not be interested anymore. I'm a man who likes clarity. Though, the lack of knowledge is definitely worrying me. Unfortunately, all that I can do is simply wait. All sorts of thoughts were running through my head, but I knew I had to be patient.

*　　*　　*

'Queen Yagi had sent me to get you,' Jihon wheezes to me as he crouched in exhaustion from running here. I gave him a very confused look not understanding why he was so worried and why the sudden appearance after not seeing any of them for many days. 'James … Princess Olnia, Beautiful, has been kidnapped by the Zolgs and taken to their fortress.'

My heart skipped a beat as the shock of such news pummelled me. I've never encountered the Zolgs, but I know that Arka is at war with them and that's enough information to tell me they're the enemy. Suddenly, my anxiety heightened even more as I remembered Jihon telling me that the last time the Arkans attempted to storm the Zolg fortress, over 100,000 Arkans died with no success. I can't see more people die, even if they're not my people.

After I had overcome as much of the shock as I could, I came back to my senses. Looking at the state Jihon was in, I told him to lie down and rest. He was puzzled by my reaction, but I could tell he needed the rest. After all, he had been on his feet for the past three days, tracking the Zolgs to where they have taken my Beautiful.

As soon as Jihon fell asleep, I got all my equipment ready for tonight's sortie into the Zolg's fortress. And just in case, I'll bring plastic explosives with me from Earth. I am grateful I had brought all of this obscure stuff with me before I left Earth. If I remembered correctly though, Jihon told me a while back that the fortress is surrounded by four deadly towers that stood at each corner of the Zolg's fortress. If I am going to get anywhere, doing some permanent damage to these towers would give me a strong advantage, not to mention it's a brilliant distraction. Even if Jihon and the rest of the Arkans believe this fortress is impenetrable, I just don't believe it. There is always a way in. I just need the Zolgs to have their guard down while I figure out the way in.

Looking in the mirror, as I'd put my gear on, with the extra weight of the explosive, I looked like a black or very dirty snowman. Everything was now ready, so I decided to get some shut eye before we took off. It would be sort of inconvenient if I fell asleep half way through sneaking around the fortress.

I had woken up long before it was dark, so I waited until the sun went down before waking Jihon up. Shortly after, I made both of us a quick snack before I told Jihon to take me to the fortress perimeter.

Once we had eaten, we gathered our things without hesitation, and hurriedly proceeded on our way to the flyer. While we flew directly to the fortress, I asked Jihon to tell me everything he knew.

Capital Ark was in uproar since the Zolgs somehow managed to kidnap Beautiful from her school in broad daylight. How is that possible? Poor Vianna. Apparently she was in an inconsolable state, she couldn't even think straight. I can't imagine the state of worry she must be in right now. High Prefect Baka did have all of the Prefect Corps looking all over the capital for Olnia, until Jihon had discovered and reported her location. The Zolg fortress is probably surrounded by Arkans by now. Evidently, that means I have to remain undetected from them too to avoid additional trouble.

Midway through the flight, Jihon asked for my bracelet and appeared to add something to this fancy-looking gadget. When he gave it back to me, he informed that he added an update that allowed me to understand the Zolg's language. Smart thinking, Jihon. My head was so clouded by the shock and worry about Beautiful that my head began rushing over important details such as this. But now, by understanding the Zolgs, I'll be able to gather any essential intel that may aid me, maybe not now, but even in future instances. He is not just my baby brother, but a very good friend.

As we flew towards the Zolg fortress, I began putting green and black camouflage paint on my face; Jihon looked at me blatantly confused.

'My white skin will stick out like a sore thumb in the dark, plus I don't want to capture the attention of the Arkan troops either,' I explained. Jihon nodded in understanding. On top that, I really couldn't afford to be wasting time to explain myself instead of helping Beautiful; it's better to be inconspicuous.

Momentarily, Jihon wisely decided to land the flyer away from the Arkan troops. As we exited the flyer, I asked Jihon to keep the Arkan troops away from me and let me do what I do best. And as an afterthought, I told him to tell his troops not to get all excited when they see the luminous green marker I'm going to put down. I need it so I know where to retrace my steps after.

Once we had exchanged final nods of understanding, Jihon left immediately. At last glance, he was talking to, what I presume, were officers, hopefully to tell them to leave me alone.

After some time observing the surroundings, I squatted down and drew a map into the ground. With this, I used some quick mathematics to work out a potential blind spot for the two fortress towers that were facing me. Putting on my night vision goggles, I left my green marker and before I knew it, I was standing by the fortress wall completely undetected. Now it was time to a find a discreet entry point into the fortress. Failing that, I suppose I would have to use the grappling hook and start climbing – which was even riskier. I really did not want to do it that way; it would mean that I'd have to kill a lot of Zolgs once I get up there.

Following my rounding off of a third tower, I finally spotted the fortress's weak point. Good job that I did or the grappling hook it would've been. The third tower was over a body of water. I hope that there aren't any zarks because I don't fancy being eaten alive once I get in it. Otherwise that'd be the end for me and Beautiful's rescue.

Fortunately, my luck was in as it had only taken five breast strokes to resurface inside the tower. Like I said, every fortress has a weak point, this one was hidden in a body of water. However, to my sweet surprise, there were no guards anywhere.

As my kit was drying off, I moulded some of the plastic explosive to the interior to make it look like it was part of the tower wall. I inserted the wireless detonator and moved on to the other three towers to do the same.

By the time I'd finished placing the plastic explosive, I must've lost ten kilograms from all the running around.

Now it was time to look for Beautiful!

I was pleasantly surprised by general lack of security around the fortress; the Zolgs clearly take plenty of pride in being known for their impenetrable fortress. When I was sneaking past an office, I had made my first encounter with the Zolgs; I heard angry exchanges inside the office. So I decided to stop and listen into their conversation. I'm not a nosey prick, I prefer the term intel gatherer. As it turns out, two Zolg commanders were very unhappy that the general ordered his elite guard to kidnap Princess Olnia.

WHAT ARE THE CHANCES?

'General Zog, this is not how we do war! And we demand that you release the princess back to the Arkans first thing in the morning!'

To be honest with you, I did not expect what I heard next. 'If there is any attempt at freeing the princess by you or anyone under your command, you will be flayed in front of all your fellow troops, just as the last predecessors who dared defy me,' the general proclaimed.

'What a prick,' I muttered under my breath. Looks like there's problems among the troops.

'Besides, the princesses' life is in some baron's hands now. But from now on, I'll have my elite guard keeping an eye on you two,' the general then dismissed them, which was my cue to dive for cover so they weren't aware that I was there.

The two commanders left the office, muttering, what I assumed, to be curses towards their general between themselves. There is no way in hell I'm going to leave this guy alone.

Furiously, I marched into General Zog's office to 'politely' confront him. This was the scumbag who ordered my Beautiful to be kidnapped and ruined my birthday. So I tasered him. Quickly, I slung him over my shoulder and made my way outside the fortress through the water. When we emerged to the outside surface, I tied him up and taped his mouth shut so he couldn't alert anyone. And just for good measure, I tasered him again. He should be out until I return with Beautiful.

I snuck back into the fortress and started looking for my Beautiful. After about half an hour, I found some mean-looking soldiers outside of a door; these soldiers didn't look like the other Zolgs I had seen so far. My guess is that they must be the elite guards that General Zog was on about. Suddenly, my impatience went into overdrive so I decided to scrap a stealthy approach and move in swiftly. I ran straight at the two guards. Before they could react, I used my katana to relieve them of their heads. They definitely looked better without their heads.

I placed my ear against the door, hoping to hear what was going on inside. My blood ran cold when I heard my Beautiful crying after one of the guards inside hit her and hit her repetitively. Then I heard her defiant words, I couldn't help but act instantly.

'Once my real daddy gets here, he's going to chop your heads and your arms off for hitting me,' she cried.

The next thing my Beautiful heard was me shouting to her to close her eyes as I stormed through the door, thirsty for their blood. Adrenaline coursed through my veins as I killed each one of the general's elite guard. But the one that hit her, I chopped his arms off, looked him in his agony-filled eyes, before I shortened him by a head.

Beautiful then opened her eyes, her brown orbs glowing up at the sight of me. She was indeed happy to see me, but still a little apprehensive, probably because of the green and black paint all over my face.

I crouched down to her level and held her hands smiling. 'It's so the bad men can't see me.' She smiled back as I rubbed her cheek before we started making our way to freedom.

When we got to the tower, I explained to Beautiful that we

would have to swim under water, but all she had to do was put her arms around my neck and hold tight.

'I'll do all the swimming, just concentrate on holding your breath while under water, okay?'

After five breaststrokes, we were outside the fortress and the general was still lying there tied up and unconscious.

I needed to quickly speak with the general. But in order to do this, I needed to borrow Beautiful's bracelet. I asked Beautiful to stand quietly against the fortress wall while I conversed with the general. I hoped this would work as her arms are obviously much smaller than his; close to skin contact is going to have to do.

I brought General Zog back to consciousness, holding Beautiful's bracelet against the skin on his arm. I told him to blink once if he could understand me, to which he did.

'Alright, General, I am going to give you two options and right this minute, I really hope that you will pick option one. Option one, I decapitate you and stick your head on a pole so when morning comes, all your troops can see your head. Option two, you stand up and walk quietly to be taken prisoner. And remember if you choose this option and try anything, I will immediately go with option one and chop your head off. So blink once for option one or twice for option two.'

He decided to go with option two. What a pity. I gave Beautiful's bracelet back to her and lifted her up onto my arm and made the general walk in front closely by the wall of the fortress. Through Beautiful, I gave the general his orders what direction to move or to stop. When walked around the corner, and I had to put on my night vision goggles so I could find the green marker that marked the fortress tower's blind spot.

Once we got to the place I stopped to find a way into the tower before, I instructed the general, through Beautiful, to turn right and walk straight forward. Just for extra precaution, I was directing him with my katana so he would not stray from the path. As we reached the green marker, I saw Jihon running towards us and right behind him was another officer. I quickly waved the katana at Jihon, insinuating for him to look behind. He did and then shouted something that caused the officer to stop immediately and turn back to where he came from.

Jihon was in awe of me when he saw Beautiful sitting in my left arm. He did, however, look shocked and puzzled by who the fellow was that I'd brought out, but once he got closer, he recognised General Zog and smiled even more. He gave my Beautiful a great hug and told her that it was great to see her highness and to have her back.

I asked Jihon to take General Zog and hand him over to the officer in charge of the blockade. Then I came up to General Zog, still holding Beautiful in my left arm, and punched him so hard that he fell onto his knees.

Once he got his breath back, he said something to me which Jihon translated, 'He wants to know why you hit him.'

I told Jihon to tell him that it was for the order he gave to have my Beautiful kidnapped. Then I turned round and made my way towards Jihon's flyer. It didn't take long for Jihon to return, and before I knew it, our flyer was taking Beautiful back to her mother and grandma at the palace.

WHAT ARE THE CHANCES?

After some time, we landed in the private port of the palace strictly reserved for the royalty and for officers under the royal command. I hugged and kissed Beautiful and told her to tell her mum that I missed her. Then, I instructed Jihon to take her safely back to her mother, but told him to remain vigilante. Jihon seemed eager to ask me something but it was going to have to wait until after he returns. Sadly, I had to admit that I felt sad when I saw Beautiful disappear from my view. But unfortunately, this is the way things had to be; the other Arkans could not know I was on their planet – not yet anyway.

I closed the flyer door before getting myself comfortable. I drew out two beers, from the backpack I had left in the flyer, for Jihon and me to celebrate a successful mission and the safe return of Beautiful when he returned. But until then, I opened my beer took a long sip and smiled.

CHAPTER 11.5

I walked with one of my hands on my weapon and the other closely shielding Princess Olnia. I didn't need to ask James why he specifically told me to stay wary. I also have figured out that there must be a traitor amongst the populace, helping the Zolgs.

Finally, we got to the main garden that led directly to the throne room. I told Olnia to walk close behind me, so we could catch her mother and grandmother by surprise. Eagerly, the princess agreed, smiling in excitement. So she trailed closely behind me. In fact she was stuck to me like glue as I walked onwards. Once we were inside the throne room, my eyes searched for Queen Vianna immediately. She was surrounded by her five generals and seven overseers. My family and I, like many others on Arka, detested the fact that King Gah, commonly known as an idiot, had allowed the overseers to increase from four to seven. I sincerely hope that once James marries Queen Vianna and becomes a king, which is bound to happen at this rate, then he will put a stop to this nonsense.

As I made my way towards Queen Vianna and Queen Yagi, I noticed, from the corner of my eye, that both of my parents were in attendance. I inclined my head towards my mother and father and then looked towards Queen Vianna. When I looked at her eyes, she had puffy red circles around them, clear evidence that she had been crying. When she looked at me, she had this hopeful look on her face, but one filled with a lot of suppressed desperation behind the hope. I tried very hard not to smile but I really just couldn't hold it back; I stepped to one side to reveal a smiling Princess Olnia. Immediately, Queen Vianna stopped talking to the crowd around her, and ran towards her precious daughter. As she neared me, I quickly said, 'I believe you lost something!'

The queen just smiled her grateful thanks to me, and tightly embraced her daughter. Queen Yagi ran up too, but not to the princess, but to me and thanked me before she went up to the princess to hug her lovingly.

I turned to walk towards my parents, seeing how very proud they were of me, but before I could take more than two steps, the generals and overseers started to shout my name and congratulate me. Not long after, everyone started to chant my name. Normally, I would've been proud of this, but I was conscious that they were all heaping praise and congratulation to the wrong guy. I definitely didn't deserve this. Even though James came from another planet, I loved him like he is my own big brother. So I'm going to set this right.

'Quiet!' I shouted. When everyone in the throne room became quiet, I looked at Queen Vianna and Queen Yagi apologetically. 'I'm sorry, Your Majesties, and I am very sorry princess, but I can't do this!'

Everyone present in the throne room looked confused, I even heard my father shout what was going on; I lifted my hand, indicating for them to all stop and just listen.

WHAT ARE THE CHANCES?

'I do not deserve all of the praise, and I refuse to accept all your praises for someone else's achievement. It was not me who rescued the princess from the fortress, just like it was not me who had found our gracious Queen Yagi in the jungle!' I heard loud gasps around the throne room; while scanning across the audience, I spotted High Prefect Baka, who gave me the reassuring nod to carry on. 'All praise and congratulations should rightfully be going to my big brother, whose skill is far beyond mine or any of our best soldiers. It was him who snuck into the Zolg fortress, and retrieved Princess Olnia, capturing General Zog in the midst to be taken as prisoner! The only reason he is not here is because he is an alien warrior, from a very distant planet called Earth. He holds a noble title as well as the rank of a commander, and his name is James!' I confidently proclaimed, putting my deep admiration for James within every word I had spoken. I also silently prayed for Vianna not to kill me. I knew this was not my place to say, but I knew Vianna wouldn't be doing this anytime soon, and I just couldn't take the praise for another life-changing event for Arka.

The gasps around the throne room were audible at this revelation. Arkans began muttering between themselves, and those who did not speak held shocked expressions. Even my own father began accusing me of illness, since I had no siblings. Suddenly, Queen Vianna declared, in a loud and confident voice, that Baron Rak must be the one that is ill.

'Commander Jihon in fact does indeed have an older brother called James.' Even Princess Olnia had exclaimed that I was correct.

WHAT ARE THE CHANCES?

My mother was always the wise one in the family, so she calmly asked if she could meet this long-lost older son called James. 'Of course, Mum!' I was just about to turn towards the door, which I had entered from, before Queen Vianna stopped me and approached me, asking me where her love was right now. 'In the flyer, awaiting his return.'

Out of the blue, Queen Vianna had kissed my cheek and ran through the door, quite obviously towards the flyer. When I looked behind me, I could see the disapproving looks, especially from General Akda. As expected, but still rather petrifying. Contrastingly, Queen Yagi was openly smiling wide, and as the disapproving voices around the throne room became louder, she ordered for everyone to shut up and have some respect for the heroism I displayed. Much appreciated, Yagi. She then approached me too, and much like Vianna, she kissed me on the cheek. For some reason, that made me feel better.

For now, they all waited patiently for Queen Vianna and Commander James to appear.

Meanwhile, I took this opportunity to come up to Chamberlain Vern and asked him if he could get someone to bring a large bowl with warm water and soap along with a towel. Without question, the chamberlain left to organise what I had asked for. Queen Yagi, still standing close to me, asked what the water and soap was for, but I just smiled and told her to be patient and wait and see.

CHAPTER 12

I've been exhausted since Olnia was kidnapped by the Zolgs. When Jihon told me the news that Olnia was taken to the Zolg fortress, it was utterly devastating. If she were somewhere around the capital, then there was a chance of getting her back, but the fortress? Getting her back is going to be next to impossible. The last time my military had attempted to storm it, it costed 100,000 lives. My sweet sweet Olnia. How could I have let this happen?

I couldn't even remember the last time I slept properly. I'd been up non-stop since I found out, and now my trusted soldier, Jihon, has gone off somewhere. I really hope that he didn't try to do anything stupid, like try to get into the fortress himself. Oh God, it just gets worse the more I think about it. Sania would kill him, and if not her, then I would do it myself.

The constant talking to the generals and my overseers was tiring me out at this point. At one stage, I almost issued an order for all of the overseers and generals to be arrested and thrown in prison. Only the intervention of my mother had spared them from this ordeal. But I couldn't just run from my problems, I had to stand here and talk to them with all of these people in the throne room.

It was early hours now, and I simply just had enough. In this moment, I just remembered I had forgotten about James. I really needed his safe and comforting arms right now. If he even knew that his Beautiful had been kidnapped, he'd most likely attack the fortress himself.

I was just about to scream at the people around me, from a mixture of exhaustion and frustration, when I had noticed that Jihon was walking towards me from the direction of my private gardens and private flyer port.

When he had finally gotten within ear shot, he stood to one side and raised his voice, asking me if I had lost something. Shortly, he revealed my smiling Olnia. Immediately, I bolted towards my daughter, closely followed by my mother. As I passed him, I thanked him before embracing my daughter in my arms closely. As I turned to look back at Jihon, still holding my daughter tightly, I noticed my mother whispered something to him before giving him a kiss on the cheek. The three of us were crying intensely, but this time, from pure happiness. In this moment, I really wanted to ask Jihon how he had done it, but my plans were disrupted when everyone in the throne room started to chant his name, praising him for his daring rescue of my daughter – and I was grateful. But as I glanced at Jihon, I knew him well enough to know that he felt positively uncomfortable with all the attention and praise he was receiving.

His head dropped, and all of a sudden, he yelled for everyone to stop. He looked straight at me, where I was holding Olnia with my mother, and apologised for what he was about to do and say. He then announced to everyone, in the throne room, that it was not him who rescued Olnia or found my mother in the jungle, but rather his big brother James. I almost burst with pride at hearing this. I should've known that James would not just sit back and let his Beautiful be kidnapped. Why I didn't think about letting him know this myself was beyond me.

Sadly, I had to admit I felt sorry for Jihon when his own father, Baron Rak, accused him of being ill when he declared he had a big brother. I looked at my mum, seeing her big knowing smile as I defended Jihon right away. I didn't even realise my sassy comment had slipped out, accusing Baron Rak of being ill himself, until after I said it. Indeed, he was not happy with my remark, but accepted the place I had put him in as I was the queen. Luckily, Jihon's mother the Baroness Mima came to the rescue, asking if she could meet her long-lost older son. I simply nodded to Jihon approvingly. Jihon was just about to make for the garden door before I had stopped him. I needed to know where James was. To thank him, but also to see him once again – he is my love and future after all. After Jihon informed me of James' whereabouts, I bolted for the flyer to see my James, to show my appreciation and how much I have missed him.

When I got to the flyer the door was closed, so I opened it and jumped inside hoping it wasn't some random stranger – although it shouldn't be, since this flyer was in my private gardens. There was my love, James, drinking one of those Earth beers he is so fond of. But what was that black and green dirt on his face? I love his handsome white face, why did he have to put dirt on it?

Without hesitation, I jumped onto his lap and firmly kissed him. I'm not quite sure why I did this, or whether I'd just lost complete control, but I impulsively asked him to marry me, to be with me and Olnia forever. For a split second, he didn't answer, my eyes widening once I realised what I'd said. He just softly smiled and kissed me soundly. I was about to say something before he started laughing at me. Because of this, I got a bit flustered as I had just declared my love for him and wanted us to be together forever, and he was laughing at me. Just as I was about to tell him off, he held out his hand, taking a small pocket mirror out of his black uniform and showing me why he was laughing at me.

Right there, on my face, lips, nose and cheeks smothered with black and green dirt from us kissing. He smiled again and told me that even though my face is dirty, that he still loves me very much and wants to be with me and Olnia. I think he could tell I was curious about his face too, so he explained the reason for his green and black face. He was trying to protect my soldiers, even when he was in the act of rescuing Olnia. He's like the total opposite of Gah.

I got off his lap and grabbed him by his arm, asking him to follow me. Immediately, he frowned and told me that it was not a good idea. So I had to inform him that his baby brother had already told everyone that he existed, and that his mother would like to meet her older lost son. He burst out laughing for a second, before he finally agreed to come and meet his mother. I was exhilarated. This was the start of a real life together. I couldn't be happier. Finally, I did not have to hide my James anymore; and finally I could love him in the open.

When he got out of the flyer and closed the door, he gave me a kiss, enthusiastically saying, 'Let's go and meet the family!' I had to laugh since my family are about sixty-two million Arkans.

WHAT ARE THE CHANCES?

Hooking my arm through his, we started to walk towards everyone in my throne room. I really wanted to shout out loud that I loved him when I entered the throne room, like in one of those Earth romance movies James lets me watch sometimes. But I figured that'd be too cheesy.

When we both entered through the throne room doors, I still had my arm hooked through James'. Basically instantly, I noticed a few disapproving looks. Honestly though, I didn't care. I loved him and nothing in this world will stop me being with him.

As we approached my and my mother's thrones, Jihon called James to one side, pointing to the wash bowl and towel. While James washed the paint from his face, I instructed Chamberlain Vern to bring the bracelet machine from my private audience chamber, so everyone present could have their bracelet updated. This'd be easier if everyone understood English.

When everyone had their bracelets updated, I introduced James, making it clear to everyone that he was also my boyfriend. And of course, my beautiful and brave daughter added that he was also her real father, as Gah was broken. We all laughed at Olnia's introduction. James scooped her up in his arms, giving her a kiss on her cheek, announcing to everyone present that he might not have been her biological father, but he did however consider himself to be her real dad now.

Once the introductions were over, Jihon took James to meet his parents. To everyone's surprise, including mine, Jihon's mother hugged James and welcomed him to their family. That was heavily unexpected. They had a very long conversation, but unfortunately, everyone else wanted to meet James too – there simply was not enough time. Uncle Baka and aunt Seline came over to greet him fondly. Uncle Baka even smiled, overjoyed for us not needing to hide anymore. And that felt damn good.

Momentarily, I introduced him to the generals and the overseers, and then I would eventually to a group of Baron and Baronesses. But my dear mother came up to James and gave him a great big hug and kiss, telling him she was proud of him very much audibly, before I could do so.

As James was mingling with everyone, I noticed that absolutely everyone wanted to have their personal meet and greet with this white alien; all the ladies were attracted to him, even. Well, they better not even think about it! James is all mine, and that's it!

*   *   *

It was now daylight outside, but that didn't make Arkans any less curious; everyone still wanted to be seen or converse with James. I was going to step in to come to his rescue, but before I could, he firmly told everyone that he needed some rest himself. James suddenly shouted for everyone to be silent when everyone remained in deep and loud conversation because of his obvious display of exhaustion. He proceeded to politely ask for everyone to return back to their homes, excluding the generals. I wondered what about.

Once my people had left, James took a deep breath before announcing a statement that changed everything, 'We have a traitor amongst the populace.'

WHAT ARE THE CHANCES?

I had to admit, logically it made sense, but I was still baffled by the statement. But since James has far more experience than I, I knew I had to trust him on this. Especially with what I know happened to him back on Earth, the reason why he is here. James informed us that, from his experience, he believes that because this traitor has had their plan ruined, they will do something rash that will reveal their identity within the next twenty-four hours, usually. To nobody's surprise, General Akda said that this theory was simply impossible, as this wasn't his planet, he had no right to make such accusations. My blood boiled at his blatant discrimination, so much so that I almost kicked that imbecile Akda, although it seemed that my mother had noticed my sudden defensive demeanour as she intervened, strongly recommending to the generals that they should listen to James and take notice. She also pointed out to them that it was him, not them, that had actually managed to get in and out of the fortress, something they failed to do for many years in fact. My mother highlighted James' bravery and expertise that were beyond question, essentially putting them into their places. Good riddance.

But of course, she couldn't leave out the bravery of James when he slayed the Garuga with a single shot to its eye in pure darkness. Sometimes I truly believe she admires him more than I, and that is truly saying something. Although, straight away, a few of the generals questioned my mother, primarily General Akda, telling her that she must be mistaken, as all Garugas were exterminated a long time ago. My amazing mother just smiled and projected a picture of herself and a dead Garuga on to a neighbourly screen, asking them while smirking, 'What is this then?'

WHAT ARE THE CHANCES?

I had to conceal my smile with my hand as she made General Akda look like an incompetent imbecile. My mother is always prepared for anything. That is why she was and is an excellent queen. I know she loves nothing more than putting people into their places – especially those darn generals.

In response, the generals shied away as Akda frowned and shot my mother a deep look of spite and jealousy towards James. He has every right to be jealous, the incompetent fool, and who made him a general in the first place?! Oh yes, now I remember, it was that incompetent fool Gah.

Speaking of James, he asked me to announce that Beautiful had been rescued and then wait and see what happens. I was just about to ask my very sleepy Chamberlain Vern to do this before I saw him already rushing for the door to inform the media of Olnia's rescue. No matter how exhausted that man gets, he never fails me. A hard-worker he is.

Though I had to admit, I was rather exhausted myself. It had been a long day, too long for my liking, so I think it would be best to retire for today. I just hope Uncle Vern gets the rest he needs.

'Let's meet late morning, since we're all tired.' I glanced at Olnia's sleeping face. 'Some more than other.' We laughed and agreed.

Once everyone had left, I took James to Olnia's bedroom where he gently laid her down onto her bed. He kissed her goodnight on her forehead before I walked him to a guest room and we kissed goodnight.

This was the most relaxing sleep I'd had in the last few days. Knowing that my daughter was safe and that my love doesn't have to hide from my people anymore was a huge relief. When my chamber maids arrived, I asked them if James was up. After much giggling between them, they informed me that he was sleeping against Princess Olnia's bedroom door wrapped in the bed cover. As soon as I heard this, I ran out in my nighty to see this for myself. I could hear my chamber maids asking me to stop and get dressed first, but I didn't care when it came to James. Plus this was a sight I simply could not bear to miss.

When I got to Olnia's bedroom door, James was indeed there, fast asleep against her door – or so I thought. When I was standing there, intensely observing him sleeping, he suddenly smiled, and without opening his eyes he informed me that he knew I was standing there and even told me to go and get dressed. How did he know I wasn't dressed yet when he didn't even open his eyes?

He then opened his eyes, greeting me with a 'Good morning, my love.' I loved hearing those words; I haven't in a while. He then opened the bed covers to reveal that he was fully armed and ready for any trouble that may arise. I chuckled at his defensive tactics; I reassured him that he was safe in the palace. But James being James simply replied, 'It's not my safety I am concerned about, I have to continue protecting Olnia, since we haven't caught the traitor yet.'

This sparked an idea in me. 'Would you like to take Olnia with you to your palace, that way she will be safe. No one can get her there.' He smile-winked at me, saying that he would love that. In this instant, I wondered if James even knew how much I loved him. He got up, folded the bed cover, and then asked if I wanted to join him in waking Beautiful up to give her the good news. I smiled and kissed his cheek, hooking my arm through his, motioning for us to go in.

Olnia was very happy to see us both there. Once we told her that she would be going and staying at James' palace for a while, she literally screamed with delight. But her happiness didn't last long as James regretfully informed her that she will also be taking her school books with her. That really made me laugh, not out of cruelty to my daughter, but because I somehow got lucky enough to fall in love with a guy like James who accepted my daughter without any reservations and always has the best interest of his Beautiful in his heart.

I told Olnia to wash and then get her things ready that she wanted to take with her while I went back to get washed up and dressed.

CHAPTER 12.5

While I was having a wash I had to smile, as Vianna really looked very sexy and smelled very nice in that nighty standing over me while I was guarding Beautiful at her door.

I began thinking on what I had revealed to the generals last night, and I really do hope that the traitors do reveal themselves within twenty-four hours – or I'd look pretty stupid. Oh well. There is no point dwelling on something I have no control over. Just have to wait and see! After I get back to my place, I'm going to find out from Jihon if he had ever come across this baron that the Zolg mentioned in General Zog's office when I was sneaking around the fortress.

Dressed, and once again fully armed, I left the room that I was given to sleep in, and made my way to the dining hall to get a late breakfast. There's plenty of new things to learn and discover, but I was looking forward to the food the most. I was curious about the standard Arkan breakfast; every time I had guests at my place, I always cooked food that people would normally eat in Great Britain, in my home country.

As I walked through the door leading to the private dining hall, my Beautiful ran up to me and guided me to my seat. She really is such a sweetheart, despite all that she's been through. My seat was right next to hers, obviously by chance! I smiled at her and chuckled, before thanking her and kissing her good morning on the forehead.

We all had finished our breakfast, which was very tasty but very similar to what I would have had back on Earth. Call it an English breakfast but substitute everything with the Arkan equivalent.

We were having a pleasant conversation when Chamberlain Vern, looking all fresh and well-rested after a late night, announced that the generals had arrived and were waiting in Vianna's throne room. At this news, I informed Vianna that once Jihon got here, I would be leaving for the house of fun. Beautiful was very eager to go and I could see that very clearly. The eager ball of excitement could barely even sit still.

Vianna, Beautiful and I walked into the throne room together. I went to one side with Beautiful as I didn't feel like chatting with the generals – sorry Vianna. Besides, I knew what they were going to ask, and I didn't feel like sharing what I discovered in the Zolg fortress.

Yagi and Vianna were in deep conversation with the generals when my baby brother arrived. I turned to Beautiful and told her that it was time to go, telling her to go give her mother and grandmother a kiss. As I was prepared to leave, my love came up to me and soundly kissed me, leaving the generals – which I do not blame her for. Without a doubt, she was very much in love with me.

The three of us were just about to leave through the door for the private gardens when Chamberlain Vern entered the throne room, further announcing Baron and Baroness Kran with escort. This announcement stopped me in my tracks. I called Jihon close to me and asked if he trusted me. Without a single hint of hesitation, Jihon replied implicitly. I told him to quickly take Beautiful to her mother and command the generals to place themselves in front of the royal family. As for me, I made my way towards the door that the baron and baroness would then be entering. I leaned against the heavy curtains, so that anyone entering the throne room could not see me. While I did this, I greeted the guard next to me and asked for his name, telling him not to get excited once I start.

Corporal Gurt smiled and assured me that he is not the excitable sort. I winked at him and told him, 'Good for you.'

As the baron and baroness entered with their escort, I could see that a couple of the generals were not happy with Jihon's crisp order to place themselves between the royal family and the new arrivals.

Alarm bells were ringing very loud in my head, almost immediately. However, my suspicions were truly raised by everyone in Baron and Baroness Kran's escort. Visors clasped down. Gloves on. In this tremendous heat?!

Having the observance skills I'd learned from being in the army, it only took me a fraction of a moment to figure out who the officer was in the escort. Although, it took me a while longer to spot the sergeant. I definitely needed him alive for my plan to work.

Taking my stun gun, I incapacitated the sergeant. Once he was down, I killed the rest of the escort. Thank God there weren't that many though. I noticed that Corporal Gurt looked puzzled at what I had just done. But nerveless, he stood firm and did not react – something that couldn't be said for most of the generals, especially

WHAT ARE THE CHANCES?

General Akda. Akda was shouting and throwing orders around, even going so far as to giving the order to have me killed. General Mass immediately countermanded Akda's order. In the instant that Akda gave that order, I knew straight away that it was him who had recklessly sent the 100,000 Arkan soldiers to their deaths at the fortress.

He was a killing officer, and a coward, and I certainly did not have the time for someone like him. A low anger drove me to go up to him and grab him by the scruff of the neck, and drag him to one of the dead bodies lying beside the shocked and motionless Baron and Baroness Kran. I told him to the lift the visor off the dead escort. He was still shouting meaningless orders, relentlessly calling me a crazy bastard. I slapped him across the face, sternly informing him that if he didn't lift the visor in the next few seconds, then he would be joining the dead.

Grudgingly he lifted the visor. To everyone's shock they saw, not an Arkan, but an elite Zolg guard. I thought I killed all the elite guards the night before. He withdrew away from me, biting his tongue of words immediately. After checking all the dead bodies and the one I had stunned earlier, the escort were comprised of normal and elite Zolg guards.

I then called Jihon by his official rank of commander and asked him to arrange for the incapacitated Zolg sergeant to be taken to prison. I made it clear I didn't want him interrogated or harmed in any way. As Jihon was leaving with the semi-conscious Zolg I also asked him if the two traitors standing in front of the queen had a child who serves in the military. Without even answering me, he contacted the commander in charge of the troops surrounding the fortress and told him to arrest Captain Srin Kran on the charge of high treason immediately. Proud with myself, I looked over to where my love was standing to see she had this great big grin on her face.

Later that day, she told me that she took great pleasure in telling all her generals that I was right again and they were wrong, again! What I did enjoy was Queen Yagi raising her voice, commanding General Mass to strip Akda of his rank and remove him from her sight. If only I felt bad for him … Not!

While Akda was causing uproar, I came up to Vianna, kissed her and told her that everything will be all right. I then asked Beautiful to get me a bottle of water and be very slow at getting it while I spoke to the traitors. Chamberlain Vern was certainly on the ball as I didn't even have to ask to have the two traitors' bracelets updated so they could understand me. He just took their bracelets off them and updated them without any word from me. Quite honestly the man deserves more credit – and more rest for sure. Honestly I feel rather wrong for comparing Akda and Vern, but they're like the two ends of a scale on extreme competence.

Once the traitor Krans had their bracelets back on, I came up to the former Baron Kran and asked him why he and his wife chose to betray the queen and Arka. He was just about to spit at me when I warned him that if anything but a confession comes out of his mouth then he would sincerely regret it. He glared at me with deep spite. It's amazing how criminals still think that they can get away with things just because they once held a noble rank.

WHAT ARE THE CHANCES?

Sadly, he chose to be just like those other criminals.

His wife screamed with horror as I swept his feet from under her husband, who had spat in my face, and then promptly chopped off his little finger. Red trickles of his blood squirted all over the throne room floor while her husband screamed in pain.

While he was on his knees whimpering and trying very hard to stop the bleeding, I came up to his wife to ask the same question. She was so terrified after what she had witnessed that she spilled it all. Good.

Vianna, her mother, and everyone in attendance could not believe what they were hearing as Baroness Kran spoke. 'Okay okay okay! My husband wanted to be crowned king of Arka. So he made a deal with General Zog for his help in getting us crowned the king and queen of Arka. And if he made that happen, then we would give the general as much of Arka's mineral resources as he wanted.'

She then proceeded to tell us that the Zolgs were able to build their fortress so fast because her husband was using his position to redirect officials so no one would get wise of what was happening in the wilderness where the fortress was being built.

'And- and,' she tried to say through tears, 'my husband provided the Zolgs with detailed plans of the capital as well as the sewer's plans, so the Zolgs could move around unnoticed and unchallenged.'

She still had plenty to say but I noticed that my Beautiful was coming back with my bottle of water and Jihon was back too, so I gave Vianna a quick kiss and told her that I would see her later.

WHAT ARE THE CHANCES?

I reassured her that she had nothing to worry about as I would protect my Beautiful with my life. Of course she wasn't satisfied with just a quick kiss so she planted her moist lips on mine and kissed me so passionately leaving everyone present with no doubt as to the state our relationship is at.

I then collected Beautiful, who just arrived with a bottle of water, and Jihon and left for the gardens where the flyer was parked.

While we walked, or shall I say Jihon and I walked while Beautiful sat proudly on my right arm, Jihon informed me that he made arrangements at the prison for my Zolg sergeant and that no one but me will take him out of there. That's my baby brother. The three of us then got in the flyer and made our way towards my place. I think I've had enough excitement for today.

*   *   *

I don't know what it was but when I arrived back at my place it really felt good. Unknowingly, I came to treat this alien palace as my own home and I was very comfortable here. It truly did feel like home.

I had to smile as my baby brother, without asking, went straight to the cooler and got himself a beer. I made a good Earthman out of him.

Beautiful sat herself in front of the television and asked if she could watch one of the kid's films from Earth. The face she pulled while asking to watch a film, I just had to give in. So cute! So I put one of my favourite cartoons on. Besides I wanted to have a chat with Jihon and we still didn't have our celebration beer from our mission success the night before.

Sadly, poor Jihon was so worn out that he fell asleep halfway through his second beer, so I made him comfortable and covered him up.

When Beautiful had finished watching her film, I took her to the dining room and persuaded her to do some school work. The poor thing didn't want to, and honestly I didn't blame her. Good to know all kids are the same no matter what planet. But I found out that if I asked her whether she really loves me or not, then she will do even the most hated task. The thing is, she really enjoys learning; she even got all excited when I asked her to teach me Arkan. She started me off with an Arkan alphabet and I was trying very hard not to laugh as she was acting like a forty-year-old professor rather than a nearly seven-year-old. But I'll give her this, by the time Vianna and Queen Yagi arrived I mastered the alphabet. Wow! I was on my way to greater things.

Vianna and Queen Yagi took a quick glance at Jihon sleeping and quickly joined Beautiful in the dining room. Beautiful told them off for interfering, as she hadn't finish teaching me yet. I did feel sorry for her as her mum immediately pulled her rank and informed her daughter that she needed some loving attention from me. What can I say? I'm quite the popular man. At that Queen Yagi suggested to Beautiful that they should go in the kitchen and have something to eat while her mum and I do some of that loving attention.

Unfortunately the loving attention didn't last long as they came back after only a few minutes to ask why there was so much wasted food in the kitchen. I was telling them that I was expecting all of them last weekend, but unfortunately our little wanderer here decided to go and explore the Zolg fortress instead. Vianna looked at me and somehow she knew that I was keeping something from everyone, so I told them all that last Sara, which is Sunday back on Earth, it was my thirty-fourth birthday and I wanted everyone who came to help me celebrate it.

Vianna was just about to say something when her mother chased her off my lap then gave me a big hug and kiss on both of my cheeks and declared to Vianna that next ferga they will hold a birthday celebration for me, fit for a king. She then looked straight at Vianna and told her that if she doesn't marry me fast then she will steal me from her.

Poor Vianna didn't take that well as she literally screamed at her mother, telling her that she will have her thrown in jail if she ever tried to steal me from her. Once again, I'm quite the popular man. From perspective, this all looked like one of the corny scenes in Earth romcoms. However, it seemed my love had taken it to heart. With slightly saddened eyes, she looked at me asking whether I would ever leave her. I gave her the biggest hug and passionate kiss and told her that I am forever hers – and hers only.

When I finished kissing Vianna, I opened my eyes to see her mother giving me a wink and a knowing smile. I definitely started to worry here and I was angry at myself as it was my flipping hand which strayed to Queen Yagi's bum while giving her a helping hand up the tree in the jungle. This whole scenario seems like an Earthman's dream, but honestly there's something about Arkan women that gives me the chills.

WHAT ARE THE CHANCES?

Luckily Queen Yagi informed Vianna that she was only joking and that she will only love one person for the rest of her life, and that is her father Herc.

The relief on poor Vi's face.

Suddenly, Vianna said that she and her mum had to go back to the capital so that they could plan my birthday party. I knew it was pointless arguing with Vianna as I did not want a big celebration, but that wasn't an option now, so both Vianna and her mother left leaving Beautiful, the sleeping Jihon and I behind.

It's amazing how fast an nine day week can go on Arka when you have Beautiful staying with you and a baby brother popping in almost every day. The week I have spent looking after Beautiful has shown me how much of an intelligent and amazing little girl she really is. Any parent would be proud of a child like this. She has taught me an Arkan alphabet and quite a few words and phrases, but I have a strong feeling that some of the words she has taught me are not very nice as every time I say them she keeps giggling to herself and Jihon did the same when I said them too. All in all I enjoyed having my little blue daughter staying with me and before I knew it all three of us were flying towards the capital, to Vianna and Queen Yagi's palace where my thirty-forth birthday celebration will take place. From what Vianna had told me, it looked like there would be hundreds of persons at my celebration. Crap! I really hate court toadies and nobles with over-inflated egos. Well, I have a surprise for all of them, and this also includes my beautiful Vianna.

I am going to wear my dress tartan kilt with all the trimmings. I love representing my Scottish heritage after all. That should ruffle feathers, maybe even start a new fashion trend on Arka. Maybe I should put a shield on my back saying 'Duncan's Galaxy Tour'.

As we landed in the private landing port reserved for the royal family and officers under royal command, Vianna and Chamberlain Vern were already waiting for us. After a long kiss from Vianna, Beautiful informed Uncle Vern that she would be escorting her real dad to his room. Chamberlain Vern tried very hard to hide his smile behind his hand but it was of no use. I turned to him and joked, 'It looks like my Beautiful will be putting you out of your job my friend.' He just smiled and welcomed me to the family. Momentarily, Jihon then told me that he would be going back to his place and that he, along with our mum and dad, will see me later.

Looks like I am in Vianna and Beautiful's hands now.

Beautiful escorted me to my room, which just happened to be next to hers, and told me that she would see me later. For now she and her mother had to get all dressed up for me for later. But for now, to my dismay, I was left alone. I had to admit that it wasn't that bad though, I could do with a bit of my own company. So I hung my kilt up and my jacket that I was going to wear. I had just managed to close the wardrobe door when Queen Yagi came in and asked me to join her for some light refreshments. For some reason she made me very nervous, might have to do something with my hand on her bum while we were back in the jungle, so I agreed immediately.

After arriving at the Royal Gardens, I saw a large table with refreshments already set up for us. As I walked with Vianna's mother down the garden, I noticed the perfectly trimmed hedges were streamlined with decorative flags, pink flags with hearts, I can certainly tell whose choice that was, Beautiful's of course. Both of us sat down, believe me when I tell you I did not even have the chance to lift my drink close to my lips before Queen Yagi started to inform me, no, more like ordered me to marry her daughter. Immediately, I placed my drink down firmly, looked her straight in her face and told her, 'Not yet.' She was taken aback by my answer, and I chose not to elaborate until I had a long swig of my drink. What can I say? I was thirsty.

Or maybe it was a mechanism to overcome the shock. Who knows?

'If I married Vianna now, your people would never accept me,' I simply stated. And to be quite fair, it was true. Marrying Vianna now would make me look like some wannabe poser, that makes me no better than Gah. I've not exactly been accepted by all of Arka, I want that more than anything else, for Vianna's sake.

'And with time they shall. But they must get to know you,' she replied.

'Oh I have a quicker way, just be patient,' I say in a light-hearted tone to ease the tension. I further explained how I intended to end the feud between her people and the Zolgs. As expected, she gasped with shock, her look of disbelief begging for me to elaborate. 'If I do things right, then I will finish this war without any more casualties or unpleasantness between Arkans and Zolgs.' She was just about to make a comment before she suddenly stopped, looking pretty wild-eyed as if she had just seen a ghost or something.

We then sat quietly for a while before she spoke up, 'I am aware of how you make Vianna feel, and I simply cannot wait for you to marry my precious daughter. We will be happy and to have a strong king by her side.'

Wait ... what?

I looked at her with an ultimate expression of realisation blurting out, 'I don't want to be a king!'

Queen Yagi looked at me, realising I really didn't have any intentions for grandeur, and asked me if I want to marry her daughter. It wasn't a trick question, so without hesitation I obviously replied with a 'Yes.'

She downed the rest of her drink before exclaiming, 'Good! Then you will be a king and, from what I heard about Gah, our people need someone like you. You are not only a leader but also a man of action. You are the one who managed to detect the treacherous plot against us, lurking outside of our vision, and you also unmasked the traitors, putting a stop to it. Something that all my generals and the Prefect Corps couldn't do. I know that you have your reservations, but trust me when I tell you that you will make an excellent king and Vianna's father would have loved you for all the qualities you have.'

She looked like she had tears in her eyes so I just decided to say nothing. We sat in silence for what seemed like eternity before one of the court officials informed us that the guests to my birthday party started to slowly arrive. I stood up, took Queen Yagi's right hand in mine and kissed the back of it, informing her that I would always protect Vianna and Beautiful. She stood up, put both of her hands on my cheeks, and kissed me straight on my mouth, telling me that she knows that I will never let her daughter and her granddaughter down and that I will always keep them safe. As much as I was appreciative of her acceptance, I think I was just violated. I gave her a confused look behind a smile before she then hooked her arm through mine and we walked back towards the palace private quarters.

As we walked away from the gardens, she asked me if I liked the pink flags.

'They are lovely, Beautiful has excellent taste,' I laughed.

'Beautiful? Honey this was all me,' she stated with a stern face, obviously insulted by my ignorance. Oops.

When I neared the door of my bedroom, Beautiful came out all dressed up and asked me if I thought she looked beautiful.

I immediately told her that she's always beautiful. She pouted a little, accusing me of being biased. I reassured her that I wasn't, I was simply being honest. She looked just like her mother when she did that. Even the cute smile she gave me after was a spitting image of Vianna. She motioned me to bend down, kissing me on my cheek and telling me that she loved me and then ran off towards her mum's quarters.

When I got inside my bedroom, I couldn't even make one step away from the door before there was a polite knock on my door. My oh my I'm a busy man today. I opened it to see Chamberlain Vern standing there. He apologised for his intrusion but he really needed to know how to announce me when I enter the ballroom. Bless this man. I told him it was okay to just say James, but he was not happy with that. So unfortunately I had to tell him to announce me as Sir Commander James Duncan of Great Britain. I might be millions or trillions of light years away from Earth, but I am proud to be British. He seemed very happy with what I said as he left immediately.

Finally I was alone in my bedroom, so I could relax and get dressed in peace.

My good friend King George once advised me to always be late with an entrance to a party by at least half an hour. I had to laugh to myself as he called it fashionably late, so I decided to take his advice and do the same. After all, it is my birthday party.

It was coming up to seven in the evening, many of the guests would have already arrived by now. Despite my party beginning at seven, I still wasn't ready. Quite honestly, I had no idea what exactly I was preparing myself for. I just knew I had to look the part. I might just start a new fashion trend and go in my birthday suit!

Flashbacks to when I was returning Queen Yagi back home in the jungle flooded my mind. I swiftly rid off the birthday suit idea.

I had just finished dressing when there was a light knock my bedroom door. So I opened it to see my beloved Vianna, standing there in the most amazing yellow I had ever seen. Human women could never look this stunning in yellow. There's just something special about the blend of blue and yellow – she looked breathtaking. Vi was about to ask me if everything was all right when she noticed my kilt and immediately snuck herself into my room with a concern and an inquiring look on her face. Quickly, I explained my heritage to her, Scottish traditional attire, informing her that no it was not a skirt, but it was a kilt to represents my family's clan.

WHAT ARE THE CHANCES?

'If anyone in the ballroom refers to it as a skirt, Vianna, then there will be many bloody noses tonight.'

She looked at my stern face, and after just a small pause, she asked me if she could escort me to my birthday party. As it was probably around half seven, I readily agreed to this amazing woman escorting me. She shook her head funnily, muttering, 'Typical James.'

It's not that I'm a violent man, but I do take my heritage very seriously and will not allow anyone, including Vianna's people, to disrespect my clan.

We left my bedroom, Vianna hooking her arm through mine, as we walked towards the ballroom where everyone was waiting for me.

'Meeting you was the best thing that has ever happened to me,' she whispered to me through her rosy lips. She gave me a quick kiss in the cheek and told me that she loved me.

As we neared the entry door, she then told me that this would be a good rehearsal for when we got married. Even though I love her, the word 'marriage' still made me nervous. After all, I did my best to avoid getting married when I was back on Earth.

The reaction of the guests were somewhat expected when Vianna and I walked through the door to the ballroom after I was announced alongside Queen Vianna. To my surprise, it wasn't the women who were tongue wagging but rather it was the men. Vianna, being the smart woman she is, decided to announce that I was sporting my Earth Highlander attire, warning anyone that was planning to refer to my kilt as a skirt they'd be immediately jailed.

WHAT ARE THE CHANCES?

Inevitably, I noticed a few disapproving looks as people noticed the queen's arm hooked through mine, but my beloved then announced to everyone that I was her boyfriend and her love and that had brought a scream of joy from none other than my Beautiful herself, running towards us with sheer delight.

My birthday party was now in full swing and after I was passed by both Queen Vianna and Yagi, from person to person, and Beautiful sticking to me like glue, I now knew how George felt and why he hated formal events so much. All the switching from conversation to conversation started to give me motion sickness.

Everyone wanted to meet me, and considering it was supposed to be my birthday bash I didn't have a second to myself.

The worst moment came when they all sang what I can only guess as an equivalent to happy birthday. I thoroughly enjoyed and found it interesting to see Arkan culture, but the music they played after singing me a happy birthday was the downside.

Let me tell you this, Arkan music was ... how can I best describe it?

It's shit!

It was total torture to my eardrums. I thanked my new mother, who rescued me from killing all the musicians on Arka, for taking me out of the ballroom and into the gardens. When we were outside she smiled, telling me that she also didn't think that Arka's music was very good. I replied, telling her that describing it as not very good is the nicest thing anyone could call it. She chuckled as I told her how I almost walked up to one of the palace guards to ask him to shoot me in the head just so he could put me out of my misery listening to that.

WHAT ARE THE CHANCES?

Then, an idea popped into my mind – a very good one at that. I took my phone out of my sporran, along with a pair of headphones, and placing one into Jihon's mother's ear, and then asked her to dance. Wow! My new mother really was a good dancer and she definitely enjoyed the music from my planet.

In the end, my birthday bash was good, but I was glad it was over since another minute listening to that ear-screeching music would've made me beat the life out of the musicians. One thing was certain, that the little girl I'd saved from those beasts many months ago has somehow wormed her way into my heart. Even now, at the breakfast table, she was sticking to me like glue. As for her mother, what can I say? Apart from the fact that for the first time in my life I was really in love! I just hoped that my love for her would not bring any misfortune upon her and my Beautiful.

After a yummy and filling breakfast, Vianna, Beautiful and I went for a stroll in the Royal Gardens. I had to admit that this is the first time since I arrived on this planet that I noticed all of these beautiful and strange flowers growing all over the garden. I've been too occupied to truly embrace the beauty of Arka's nature. The sweet and almost tangy scent made me feel content.

Later that day, I broke the news to Vianna and Queen Yagi, I'd be returning to my place soon. That announcement did not go down well with both of them, but trying to reason I told them I needed to think things through so I could end this war with the Zolgs, without any or minimal causalities. For some reason, that information made my future wife and future mother-in-law suddenly very agreeable to me leaving tomorrow. I have a feeling that they are not telling me something.

After hours of deep thought and packing, I collapsed onto my bed, falling into a deep sleep for a day of hard work tomorrow. Soon the next morning had arrived, and after taking Beautiful to school, I met with my baby brother to fly back to my place.

CHAPTER 13

Over the past few weeks I remained at my place, Jihon informed me that all four of the generals were bugging him about my intentions for the captured Zolg sergeant. Right now, on my orders he was just jailed with strict instructions for him not to be interrogated or harmed in any way. I supposed it is time to follow up on that.

On the brighter side, the good news was that the Zolg fortress was locked down, so there was no unpleasantness from either side. This was impeccable news for me as this would help my plans to end this conflict peacefully.

It had now been three and a half weeks since the Zolg sergeant was put in prison and this was enough time to complete my plan of action.

But for tonight, all my usual friends and I were going to have dinner at my place. But this time, my new mother and father would be joining us, so I had to pull all the stops to prepare something delicious and filling from my planet – I wanted everything to be great. After all, I do want to impress my new mum and dad. And as luck had it, the strawberries and raspberries were ripe, so fresh fruit from my planet should go down well with my guests. If I remember correctly, they're arriving at seven-thirty but I bet my life that Vianna, Beautiful and Yagi would arrive early, just to make sure that I've prepared everything for our guests. It didn't go unnoticed that Vi's mother is always checking on the food I cook like some chef executive.

Vianna and her gang of two arrived at half-six as I predicted; Queen Yagi went directly to the kitchen to sample the food I prepared for tonight. She must've tasted something 'funny' because she sampled the same dish so many times she might as well have scoffed the whole darn thing.

The rest of my guests arrived a while later. We all did some catching up before I asked everyone to come and take their seats in the dining room. The meal went down well with everyone, but not as well as the fresh fruit from my planet. I have never heard strawberries and raspberries described so eloquently as tonight. My baby brother and my new father kept on and on about the fruit, I eventually leaned towards Jihon and whispered in his ear that Dad really needs to get a life. That is when he told me that his family, or shall I say our family, are famous for growing fruit and vegetables for all of Arka. Maybe when I have time I could make some money! Or in this case, credits, as they don't use money on Arka.

After dinner when everyone was relaxing. Most of us were flopped down onto our seats, a little belly pudge poking out from eating too much. I decided to drop the bombshell by casually asking Vianna and her mother if I could have a private meeting with all her generals. High Prefect Baka was the first one to enquire. So I bluntly told them that I had a way of ending the war peacefully. But this meant that I needed some concessions from their generals before I could proceed with my plan. Queen Yagi made it clear that they'd be at my disposal, making it absolutely known that I would be in charge and not them. Thank you, Yagi. I smiled at her. 'It's a good thing that you and Vianna have four generals.'

Everyone in unison asked me why. 'I only need to kill one of them to make my point,' I said with an indifferent expression. I was only joking, but everyone seemed to take it pretty seriously.

Oh well, maybe if this gets back to them, it'll be easier to deal with them that way.

A while later, I put an animated children's film on for Beautiful for her to enjoy. What made me laugh was that everyone had watched and thoroughly enjoyed it. I suppose everyone has a bit of a child deep inside of them. After the film had finished, I introduced a few games to everyone; they were enjoyed by all and before you knew it, it was time to go. Time really does fly by when you're having fun, no matter the planet. So everybody but Vianna, Queen Yagi and Beautiful went home. For tonight, these three stayed at my home and slept soundly.

After breakfast the next day, I travelled back with them to the palace in the capital, Ark. When we all got off of the flyer, Vianna and her mother headed for the throne room, but I decided to stay back and ask Beautiful if she wanted to show me around the gardens. And of course, with bright eyes glazed over with pure excitement, she said yes.

Beautiful and I were trotting down the gardens together, enjoying ourselves as we embraced the beauty of Arka's nature. Back on Earth, you'd never see anything like this. Most of the greenery was brown and limp from pollution; if you wanted to see anything to match the sole beauty of this garden, you'd have to pay much to venture out for it. Unless you were one of those lucky sods that lived by adequate landscapes in holiday destinations. As we journeyed deep into the gardens, Chamberlain Vern found us and notified that our presence was required in the throne room. Naturally, we nodded and obediently followed Uncle Vern to the throne room.

Finally, we arrived. The four generals were already waiting for me. Chamberlain Vern is always very prompt with his duties. When I marry Vi and I must become a king, and I am able to save Arka from this war, he will be one of the first people to receive my gratitude. And with that, I was whisked off to a meeting room with a kiss from Vianna and the clear instruction of, 'No hitting, and definitely no killing.' How boring.

I completely understand why she ordered that with desperation, I mean I did say I was going to kill one – jokingly, of course. My joke was even missed by my future wife. As I settled into the meeting, the generals look apprehensive at hearing Vianna's order. Before I left, I asked Vianna to get High Prefect Baka to join me and the generals at the meeting.

The generals and I were going through the pleasantries when High Prefect Baka arrived. General Mass questioned my intentions for High Prefect Baka's presence. I informed him that I needed a witness to this meeting and what will be agreed on, so if any party decided to go back on the deal, then I will make the guilty party suffer.

It seemed that Vianna's parting message about no hitting and no killing definitely got them rattled. Good. Now I can get straight to the point.

WHAT ARE THE CHANCES?

'Gentleman, I can finish the unpleasantries between Arkans and Zolgs and wish to do so in a right manner, without a shot being fired and with no casualties on either side!'

Immediately, General Kur pointed out that they had already lost 100,000 soldiers by attempting to storm the fortress.

I looked at him and simply stated, 'I am not Akda, the murdering idiot who send troops to a certain death! And as far as I am aware, I am the only person in here who actually successfully entered, unnoticed, the Zolg stronghold with them being none the wiser. If you agree to my demands, then I will send the Zolgs home without a shot being fired in anger!'

After a spirited discussion between themselves, they finally got round to asking me what my demands were.

'I want a solemn promise that once I destroy the four gun towers, and the Zolg soldiers are standing or keeling with their hands up and unarmed, none of them will be harmed, and as soon as you can arrange for their transport to come and pick them up, you will let them go unmolested and unharmed.'

I did notice that Baka was listening intently, watching the generals discussing my demands like a hawk. Baka was definitely on my side, and for some reason I had this feeling like he knew something that I didn't. And when I have a hunch, I am always certainly correct.

Finally, after about twenty minutes, the generals responded. Generals Mass asked me for details on exactly how I expected to proceed and how on earth I would manage to destroy the four towers that decimated their troops last time they attacked the fortress. In a way, I understood their concern. From my own experience of losing so many troops of my own on Earth, I cannot fathom the nerve these generals have in trusting a racial foreigner over one of their own.

To put their mind at ease, I explained, 'When I was rescuing Queen Vianna's daughter, I had already taken care of the towers. This means I am able to destroy them any time I want, and the only person that terrorised their troops was General Zog, and as you know he is in your custody.'

I then outlined my plan to send a fifth columnist back, so when we enter the fortress, the Zolg troops would surrender without any violence.

Understandably, General Kur asked how I was going to manage that when all of the Zolg commanders are inside the fortress. I simply smiled and told the generals, 'I do not need a commander. Just a Zolg sergeant, who happens, right now, to be in your prison!'

All I have to do is tell him that if his comrades surrender peacefully, then they can all go home back to their families. General Mass did point out that my prisoner is only a sergeant and that does not give him the experience to influence others. I then looked very sternly at the four generals and said, 'Are you really that uninformed about who really is in charge of the troops?'

It is not the generals or the officers who run the army only, it's the sergeants. Apart from Baka they all laughed at this, so I decided to call in the sergeant who flew us here for this meeting. The sergeant who came in was an experienced soldier whose name was Tus. Once he saluted he asked how he could be of help. So I told him to inform the generals who really was in charge of the troops. I could see that he wanted to say something, but he was holding back, mainly because of the generals, or maybe even me, so I decided to properly introduce myself to him.

'Sergeant Tus, I am a commander of His Majesty's forces on my planet, but before I was promoted to my current rank, I was sergeant major and I worked damn hard to achieve this rank!'

As my words were translated, to my surprise, sergeant major was equivalent rank to the chief of sergeants on Arka; this happened to be the rank that every Arkan in the military aspired to be. At this news Sergeant Tus relaxed, and without hesitation he informed the generals that I was quite correct; the sergeants are indeed the ones who run the army. And expected, the generals obviously did not take a liking to that news, but once it was explained to them in laymen's terms, they begrudgingly conceded.

Once that was sorted out, I said that if I did manage to do things right, then there was absolutely no reason why this war shouldn't end peacefully.

Our meeting would have been going for many hours more if it wasn't for Baka, who backed the generals into a corner and into agreeing to my demands. As Sergeant Tus was still present, I asked him to remind the generals of what was agreed on, if the generals suddenly had a bout of amnesia once we get started. I also told them without a hint of smile that if Arkan troops attack the surrendering Zolgs, then I will make them all suffer.

My baby brother already had the flyer ready for me when the meeting ended and he wasn't at all surprised when I asked him to take me to the prison my sergeant was being held at.

As the Zolg was my prisoner I had no trouble getting him released. But what surprised both Jihon and the Zolg sergeant was that I, instead of taking the prisoner somewhere to be interrogated, asked Jihon to take us to a nice bar where they served good food.

Once we got there I put the translating bracelet, which Chamberlain Vern had given me earlier, on the Zolg's wrist and told the confused looking sergeant to just relax and have some nice food that wasn't an army ration.

As the waiter was taking our order, he exchanged some very confused glances across the table. I mean, who could really blame him? You had an Arkan, a Zolg and an Earthman sitting at the table ordering food together like a boy's night out. Despite the waiter's obvious curiosity, he remained professional and took our order without any complications. As we waited for our food, the drinks got delivered and finally, when the sergeant spoke, he said, 'I don't understand what is going on.'

I told him to relax and have some food, and once he was fed, my baby brother and I would take him back to the fortress.

'So I am not a prisoner?' he said.

'Not anymore, my friend,' I replied.

He really didn't know what to make of all of this, so I told him that I spared his life so he could deliver a message to his troops. This way, the war can be brought to a peaceful end. His eyes lit up at this news and quickly asked if his comrades and he will be allowed to go back to their planet. I told him that I was inside the fortress, so I was aware that the commanders and many of his friends wanted to go back. Only General Zog and his elite guards were stopping them, but I removed that obstacle when I kidnapped Zog and killed all of his elite guards when I was rescuing the princess and the ones in service of the traitor Baron Kran. He was happy to hear that the princess was back with her mother and then informed us that everyone at the fortress, apart from the general and his thugs, did not like the fact that the princess was kidnapped and held hostage. He also told us that many of them remonstrated with the general, but all they got was the threat of being flayed if they didn't fall into line. The elite guard made it clear to everyone that the next person who remonstrated would be made an example off.

I told the Zolg that I had to secure their passage home if this war was to finish peacefully. He then told me that he knew everyone in the fortress wanted to go home to their families, he himself hadn't seen or heard from his wife and two kids since they arrived on Arka. As a man who had been in the army, I know what that is like. To go to war independently is one thing, but to subject yourself to war and leave everything you love behind is heart-rending.

But the problem now was that the gun towers were on automatic fire mode, and the only person that could cancel that mode was General Zog himself, but he would rather die than disclose this.

I smiled at him and asked him for his name. He introduced himself as Cos. I told him my and Jihon's name then asked him if I could destroy the gun towers. Once the Arkan troops are inside if his soldiers are all kneeling, unarmed with their hands up, then they will only be prisoners for as long as it takes for their ships, which are orbiting Arka, to land and pick them all up and take them home. My next news made him really happy; the only Zolg that will be staying on Arka as a prisoner till the day he dies was General Zog.

After our meal came, as we began eating we were making polite conversations about food and family. He did enquire about my skin colour eventually. After all, it's clearly not sky blue as the rest of the Arkans, but Jihon informed him that I was from a planet called Earth where the people take war to an art. I almost choked at that, but I had to agree with what Jihon told him and added that the people on my planet were nothing but a bunch of homicidal maniacs who loved nothing more than war.

Once we finished eating, Jihon piloted the flyer to the Zolg fortress and Sergeant Cos told me that he couldn't wait to see his wife, son and his newborn daughter, but since it was a long time since he left, his daughter was not a newborn anymore. Then out of anger he exclaimed, 'We should have never come here in the first place.'

Even though his sudden outburst drew some attention to us we didn't need, I understood his frustration. Between controlled and threatened to obey and risk your life only to be isolated from your family getting nothing in return would anger me too.

*   *   *

When we got to the fortress, Cos told us that the reason he and his comrades could go in and out of the fortress is because of the silver disc they all had that sends a signal to the gun towers, marking them as friendly entities.

WHAT ARE THE CHANCES?

Before he left for the fortress I told him to stay away from the four gun towers; I did not want to kill or injure anyone when I destroyed them. Cos smiled and told me he wanted to make sure that everyone was safe and told us that by the time the Arkan troops entered the fortress, their soldiers would all be kneeling and packed ready to go home.

Jihon and I waved him off before we returned back to the palace to inform Vianna and her mother that all was set to end this conflict peacefully.

Vianna greeted the news in her usual way, by embracing me and giving me a loving kiss. But as for her mother Queen Yagi, well she just said that it was great news before smiling and casually smacking my arse. This woman …

Today is the day that everything will come to an end. Strongly I prayed things would go smoothly as I really didn't like the idea of breaking a promise I made to the Zolg sergeant, Cos. I just hope that he wouldn't let me down.

CHAPTER 14

It's been three days since I had sent Cos back to the fortress. That should have given him enough time to get everybody in there on board and ready to fly home back to the their families.

In fifteen minutes, it would be time for me to order the assault on the fortress. At exactly 0800 hours, I will blow up the four gun towers, which will signal to the 50,000 troops to attack, but only open fire if they are fired on first, and I ensured that the generals made it clear to everyone of the attacking force that no violence was to be used unless the Zolgs initiated first. All the generals are close by, so if any of them gave conflicting orders to mine, I could get my hands on them pronto.

I positioned Jihon on the other side of the fortress, so he could easily step on any Arkan soldier who tried to commit an atrocity once we were inside.

Vianna wished me good luck, and after telling me to be careful about a thousand times, she kissed me about the same amount of times. I could really tell she was worried, not just as my partner, but as a queen for her people. Honestly, I understand why. Everyone of Arka fears a loss of another 100,000 soldiers. While I'm no Akda, I am an alien, a foreigner commanding their troops, and the apprehension of such circumstances is reasonable. But I shall not let doubt get to me, I will do this.

Finally, 0800 hours came, and with one press of my thumb I disintegrated all the four gun towers. It was quite a breathtaking display of carnage. As soon as these towers collapsed and crumbled into rubble, we carefully moved forward towards the four gaps where a moment ago the gun towers stood, and as yet not a single shot was fired by the Zolgs or the Arkans.

As it happened, Sergeant Tus and I were one of the first ones through the gaps in the fortress. We simply had to smile as every one of the Zolgs was kneeling, unarmed and with their hands up in surrender. After the Zolgs were completely encircled, I could see the relief in the Arkan soldier's faces that finally the war had ended and without a single shot fired on both sides. I quickly glanced towards the generals' direction to see that they were busy congratulating themselves.

I instructed everyone to be quiet and then loudly issued an order to the four generals to start making contacts with the Zolg warships above Arka then make the arrangements to take their soldiers home and also to inform their allies the Alphians and the Morrins to let the Zolg ships through to pick up their men.. That was greeted with a loud cheer from both sides.

After a few hours, the first of the Zolg ships landed, which started the exodus of the Zolg troops.

About half of the Zolg soldiers were already gone when Sergeant Cos found me; he was accompanied by one of the Zolg commanders. After Cos introduced us, the commander asked me if we could step to one side as he wanted me to have something.

WHAT ARE THE CHANCES?

Obviously I was intrigued, so I followed him and Cos to one side. The commander gave me what looked like a recording chip and then dropped a bombshell.

'I was the one with my squad who captured King Gah, but I was ordered by General Zog to hand him over to Baron Kran. When I did this, Baron Kran started stabbing him in the stomach, and while the king lay there dying, Kran was telling him what he intended to do to Queen Vianna and the princess Olnia when he took them prisoner.'

I was certainly not expecting this.

He also told me that Kran intended to be the new king of Arka and that he wanted to eradicate the Ark name once and for all. He was even going to rename the capital after himself. 'Everything I have just told you is on this chip recorded, so please tell the Queen that no Zolg has killed him.'

He was very happy to hear that Kran was now a prisoner. He then told me that when the troops inside the fortress found out that Princess Olnia had been rescued and General Zog was gone with all his thugs chopped to bits, they threw a party. He admitted that he and his soldiers had a lot to thank me for. After all, they all wanted to go back home the same day they saw 100,000 Arkans slaughtered by the gun towers. Opening up, he admitted he wasn't originally commander, but since all of the original commanders who remonstrated with General Zog were flayed in front of all the troops, he was promoted.

I always carried some chocolate and caramel bars from back home on me, all thanks to the replicators at my place, so I gave the commander one and Sergeant Cos two for his wife and himself and two more for his kids. They have never seen anything like a chocolate bar before so both of them had this enquiring look on the faces. 'It's something tasty from my planet. Once you try it they will understand what happiness in their mouth really is.'

And with that, I hope I have returned their lives back to them now. And a great way to celebrate was the easy-going approach of an Earth chocolate bar.

As the commander and the sergeant were now the last ones to leave, I walked them to their ship and as we parted, I wished them good luck.

*   *   *

By 1500 hours, all the Zolg troops were gone and the fortress now only contained Arkan soldiers. As it was coming to the time when my Beautiful would finish school, I asked Jihon to fly me there so I could meet her after.

When I got to the school, Vianna and Queen Yagi were already there awaiting Olnia. I was still in my military uniform so Vianna cautiously asked me how it went. Now imagine being able to inform the queen of a planet that you managed to end a war between two alien races with not a shot fired and all of the Zolgs on their way home back to the their families. Now I knew she'd be overwhelmed with exhilaration, but to my surprise, she physically launched herself onto me, knocking me to the ground and proceeded to passionately kiss me as she sat on my stomach.

What are the Chances?

Of course this type of behaviour was not unusual for Vianna; only her behaviour was displayed among a plethora of parents waiting for their children outside the school. If anyone on Arka was not aware that Queen Vianna had a new love interest, then they would definitely know about it after what they had seen. Heck! Even I was quite embarrassed – and I'm not easily embarrassed at all.

The only reason Vianna stopped kissing me was when a well-rehearsed announcement by the four generals was made and transmitted to every informative screen around Arka. Queen Yagi helped me up and then, while smiling, almost accusingly asked me why I couldn't kill at least one of her generals.

'Tempting. But I wanted to maintain a good impression, so I decided to forgo the pleasure,' I laughed with an utterly serious expression.

Finally, when Beautiful came out of the school and saw me standing there with Vianna, she went crazy. She leaped into Vianna's arms as she told her mum and grandmother that this is what she wanted from now on: her mother and her real dad, James, picking her up from school. I had to smile as she then jumped onto me just like her mother did earlier and kissed me, announcing to everyone loudly that I was her real father.

The walk back to the palace felt like centuries, as my Beautiful had to stop and brag to every single passer-by, and this included the palace guards, that I am her real father. I was so sure that some of my hair had faded to grey by the time we got to the main palace doors.

After we got inside the place, I skilfully persuaded Beautiful to draw something nice for me while Queen Yagi, Vianna and I slipped off to talk in private. I needed to relay what I'd learned from the Zolg commander.

When the three of us were in private, I summarised what I had been told then proceeded to pass the chip that I was given by the commander to Queen Yagi.

She inserted the chip into a device and watched as everything we once believed about the incident with King Gah was false. Now Vianna and Yagi knew what really happened once King Gah was captured. I had to cover my mouth as Vianna declared, after watching what had happened to her poor excuse of a husband, he couldn't even die properly. I couldn't tell if she was amused by his incompetence, as she was very upset when Kran stated he would feed both her and Olnia to the Lugii. Though it was probably a bad time, I asked what this entity called a Lugii was. Queen Yagi didn't leave anything to my imagination as she explained that it was a humungous, horrid beast that rips apart the flesh of its victims while they were still alive.

'That is where Kran will be going once the trial for high treason, and now regicide, will conclude,' she furiously stated.

As there was a bit of tension in the room I exclaimed, 'Nice people you have on your planet!'

Both of them looked at me frowning, before letting their burst of laughter fill the room.

Maybe this was because my training, but I had this instinct to turn around. So I spun around to see the door of the room we were in slowly closing. I distinctively remember that this door was closed. That meant someone was there a second ago, but now it was an empty space. I've decided to stay vigilant for this phantom eavesdropper. Might be nothing or it might just be a new threat.

While I was still trying to assess the new development of potential threat, Queen Yagi suddenly asked – I say asked – she actually declared that she would be announcing Vianna and my betrothal this ferga. Vianna was very happy for her mother to make the announcement but as for me, well I did try very hard for the past thirty-plus years to avoid getting imprisoned – sorry, I meant getting married. I had to think quickly.

And then it came to me. 'Your Majesty! I feel that it would not be a good timing of the betrothal as the war with the Zolgs has just ended and their people haven't digested this fact yet. Let them enjoy the victory and get uses to the idea of a white man being with their queen!'

Vianna looked crestfallen, as if she could she would have married me the second I stepped foot on her planet, but Queen Yagi was a diplomat to the core and very calculating, so she smirked, and it was definitely a smirk, and told us that she will leave it for two weeks before she would make the announcement of our betrothal. And then she added, 'Unless you don't want to marry my daughter?'

I swear Yagi has a mind of a mischievous, troublemaking teenager more than Vianna does. Dear, I hope Olnia does not inherit this …

Just that statement from her mother was the first time that I saw real fear in Vianna's eyes.
So I replied, 'I most certainly do want to marry Vianna! But not if it will cost her the loyalty of her people.'

What are the Chances?

Since I'd already used that excuse, I decided to point out a plot we have just discovered against her and the cold-blooded murder of her husband. This way, maybe Yagi will definitely stop pestering me about it. They both had to agree, I was right. But in two weeks, I'd have to go through the betrothal ceremony.

And right then, it hit me.

It wasn't the act of getting married that scared me, but the ceremony of it. After all, Vianna is a queen and I am just an alien who fell in love with her and her daughter. I simply just can't handle the excess stress of a wedding alongside everything else right now. Why can't she just get married to me while I'm away somewhere instead, and then tell me about it after? I had to admit that I would definitely prefer that as I had to be honest, I am scared.

Back on Earth, being part of an organisation concealed from the rest of the world, I had no family or friends I could really see anymore. The closest thing I had outside of the organisation was King George. Then again, we only became close because of our contact during my receiving of my medals and Victoria Crosses. But with romantic relationships, definitely not. I avoided them like the plague. Not just because I wanted to, but because I had to. My identity had to always be unknown in order to work efficiently, and Mia … I don't know what we could have been. She was also part of the same organisation, working as a doctor, but truth be told, we could never have had a meaningful relationship. Vianna is my first relationship I felt had meaning that I wanted to keep forever. But the thought of that scares me; I could never deal with losing her or her losing me.

WHAT ARE THE CHANCES?

*   *   *

The sun was shining as bright as usual alongside the day moon, and the charges against the Krans had been announced. The majority of the Arkans demanded a swift death for the traitors, but High Prefect Baka declared that everything would be done by the law.

When Baka discovered it was in fact Baron Kran who had murdered King Gah and not the Zolgs, he immediately let it be known across Arka that Kran committed regicide. This was received well by some of the Arkan nobility that originally frowned upon our choice to allow the Zolgs to leave. Now they knew that the Zolgs were innocent of regicide as they all came on board with the peaceful victory over the Zolgs. The fact that many of the soldiers vocally gave me the credit for ending the war peacefully went down greatly with the Arkans, and especially with Queen Yagi and Vianna.

I had skilfully managed to get myself back to my place, so I could finally get out of the limelight and seriously prepare for the betrothal announcement in two weeks. I am really panicking about that! When I originally got back to my place, I thought that I would get some peace and quiet and maybe think of something to delay Vianna and my betrothal ceremony, but Jihon with Sania was a frequent visitor and he brought his parents, or shall I say our parents, and then Vianna, Queen Yagi, Beautiful and Baka with his wife. I love them all, but can a guy get some rest? The two weeks, an entire eighteen days, had not only flown by quickly, but I could not come up with anything to delay the betrothal ceremony. Why was this ceremony and the wedding so terrifying?

WHAT ARE THE CHANCES?

Right now my baby brother Jihon was flying me back to the capital and to my doom. Sorry, I meant our betrothal ceremony. I wish that she and her mother would just get on with it and then tell me about it after it was all over. Sadly, even on Earth, it doesn't work like that.

When we landed I was met by Chamberlain Vern, to be escorted to my room where a host of tailors were awaiting me to design my betrothal suit. What was wrong with my rags? They are very strong and I can run in them faster!

Jihon was not even in my room with me to give me bit of moral support, but I don't blame him as I knew he was totally in love with Sania, so he spent every minute he could with her. And her being in the palace just gives him an extra excuse to be there.

After the tailors had finished taking all of my measurements, I arrived shortly after followed by Vianna. Even so Beautiful was climbing all over me to get a hug like a kitten, I had to admit that Vianna looked great and I would be proud to be her husband.

The evening meal was for family only. I supposed I better get used to it though, since the second I say 'I do' I will be with them forever. Queen Yagi was telling me what will happen tomorrow night at Vianna and my ceremony, but I could not help but look bemused at the smug smirk my Beautiful had on her face all evening. She looked like she had won the lottery and she was congratulating herself for all its worth. In spite of myself, I really love that little girl who wormed her way into my heart. I will be proud to be her father once I got married to her mother and as for Vianna, well she didn't just steal my heart, she smacked my face with a host of frying pans and before I knew it I wanted to be with her for eternity.

The next day was pretty much a blur. The last thing I remembered was when Vianna and I were saying goodnight to Beautiful in her bedroom.

When we left Beautiful's bedroom, Vianna and I went for a walk in the Royal Gardens. When we sat down under this amazing tree that looked a lot like a weeping willow back on Earth, she poured her heart out to me.

'You know, James, almost nine years ago my life took a turn for the worse. I lost my father and my mother and I was left alone and before I knew it, I was married to that idiot Gah and very much pregnant with Olnia. You need to know that that I was actually glad and relieved when Gah was killed. Believe it or not but Sania and I actually celebrated his death, and I wouldn't be surprised if the rest of Arka did the same.' She took a deep breath before she continued, 'Also the Zolg invaded and we didn't even have a clue what was happening, but things started to turn for the better the day you saved my, sorry I meant our, daughter from the sarks and then meeting you. But you didn't just bring me love, you also somehow managed to bring my mother back to me. I am the luckiest person in the galaxy and it is all down to you. Thank you, darling.'

She then soundly kissed me. I had to admit that I really loved this woman, and even though the wedding ceremony terrified me, I am more than willing to go through with it so I can call this extraordinary woman my wife.

WHAT ARE THE CHANCES?

I hold her close and asked her about the last day she saw her father and her mother, as I was curious about something.

'Oh James, it was really horrible to wave off your parents just after you had exchanged angry words, only then for the flyer to later crash, leaving me feeling totally empty.' And then she added that she was supposed to be on the flyer with her mum and dad, but because she and Sania got into trouble the night before her parents barred her from travelling with them.

Now that got the alarm bells in my head ringing at this news, so after a few more passionate kisses and comforting hugs, I asked Vianna if she would be all right as I really had to speak to Jihon urgently. She was bit shocked, as it was now 10pm, but she knew that Jihon and I were very close, so she didn't kick up any fuss when I told her that I needed to see him.

By the time I knocked very loudly on Baron Rak and Baroness Mima's – my long-lost parents – front door it was almost 11pm. The servants answered and upon seeing me immediately escorted me to see Jihon. And mothers being mothers, Baroness Mima was also up and offering to make me something to eat and drink. I apologised for the late intrusion but I told her that something urgent came up so Jihon and I had to go out to see someone. Jihon was a little puzzled, but by now he knew me well enough to realise that something was up, so he quickly got dressed before we left the house.

As we left the house he asked me what was so urgent, so I told him to take me to Baka's house. He almost protested as it was late, but one look at my face told him that I was not ready to be argued with. We arrived at Baka's house just before midnight and, although very sleepy, Baka invited us in and ordered his servants to bring us something to drink.

Once the three of us were left alone I quickly told Baka what Vianna told me tonight and about the alarm bells going off in my head. To my sweet surprise, Baka told me that he also thought that something about the flyer accident didn't sit right with him. This is why he has all of the flyers parts safely locked up as he regularly goes through the accident reports to see if he can find anything that will point him to foul play.

I asked him if Jihon and I could look at the incident reports and the flyer. I really needed to look into this. Baka asked me why I was so curious, so I told him that I wasn't really sure myself. It could just be my natural curiosity or the fact that I was very close to my sister, who was a coroner back on my planet. Habits pass on. Looks like that got Baka's attention, but what I was not aware of was that coroner in Arkan translated to prefect; that simple fact got me the approval from Baka to look into the flyer crash.

Baka told me that first thing tomorrow, he would give instructions to the Prefect Corps to assist me in any way I require and since he was the only one with the code to the door where the crashed flyer was, he would be there to open it for us.

After several long conversations, it was now late at night and time to leave Baka's home. Even though I longed for the comfort of my bed, I was far too tired to travel all the way back to my palace, so I decided to sleep at Jihon's. Unfortunately, I found it difficult to drift off as my mind was working overtime. The fact that every time I had a hunch I was always right; this kept me awake for majority of the night.

In the morning, Jihon and I had a quick breakfast and we left even before Mum and Dad were up. When we got to the Prefect Corps' building, Baka was already there waiting for us. He introduced us to the chief of the Prefect Corps and instructed him to give us any assistance we may require. Baka then took us to the hangar, where the crashed flyer was stored, and after showing us everything he left us to our devices.

'Keep me informed of anything you find,' Baka asked, and with a simple nod, he left.

Honestly, I had to feel sorry for Jihon. I couldn't read any Arkan so he had to read all of the accident reports out loud so the bracelet could translate it for me.

After twenty-four hours of reading, or in my case listening to Jihon reading them aloud, the one thing that I kept going back to over and over again was the chief engineer's report of the accident. Jihon didn't see it, but once I had told him that I felt that for a chief engineer to do such a short report, and a not very technical assessment of the flyer, was very suspicious. That is why tomorrow, Jihon and I would be going to the university to get us our own engineering expert.

'Brother, you do know that anyone we get from the university will not be an expert,' Jihon said.

'I don't need them to be an expert. I need them to be eager and have a hunger for knowledge,' I then winked at him and told him that we would be getting ourselves a top engineering student.

What are the Chances?

So after spending all night in the hangar, Jihon and I went to the University of Ark to get ourselves an expert. What I need was someone with the passion of learning, and not someone who was all skill.

Once we finally arrived, Jihon took me to meet the university dean so we could get his approval for taking a student out of class in order to help us with our investigation. The dean took us to the final year of the engineering degree class and introduced us to the professor and the students. I was not in the mood for long greetings so I cut across the pleasantries and asked who the best student in this class was. Unanimously, the class and the professor shouted out the name 'Matt'.

'Alright Matt, can he step forward?' I exclaimed.

On my planet, the name 'Matt' is short for 'Matthew' – a boy's name. But instead of a boy stepping forward, a very pretty girl stood up. 'I am Matt, Commanders!'

After letting a look of shock slip out, I brought myself quickly out of it as I wanted to get going. I turned to her and told her to get her stuff. For now, she is in my service until further notice. The professor wanted to object, but the dean quickly pointed out to him that Jihon was under royal command and that I was the queen's betrothed. There shall be no objections today, my friend.

The three of us left the university without delay. First port of call: food. Jihon and I haven't had a chance to eat anything yet.

As the three of us were scoffing down our delicious food, I quickly explained to Matt what we needed her for and that from now on, she was our engineering expert. When we got back to the hangar, located at the Prefect Corps site, we were informed by the Prefect Corps sergeant that if we needed anything, then we just had let them know and they would get it for us. We thanked him before entering the hangar. Throughout the whole journey, Matt was squealing, clearly excited to be working with us. I could not fault the young girl's excitement though, this is a rare opportunity that will look quite adequate on her record.

Before Matt could even put her things down, I asked Jihon to show the chief engineer's accident report to her. We didn't say anything to her as we wanted her to take in what she read clearly. Instead, we waited patiently for her to finish reading.

When she did, she had this expression on her face that showed she was very unhappy with it. Suddenly, all of her bubbly energy seemed to drain out of her. That was one unhappy engineer. Jihon asked Matt what she thought of it, and to our delight she came to the same conclusion as us. The report is unsubstantial and it showed to anyone with engineering knowledge that the flyer was not investigated thoroughly.

'Can I inspect the flyer and the parts myself?' she asked. So we invited her to be our guest.

She opened her bag and took a pair of anti-static gloves out and put them on. She started her investigation while Jihon and I went back to the paperwork from the accident.

Baka came around on his way home to see how things were going and to inform me that Vianna was looking for me. I asked him to cover for me and tell her that he had sent me to check something. I stressed the importance of him being very, very vague about what it was.

What are the Chances?

Jihon and I have been at the paperwork for almost two days, it was not a surprise when both of us just fell asleep.

Both us were in an amazing, comfy deep sleep. That was until Matt decided to give us both a heart attack in the early hours of the morning. She was all excited, jumping around as she wanted to show us what she had uncovered.

So half asleep, Jihon and I trotted towards the wreckage of the flyer that cost King Herc his life. Matt showed us this part of the flyer that she called the 'energy runner'. Even with her simplified terminology, Jihon and I didn't have a clue what it was for or what that even did, but we did stare at it intently.

She then asked us very carefully pay attention to what happens when she charged the energy runner. What we saw was impressive, but we still didn't have a clue. But what did shock us was how, out of the blue, the energy runner that was once full of blue-coloured energy, suddenly extinguished itself after something black shot out from under the energy runner's guard. Both of us looked inquiringly at Matt, so she explained in layman's terms what has transpired.

Matt informed us that the black part that suddenly shot out from under the runner guard should not be there. 'The only function of that part is to prevent the energy from getting to the flyer's engine.'

She then showed us the energy runner on the other side of the flyer and after she powered it, the same thing had happened. Because she knew that this flyer was the one that King Herc died in, she lowered her eyes and told us that this flyer was sabotaged and that whoever did this killed King Herc. I had to admit, to see such a lively girl suddenly exert an aura of death so suddenly was very scary.

What are the Chances?

Well, this news got us both wide awake. Jihon was planning some serious deaths for the person who did this, but as he was planning, I took Matt to one side and asked her if she could remove both of the energy runners without damaging the evidence. She simply smiled and told me she could without a problem.

I asked her to go ahead and remove them both and then told Jihon to stop inventing different ways to kill a person so he could get some sleep instead. Jihon got himself under control and got back into his chair and promptly fell asleep. Once Matt safely removed the energy runners and we stored them near us, I told her to get some sleep and then I too went to sleep.

We were all awoken by Baka with some delicious hot breakfast, so after the pleasantries all four of us got some food inside us before I realised that the three of us were so completely submerged into a pool of investigation, we all hadn't actually eaten anything since 2pm yesterday.

Once we finished our breakfast, we informed Baka that his dear friend King Herc was murdered. After Matt explained in detail what was happening with the energy runners, Baka was ready to not only arrest the chief engineer for not spotting this, but he was also ready to castrate him to for this serious oversight. I asked Baka to keep this all to himself for the time being as I wanted indisputable evidence on who the culprit, or culprits, were before we make our move. I made it clear that I didn't want him to go anywhere near the chief engineer. If he really wanted to do something, then I instructed him to go to the palace and do some discreet snooping – as in asking the garden staff who was in service during the sad times of King Herc and Queen Yagi's last trip.

He agreed immediately but was inquisitive about my plans. I told him that Jihon, Matt, the energy runners and I will be going back to my place so I can collect some DNA off them. He wanted to know what DNA is, but I told him it would be far too long concept to explain. So once I find if there is any DNA on the energy runners, I will collect it and explain it to him then.

Twenty minutes later, the three of us were in the flyer heading towards my place and the truth.

CHAPTER 14.5

Why have Mummy, Daddy and Grandma snuck off? I think they went into a closed-door meeting. It's not fair! I never get to come! I looked at Uncle Vern to see him surprisingly invested in the drawing I was supposed to be doing for my real daddy. I quickly make some excuses to Uncle Vern that I need to get some extra materials for this drawing.

If I'm sneaky enough, maybe I can listen in.

Quickly, I ditched Uncle Vern and made my towards Mummy's private audience chamber. Once I got there, I carefully opened the door so that Daddy, Mummy and Grandma wouldn't notice. I squatted so I could be less visible.

The longer I peered through the small gap, the more shocked I became. I actually saw my fake dad, Gah, being murdered by the traitor Kran. Daddy was right, Kran really is a bad man!

Even worse, Kran told Gah that he was going to feed me and my mummy to the Lugii. I am old enough to know what the Lugii is now, no matter what Mummy says. I even learned in biology how dangerous the Lugii really was. I did not want to end up as Lugii food! I have to be a big girl now!

I didn't want to get spotted eavesdropping by Mummy, Daddy and Grandma so quietly I slipped away, making sure to keep my footsteps light, slowly closing the door to the chamber behind.

I went straight to my room and began hatching a plan to get my revenge on the traitor Krans. The question was, how exactly was I going to do this. Sure I am Princess Beautiful, but who would listen to me?

It had been three days since I eavesdropped on the conversation. As of yet, I hadn't come up with anything to form my plan. But by sheer chance, I do recall hearing Grandma telling Mummy to hide the evidence video chip in her room.

'Weak,' I muttered under my breath with a small smirk.

I am a little girl. Finding and knowing all of the hiding places in Mummy's room is practically my job. I basically knew all of them – I think. I cracked my knuckles, as what my plan of action would be struck me.

As soon I was sure that Mummy was busy, I snuck into her bedroom and then systematically went through every hiding place I already knew existed in the bedroom. I was a little disappointed with my mummy when I found the video chip after only investigating the second hiding place. Weak, Mummy, very weak.

I giggled as I ran with the video chip in my hand to my room where I copied it before promptly returning the original video chip to its hiding place in Mummy's bedroom. Lesson number one of theft, always replace the original with the original – or a very good dupe.

Now, the second part of the plan would be a bit trickier as it involved getting Uncle Strah, who was Gah's cousin, to do my bidding. I knew that Uncle Strah and Gah did not get on, but I also knew that Uncle Strah loved me and always comforted me every time Gah was nasty to me.

I decided to take a moment to think really hard about my approach to Uncle Strah. What would I even do or even say? I just needed him to help me carry out my plan.

What made it so difficult to think was the fact that Daddy James was leaving for his place, so I wouldn't be able to see him for at least three days. Why can't they just get married now, so Daddy James doesn't have to leave her? I'm going to have to speak to Mummy so Mummy can get really serious about marrying Daddy. Why is this taking so long?! I can't think properly without being so distracted.

Over the next two days, I could only develop my plan when I was in bed because I wanted to spend some quality time with my daddy before he goes back to his place. But after he had left for his place, it became easier for me to think as I had more time.

I was walking with my grandmother in the Royal Gardens when the next step of the plan struck me with the force of a thousand lightning bolts. 'Grandma, what will happen to the traitor Kran?' I inquired innocently.

The information I got was a true goldmine. Now I knew that I could never get at Baron Kran himself, but his son was a very different story. I now had my target, and that target will pay with his life for his father's treacherous decisions.

Nevertheless, I had to think on two very important things to be able to succeed with my plan: how to approach Uncle Strah, and then how I would convince him to help my carry out my plan of revenge.

WHAT ARE THE CHANCES?

The next three days had just flown by, and as hard as I tried to think of a way to approach Uncle Strah I just couldn't think of anything. I decided that what I needed was a break and a bit of a distraction. After a little bit of brainstorming, this ferga would be perfect because I can spend all of my time with Mummy and my real dad at his place. Every time I'm there, there is always lots to do; Daddy James always thinks of something exciting to do. Plus, I love those Earth-films for children!

Although, I get so upset when the films are clearly stated as for children, so why are the adults always watching them and spoiling the fun? It's no fair! Once Daddy James is married to my mum, I will have to talk to Daddy about this. Films for children should only be for children and the adults need to go away and stop interfering.

Despite my annoyance though, I had admit that I really did miss Daddy James in times like these.

I couldn't wait to step off the flyer and run straight into my daddy's arms when we got to his place. It had only been around four days since he left, but I still missed him immensely, even if I was scheming behind everyone's back. I had already made up my mind that I would try to talk to Daddy about my problem, but I also had to make sure not to give too much away. After all, I did not want to give away my plans for Kran's son. The problem was that Grandma Yagi was here too, and she is always watching Daddy as if she were up to no good. Maybe I'm imagining it, but Grandma Yagi is known for her mischievous nature. I might even take after her.

First day of ferga was fantastic as Daddy made some of that delicious food from his planet and I had my favourite drink, 'hot chocolate'. Yummy! Daddy made us all skate in thick socks on the floor. Although Mummy slipped a few times, Daddy always caught her in his arms. It was fun, but I think he secretly wanted us to just polish the floor as he is always a very clean and tidy person. He even somehow persuaded me to tidy after myself all the time, even Mummy and Grandma can't do that. He must have a magical touch.

Tomorrow everyone from Mummy and Daddy's group of friends would be arriving; it's always a lot of fun as Mummy and Daddy always make up lots and lots of fun games. Even the food that Daddy cooks is wow!

But before I knew it, ferga was at an end, which meant that in a few hours, I would be flying back with my mum and grandma. This was my chance to test the waters with Daddy about my plan. Without details of course.

'Daddy!' I called out, putting my cutest facial expression yet. They fall for it every time.

I asked to talk to him in private, so without a moment's hesitation, he took us to the gardens where we could discuss freely. 'Somehow, I need to speak to my Uncle Strah, but I didn't want to make it sound like a command. Can you please help me how to approach him without upsetting him?'

Daddy James looked at me very intently; his aura of suspicion reeked. 'Why do you need to speak to the captain of the prison?'

Heck! I did not know that Daddy knew this. Quickly, I had to come up with a lie, which I did, although it did have a bit of truth in it.

What are the Chances?

'Uncle Strah was always very nice to me, especially after idiot Gah was nasty to me, and as he is Gah's cousin, I really want him to be okay with you marrying my mum and being my official dad and not that Gah person.'

Daddy took some time to think on what I said, and then advised me just to call him and tell him that I really needed to speak with him and that it is important to me.

Wow, my real daddy is very clever! Now that was some good advice – simple, but good. And it definitely didn't sound like a command from a princess. I gave Daddy James a big hug and kissed him thank you for his guidance.

Now I knew how to approach Uncle Strah and present my proposal to him, and all thanks to my Daddy James.

After smiling to myself, I thought about an ideal world, if I had my own way, then my mum and James would be getting married now! And not in two weeks' time! It's not fair, not fair, not fair!

Unfortunately, as was I thinking I realised I had to carry out my plan within a week because after, I'll be too busy getting ready for the royal wedding. I am so excited!

*   *   *

I must've been really tired as I didn't even remember getting back to the capital and the palace. I had woken in my bed somehow; Grandma was there getting my clothes ready for school. I love Grandma Yagi and I hated the fact that she was absent from my life for so long. But I loved that she was back, and that baby brother

WHAT ARE THE CHANCES?

Jihon and Daddy James brought her back from the wilderness and all its dangers. That must've been so scary! I'm internally squirming just thinking about it! But it is okay. Grandma Yagi is a strong, brave woman.

This morning I made sure to be a good girl as I didn't want to be making any mistakes. Today was my day of action and if I did this right, then Uncle Strah will help me get rid of traitor Kran's son.

During school, I made sure to be a very good student too. I even put my hand up and answered many questions correctly. I went on to the school director's office at lunch time and asked her to contact Captain Strah as I had to speak with my urgently. As I was a princess, the director contacted Uncle Strah with limited hesitation and he arrived at the school within an hour. No matter what, I could always rely on Uncle Strah, especially before my real daddy came onto the scene.

When he arrived, he had this curious look on his face and asked me what the problem was. If I were him, I'd be rather suspicious too. I need to play this smartly. I asked him to wait until they were in private as I definitely didn't want to be overheard.

Once we were in the director's office alone, all I could do was blurt it out. It was now or never, Beautiful. 'I want you to send Kran's son to the Lugii!'

Expectedly, Uncle Strah was taken aback by this, but calmly asked why I wanted this. So I showed him the video chip that I copied and asked him to watch it. As he watched the video I carefully watch him and his expression. When the bit came up when traitor Kran was telling Gah he was going to feed me and my mum to the Lugii, he definitely did not appreciate this. He even yelled, 'Over my dead body!'

He then went very quiet and gave me the video chip back. After what seemed like years, he finally told me something I've been dying to hear for weeks now. He will do it for me. 'No one that threatens my niece lives.'

But what I asked him next made him go very pale, which wasn't easy when your skin colour is blue. I asked him to record the Lugii ripping Kran's son apart and then make his father Kran watch it.

After some time he told me to remind him never to upset me, as he definitely didn't want to be Lugii bait. I smiled cutely and asked him sweetly if he will do that for me. He simply nodded and then stood up, which made me a bit confused as I didn't know what I should do or say next. But thankfully I didn't have to as Uncle Strah informed me that it will be done by tomorrow and then he gave me a hug and a kiss and left the director's office.

Well, that was easier than I thought! I huffed out a great sigh of relief. One point to Olnia Ark! I really thought that he would object and even go as far as to tell my mum or grandma, but he didn't. Uncle Strah, you are the best of your family.

I was on edge all evening as I was convinced that Uncle Strah would tell on me to my mum. As a matter of fact, I was so concerned about this that my grandma even asked me if something was bothering me. Of course I said no, but I had learned by now that Grandma was very shrewd, even so more than my mum, so I was mentally prepared for the bombardment of her questions that always led to more questions.

WHAT ARE THE CHANCES?

Wow, she was really relentless, she even popped in to say goodnight and asked me more questions. I endured every question she threw at me; I had to play innocent to a core. I had to admit that tonight was the first time that I could not wait to go to bed.

Morning came and I was all excited but a little scared, just in case Uncle Strah did decide to tell on me, but today I will get my revenge for my kidnapping and Kran's intention towards me and my mum if he succeeded. Deep down inside I felt that today would be a day of reckoning.

After breakfast Mum took me to school as usual and all throughout the lessons I could not concentrate as I was really hungry for the news of my revenge.

Finally, Uncle Strah arrived at lunch time to inform me that it was done, but when I asked him to show me the recording of the Lugii being fed; he told me off and said that beautiful little girls like me should not be watching horrible things like that. Then he added that both of his children are much older than me and he would still not let them watch an execution.

I smiled at him and told him that execution is a dirty word and in this case I would call it retribution for his father's crimes. I knew no matter how much I tried though, he would never let me see. In a few years maybe. Okay, Maybe in ten or twenty years or so.

Before he left he told me to be good to my new father as Daddy James was very special. When he said that I jumped up to give him a great hug and a kiss and told him I know – I'm glad everyone knows it too.

CHAPTER 15

When we got back to my place, I told Matt to make herself at home and relax, and as for me I quickly refreshed myself and went into the kitchen to cook something up for us. But for the mean time, I gave her a little snack as she waited patiently. She definitely enjoyed the strawberries and raspberries from back home.

As always the food from my planet went down well. What can I say? I take after my Grandma Lucy who was an excellent cook. And after dinner when we all cleaned up, I introduced them both to my DNA briefcase which would help us identify the murderers of King Herc. I didn't even get a chance to open it and Matt threw so many questions at me that if I were to answer all of them, then we would never get to the part of catching the killers. Plus I really don't know exactly how the DNA briefcase works; the training I received from Professor Mia was to collect the finger print, actually not really the finger print but rather the fat from it, add it to a solution then shake it well and then put a drop on what Mia called the filter and then wait for the computerised bit of the briefcase to do its job. On all my missions in the past every time I had to use the DNA briefcase I always got the correct result, which was very important as I definitely did not want to kill any of Andy's or Mia's or any of my ancestors when I was in the past on a mission.

WHAT ARE THE CHANCES?

So what Matt got out of me was, 'Just wait and see!'

I instructed Matt to remove the black thing that was extinguishing the energy to the flyer engine and there we got lucky because where the black thing was housed, we got some finger prints and that is not the only thing we got. One of the black things had dried blood. Looks like whoever fitted this so long ago had cut themselves; must have been badly as there were more than just few drops.

I like when things go my way, as it is less complicated. Especially since this is a brilliant piece for the trial of the Krans.

While the years-old fat from the perpetrators and dried blood were safely dissolving in the solutions, I gave Matt and Jihon a demonstration of how the DNA system works. First it took me only a few minutes to explain to Matt what DNA is and what a double helix carrying genetic instructions for the development, functioning, growth and reproduction of all known organisms and many viruses. Unfortunately it took a lot longer to explain it to Jihon. I did feel sorry for Jihon as I remembered being in Jihon's shoes when Professor Mia first explained DNA to me, and to be honest if she didn't develop this magic DNA briefcase I still wouldn't have an idea. I think that the reason Mia invented this DNA briefcase was so thick idiots like me would be able to do my job better and easier.

What?

I never pretended that I was a genius. Basically I am a Mensa reject and most probably my IQ is the same as my shoe size. ELEVEN!

WHAT ARE THE CHANCES?

Anyway, I took some saliva samples from Jihon and Matt and then after adding the solution to them and doing some nifty shaking, I entered their DNA in the briefcase by putting a drop from each of the two test tubes that I was shaking like mad. Now both of Matt's and Jihon's DNA were in the system. I then asked them to each pick a glass and that enabled me to collect the fat from their finger prints and I repeated the procedure. Once I put a drop of it on the filter, the system quickly matched Matt's and Jihon's DNA that I entered only about thirty minutes before.

Despite my display of confidence, I had to admit that I was worried because Matt and Jihon are not from Earth, meaning the whole DNA process could not work.

What could I say? When Mia invents something, it really does work no matter what planet it's used on. Well done, Professor Mia!

After the fat from the fingerprints and the dried blood got a good soaking in the solution I put a drop from each vial onto a filter, after cleaning it each time of course, and we ended up with two different DNAs.

Now all we had to do is match them up, and we already had one prime suspect. What made it even more solid was when Baka contacted me and informed me what he'd found out. And what he found out was who messed with, sorry I meant serviced, the royal flyer on the day of the ill-fated flight. Our first murderer, sorry I meant suspect, was none other than the chief engineer, as Matt and I had deducted already.

Tomorrow, after a good hearty breakfast, Jihon and I will obtain a sample of DNA from him and another from someone I suspected had a hand in it – or in this case, a fingerprint in it.

After breakfast I made arrangements to be met by Sergeant Tus and a few other sergeants so they could protect Matt. I wanted Matt to be safe while Jihon and I would go and obtain the DNA samples from our prime suspect, plus a surprise guest that is a strong candidate for the other DNA sample we discovered. When the three of us landed at a military flyer port, we were met by Sergeant Tus and three other sergeants whom Tus trusts. I explained to them that they had to protect Matt at all costs and to take her to the Prefect Corps' hangar and wait for us there.

Once Matt was escorted to safety, Jihon and I went looking for the chief engineer, whose name is Brud.

It took us some time to find him as he wasn't easy to find, since he was the only chief engineer on Arka and he moved around a lot. I was bit annoyed that it took so long to find him so I didn't have the energy nor the patience to be friendly. Basically, I came up to him and told him to open his mouth so I could take a DNA sample. He was taken aback by my request and refused to open his mouth at first, but I informed him that if he didn't comply with my request then I would break his nose and few other parts of his body. That got his undivided attention and he immediately opened his mouth for me to take a DNA sample from him. One thing that struck me as we were walking away from him was his worry-struck face; he looked as if he was ready to run and hide, so I got Jihon to contact Baka and I was sure that his Prefect Corps would be picking him up soon.

As we were making our way towards our transport Jihon asked

me where we were off to next. I told him prison where that traitor Kran was housed; he looked genuinely puzzled, but not shocked.

When we got to the prison both of us were escorted to Captain Strah, who was in charge of the prison. He was a very friendly and very reliable fellow, so after the niceties I asked if we could see traitor Kran. He was very polite but refused us immediately. He did explain that because Kran's trial was in progress, he could not allow anyone but High Prefect Baka or Kran's counsel to see him. I told him that I needed something from him, but straight away he asked what it was. I know that Beautiful loves him and he always looked out for her so I decided to trust him with this information. 'Look, Captain, I don't really need to talk to him, but what I need is either some of his saliva or some blood on this bit of cotton bud without you touching any part of the bud yourself!'

He didn't even ask for an explanation why. He simply took the bud and asked us to wait here and enjoy the drinks he had made for us while awaited his return.

A few minutes later, Strah walked in with my sample, but it wasn't saliva but blood on it, safely sealed in the container with the cotton bud. I thanked him and asked him how it went. Without a hint of smile he told me that he came up to Kran and smacked him in the mouth, then when he was on his knees bleeding, he dipped the cotton bud in his blood and here we are. Jihon and I both burst out laughing at this news, as we got what we needed and it was easier to get than expected. I thanked Strah and after telling him he is a good man, I told him that if he ever needed something from me, then all he had to do was ask.

WHAT ARE THE CHANCES?

We were just about to walk out of his office when he said he actually really needed our help. Jihon and I stopped dead in our tracks, closed the door and sat back down.

'What's on your mind?' I said to him. He looked carefully at me then at Jihon and then told us that he was in big trouble. 'What's going on?' we asked him.

And what he told us shocked us with the impact of a thousand storms.

'You know traitor Kran's son, Srin?' Jihon replied agreeing, adding that he will face High Prefect Baka with his treacherous father. 'Well ... ' he cleared his throat. 'No, he will not,' Strah insisted and then he added that he fed him to the Lugii.

Now I know I call Jihon my baby brother, but what happened next made me smile and I even burst out in open laughter when he shouted at Strah, asking him if he was out of his mind. He sounded like a seven-year-old rather than a twenty-something-year-old.

Then, Jihon informed him that only a member of the royal family could give the order to send someone to the Lugii and he knows that neither Queen Vianna or Queen Yagi would give this order without going through trial first.

Strah agreed, but added that it wasn't them that gave him the order. At this point, both Jihon and I looked at each other and simultaneously widened our eyes before shouting, 'Olnia!'

Strah told us what Olnia did and I couldn't help but laugh at the way Beautiful went about all of this. Now I know why she asked me how to approach Strah. And then it struck me: the open door slowly closing to Vianna and Yagi's private chambers. The eavesdropper was Beautiful! There was me all stressed thinking it was a wild threat. She managed to outmanoeuvre me, Vianna and, I bet, Grandma Yagi too. Quietly, I was very impressed with her, as I know what Kran had in store for Vianna and Beautiful if he succeeded.

Olnia is a smart little one.

Jihon didn't have any words for what we had just learned, but I am very good at thinking my way through a problem under pressure. So I told Strah that I would sort it with Vianna and Yagi and to leave everything to me. Then I added that Olnia might be grounded for all of her life after this, but I will take care of it as even Jihon had to concede that Strah was following a royal order, and he should know as he was also under royal command.

I think that next time I see Beautiful I don't know if I should hug her or scold her.

Now that Strah told us about this, I could see the great relief on his face, but what it showed to me was that he will always have Beautiful's back and that makes him trustworthy in my book.

After leaving the now relieved Strah at the prison I asked Jihon to take us back so I could start the DNA test for Kran. I don't know why, but I bet my life that he was involved in Vianna's father's death. It's regicide.

It took us about an hour to get back but it was nice to see that apart from the Prefect Corps' troops outside the door to the hangar, there were also two of the sergeants with them whom Tus trusted. Smiles were all around as we didn't come back empty handed. Jihon and I brought food and drink for all of them, so they were very much appreciative.

WHAT ARE THE CHANCES?

After giving them their food, Jihon and I went inside to feed Matt, Tus and his friend, as well as us of course.

After we had been fed and watered, Matt and Jihon and I went apart to start the DNA testing.

First we used the saliva from Chief Engineer Brud and after introducing the solution and shaking it like I was dancing at a disco rave, I put a drop of it on the DNA briefcase filter. It took less than a minute to get a result as the dried blood droplets that we got from the black thing that extinguished the energy to the flyer engine were a match for Brud – there was no denying it. I think that Matt and Jihon were more excited about this than I was, but what I wanted was the confirmation of my suspicion about Kran. But as I just introduced his blood to the solution for the second DNA test, I needed to be patient and after all, Jihon and I wanted it to be a surprise to Matt as we did not tell her whose the second DNA sample was.

Once I cleaned the briefcase filter and introduced the new DNA sample droplet onto it, I was as excited as a little kid who was taking the tour of a cream egg factory.

If Tus or any of his friends looked at us, they would have seen three faces staring intently at a screen of an unusual looking case for some crazy reason.

And then it happened … the DNA matched the blood sample that Strah obtained for us from the traitor Kran. Jihon just smiled and told me that when I am right, I am right. I have trained my little brother well.

Matt was shocked that one man could cause so much sorrow.

WHAT ARE THE CHANCES?

She then told us that her and her parents loved King Herc. She couldn't believe how anyone could do this. Jihon decided to comfort her while I went to open the door, commanding the Prefect Corps officer to go and get High Prefect Baka immediately. He argued that Baka was in court, but Tus' friends pointed out to him that as I will be marring Queen Vianna, it would not be fit to disobey their future king. As expected, this got the officer sprinting towards the court.

Although I appreciated the support of Tus' friends, hearing other people state that once I marry Vianna I will be a king shocked me. But more like a spaceship's-worth of frying pans slapping me in the face all at once kind of shocked.

I don't want to be a king! I hadn't even thought about anything like this. I just loved the thought of being a husband and that's it! I wonder if that be possible and if not, I will have to see if I can persuade Vianna not to make me a king.

Crap!

This is another thing I have to worry about, and I bet if Yagi had her way she would slap that crown, or whatever they wear, onto my head the moment I say I do. But even with all these racing thoughts in my head, it was no time to figure out a solution now. So I turned round and went back inside the hangar.

When I got back I didn't know what Jihon did but Matt was now openly crying as he was getting some disapproving looks from Tus and his friend. Once I came up to Jihon and Matt, he told me that she is very upset about what we have just found out.

Thirty minutes later, Baka walked in and the look on his face showed that he was ready to start decapitating the people that were responsible for the murder of his dear friend. Believe me, I did feel the same way.

Before I told him who they were, I quickly explained to him how the DNA test worked and made a point of their accuracy. Once he processed all of this he asked whether Chef Engineer Brud was one of them. Straight away Matt confirmed this, but what he did not expect was when we told him that the second DNA sample that we recovered belonged to Kran. This flew Baka into a spiral of rage, which he took out on a perfectly innocent chair he sat on a few seconds ago. Once he finally composed himself, he went to the hangar door, opened it and commanded the squad of his corps to go and immediately arrest Chef Engineer Brud. When the officer in charge of the Prefect Corps asked him on what charge, I had to step in as Baka was ready to rip the officers head off with his bare hands. Quickly, I stepped in and told him in the charge of regicide. That got him and his squad running off to arrest Brud.

Baka then went back in and sat on the nearest chair, putting his head in his hands and began to cry.

CHAPTER 16

Baka was still crying when the officer charged with arresting Brud came back to report that Brud was now in custody. Once Baka got himself under control, he asked me if I could come with him to tell Yagi and Vianna that Herc was murdered.

As Matt was the most important witness to this case, I asked Jihon and Tus to protect her and keep her safe until we knew that only those two were involved in this for definite. Both of them agreed without hesitation and even Tus' friend said that he would also protect her at all costs. After that, Baka and I left the hangar and made our way towards the transport, which would take us to the palace.

When Baka and I arrived he was still in the sombre mood he was in before we left the Prefect Corps' hangar. Baka requested for me to take over if he broke down again and cried. I am angry and sad at the situation, but I cannot imagine Baka's pain. He believed all these years the death of his dear friend was a mere accident when in actual fact, it was cold-blooded murder. And for what? For power?! I guess evil is uniform on every planet. But deeply, I admired him as his friendship with Vianna's father must have been something really special.

After comforting Baka, we entered the throne room. It happened that both Vianna and Yagi were there, so I motioned Chamberlain Vern over and asked him if he could free both queens from their duties immediately. One look at Baka told him that this must happen now, so he cleared his throat and declared to all the barons and baronesses that both Queen Yagi and Queen Vianna were done for the day. I shifted my gaze to Vianna's face and saw that she was grateful for this. Since our betrothal was announced, everyone wanted to make themselves known to her and Queen Yagi so they could weasel an invite to our wedding, but my future mother-in-law definitely had this 'what's going on?' look on her face.

Vern was great as he didn't stand for any nonsense. This meant that he quickly dismissed everyone waiting to speak to the queens and made it unequivocally clear that he was not to be argued with.

Before Baka could speak, I stepped in by asking Vianna and Yagi to accompany us to Vianna's private audience chamber, and shortly after I asked Vern to make sure that we would not be disturbed.

Once we were in private, I suggested to both Vianna and Yagi that they might want to sit down. They did that without a moment's thought as they were both astute knowing that a bombshell would be dropped within a few moments. Once we were all sitting comfortably, I turned to Baka and asked him to convey what we had discovered. I felt that this news should've come from Herc's best friend rather than some white dude from another planet.

For about five minutes, Baka remained quiet and when he finally spoke his voice was shaky when he informed them that his best friend, Vianna's father and Yagi's husband, was actually murdered.

WHAT ARE THE CHANCES?

In all my time that I have known Vianna, she was always the cool-headed one while her mother was the impulsive one, but the second Baka stopped talking Vianna exploded with anger and Yagi was not too far away. Those two were definitely related. Once their anger subsided, but not by much, both asked if we knew who the murderers were and if we had proof. I then explained what I had been doing for the past three days and how DNA works and how we obtained it. Baka also discovered that both Brud and Kran were good friends at the academy. I was still trying to think of a way to inform them about what Beautiful did when Yagi began telling us that she was going to send Kran's son to the Lugii and make Kran and his wife watch while the Lugii was ripping his son's flesh apart. This that was my cue to drop my bombshell.

I leaned back in my chair and with straight face I told Yagi, 'This is a good idea, but you can't do that.'

Yagi got out of her seat came up to me, stuck her face red with rage into mine and asked me, 'Why not?' She then added, 'I am a queen and if I say this will happen, then this will happen!' She went back to her seat.

I let her sit down before I informed her that she still couldn't do that as Kran's son has already been Lugii lunch. Vianna then jumped out of her seat, demanding to know who did this as he could only die by royal command. She knew very well that her mum and herself did not issue this command until now. I love Beautiful and I really wanted her to see her eighteenth birthday, so as gently as I could, I informed everyone present that this was done by royal command. Only the royal command did not originate from them. Both Vianna and Yagi wanted to know who then as they were the only ones with the power to issue that command. Being extra cautious with my tone, I reminded them that there was also someone else who had that power and that she liked to eavesdrop on private conversations.

My poor Vianna still didn't get it when Yagi slumped back in her seat and started to laugh uncontrollably. Both Vianna and Baka looked at her when she stopped laughing just to say one word and then went back to laughing. When Vianna and Baka heard Olnia they both looked shocked, but not because she was only seven years old, but by her maturity to be able to give this order and understand it. Heck! Even I would never have expected such an action from such a sweet seven-year-old girl.

While they were still digesting this news, I told them that great minds think alike. I made sure to tell Yagi that Beautiful also got Kran and his wife to watch while their son was being de-fleshed. However, saying this aloud makes me think the whole Ark family were sadists. Sadistic minds think alike? Once Baka, Vianna and Yagi processed this news, they all started to laugh, but deep down inside I think that it was a way to deal with the fact that their loved one was murdered.

After all that laughing came silence and it seemed like ages had passed when Baka spoke in a quiet voice. He told us that tomorrow new charges would be read out in court and that Brud would be standing with the Krans, also charged with regicide. He then turned to me and asked me to be a witness for the prosecution and also to explain to everyone in court what this DNA was and how it worked. I agreed readily until he told me that I would have to wear my 'best uniform' as he put it. Well, my best uniform, which I just happened to pack with me when I came to Arka, is my Number 2s with all the trimmings: military flashes, ribbons, medals. And I have a lot of them. But if Baka wants to dazzle everyone in court, so be it!

Vianna then asked her mum what she should do about her daughter, giving the order to send Kran's son to the Lugii. Before Yagi could answer I stepped in and asked, 'Why should you do anything?'

Then I added that we should not give her any more stage as it is. She made a grown up decision, and that is it. Then I smiled and told Vianna, 'Maybe you should tell her off for eavesdropping to private conversations instead.'

Without a hint of a smile Vianna, looked straight at me and asked, 'Why?'

She did it when she was younger many times; that way she could stayed abreast of situations in the palace. At hearing this I shook my head and then I said, 'Like mother, like daughter!'

Vianna beamed a great big smile in my direction, so I decided to respond to that cheeky and challenging smile.

'That might very well be fine, my love, but she better not be doing any eavesdropping when I am telling you what I intend to do to you on our wedding night!' Straight away she wanted to know, right in front of Yagi and Baka, what I intended to do to her on our wedding night. I just smiled at her and told her, 'Now, that would be telling! Wouldn't it, my love?'

WHAT ARE THE CHANCES?

Vianna still had to have the last word when she asked her mum if we could get married tomorrow. Yagi came to my rescue for once when she told Vianna that the royal wedding date has been set and that's it!

Then she gave me that great big knowing smirk, but you have no idea how much that worried me. While we all were in an entertaining mood I decided to ask Vianna if, after we got married, I didn't have to be made a king. Expectedly, this got Yagi, and even Baka, on their feet. I was informed by all three of them that once the royal wedding takes place, I will be anointed as king immediately and that was the end of the matter.

This is not what I wanted to hear. But I knew that this was the only way.

But wow! That had a note of finality from all three of them, and I was only marrying Vianna. You have no idea how much I wanted to respond to Yagi by telling her to relax and keep her knickers on. Knowing Yagi, she would have interpreted this totally different to what it meant.

I looked bit uncomfortable after being put in my place by not one, but three people! So I came up with the old and tried Earth-trick.

Never mind that it was almost two hours early, so I said 'Look at the time! Vianna, we have to go and pick up Beautiful from school!' After that Vianna and I withdrew from the room, leaving Baka and Yagi to talk about tomorrow.

After we picked up Beautiful, I made my excuse to Vianna and went looking for Jihon as I knew by now that Jihon would be in the palace talking with Sania. I found both of them in deep conversation in the Royal Gardens. I thought that I'd be a bit mischievous and point blank ask them when they were getting married. So I did.

Jihon just didn't know what to say, or how to even answer, and Sania's face turned so red that you could not see any blue on her face. I know that Jihon loves Sania very much and that she is into him, so after getting no answer from any of them I said, 'Two weeks after my wedding it is then! Make sure that my wife, my daughter and I get an invite!'

Both of them just stood there staring at me, utterly flustered. I know I was interrupting and I just stirred some trouble but I needed my baby brother, so I asked Sania to excuse me while I stole her future husband from her for a while.

She smiled and nodded, so I took that as 'I can have Jihon's attention'.

Come, baby brother, as you need to fly me back to my place to get something for tomorrow. After kissing Sania he quickly followed me towards the flyer.

As Jihon and I were entering my place, Jihon suddenly asked me why I was telling them to get married so soon. Since I was still feeling very mischievous, I told him that once I get married he would still be single, so why should he have better life than me?

We were halfway through our hot chocolate when Jihon finally got the meaning of what I said about him getting married.

All I could do is shake my head that my baby brother was so slow.

After our second cup of hot chocolate I had to get my Number 2s uniform and get myself ready for my court appearance tomorrow where I would be presenting the indisputable evidence in the regicide of King Herc. From what I had heard, King Herc was much loved amongst the Arkans. So once High Prefect Baka read the charges of regicide levelled at Chief Engineer Brud and traitor Kran, and I provided the DNA evidence, then the court could turn into a free for all as Arkans will not sit back when someone they love has been murdered.

I remember what happened when the Krans were found to be traitors. For weeks after, Captain Strah had to have extra military personnel just to deal with citizens trying to get inside the prison and decapitate Baron and Baroness Kran themselves.

But by now, I had already decided to be concise with my statement and be ready for any questions that the defence might throw at me.

I still can't believe that me, Sir Commander James Duncan, is getting married soon either. Me of all people! I still remember saying to Andy that if I was meant to have a wife, like him, then the army would have issued me with one!

While Jihon was watching one of the children movies that Beautiful enjoyed so much from my planet, I realised that I'd be leaving this place soon and taking up a residence in the capital, Ark. And married of all things. So much will change, more than I actually realised. To say I was overwhelmed would literally be an understatement.

Out of the kindness of my heart, I decided to let Jihon finish the movie before we made our way back to the capital, so I cleaned my shoes and got my uniform ready for a court outing tomorrow.

WHAT ARE THE CHANCES?

It was late by the time we got back to the palace and Vianna was waiting for me at the flyer landing pad and once I stepped off it was a case of 'Jihon, Sania is waiting for you in the throne room' and once he was gone Vianna soundly kissed me and told me that my daughter was waiting to speak to me. Then she dropped, as an afterthought, that she had also spoken to her about Baron Kran's son and the … little incident. And I bet that she made it plainly clear to Beautiful that it was me who told on her.

I walked into Beautiful's bedroom and straight away I was met by a harsh 'I am not speaking to you' pout with each eye shut. A few moments later, Beautiful's face contorted itself until her wide smile broke free from her baby spite as she said, 'I love you, Daddy.'

I smiled and replied, 'I thought you weren't speaking to me. Would you like to make your mind up which one it is?'

She looked like she was thinking it over, and finally, when she spoke, she told me that she was upset with me because I told on her. I decided to be all grown up about this so I asked her what Captain Strah meant to her. She looked puzzled at my question, but told me that she loves him and that he is second best uncle on the entire planet, straight after Uncle Vern, she added.

'I am glad to hear that Strah is important to you, but your little escapade almost got him beheaded as your royal command was NOT an official one, like the ones your mum or grandma issue. If I hadn't spoken up for the both of you, you would have been grounded until you were one-hundred years old, and Strah's kids would have been without their daddy as he would have been killed. Remember this, darling, every action has consequences.'

What are the Chances?

Beautiful cutely nodded before I told her to give me a hug and a kiss and then go to sleep as I had a date in court with Uncle Baka and hundreds other. She gave me a strong hug and a kiss on my cheek and then, as I was leaving, she said that she loved me. I winked at her and told her that I loved her too and then I left her room to make my way to mine.

When I entered my room I was met by Queen Yagi, who was sitting at the table sipping the local tea. I almost did a U-turn out of the room as she really makes me very nervous, but she stopped me in my tracks by asking me why I was so difficult when it came to titles. I looked her straight in the face and informed her that I had no problems with titles, as long as they are not mine. She told me to sit at the table and told me to listen.

'Very soon you will be a husband, a father and a king,' she began, though as much as I respected Yagi, I did not like hearing the last part. She took another sip from her tea before drawing another breath to speak, 'From observing you over the months, you will make a great king. It is not in your nature to do things badly, and the fact that you care tells me that you will be a very popular king with all the Arkans – especially with Vianna and I.'

I honestly did not know how to respond. Me. A king. I bet that my father, who was a mining engineer, and my mother, who was a nurse, would never have imagined me being made a king. Being trouble yes, but a king?

A definite NO!

Yagi then told me that tomorrow, when I would be giving my testimony, people would not be looking at me like just another man, but they would be looking at me as their future king. 'So testify in calm voice and don't take any lip from their defence.'

I chuckled slightly and asked her if she genuinely believed I would allow them to rattle me. I would testify to everyone in court what the truth is and with the DNA evidence, there is no argument about it. They did it and that's it!

Yagi slurped up the rest of her tea stood up enthusiastically, clearly extremely happy. Just as she was leaving my room she exclaimed, 'See, you are already a king!'

Heck, I can never win with her. She always has to have the last word. But I couldn't help but laugh when I realised that Vianna and Beautiful were just like Yagi.

I hung up my uniform then went straight to bed as today was a long day and since the past few days were starting to catch up with me.

I wasn't kidding when I say it felt like I had just gone to sleep when Vianna and Beautiful woke me up with a hot drink. When I asked them what time it was, I was shocked to hear that it was eight-twenty already. I must have been really tired. I chased them out of my room before having a quick shower, putting on some casual clothes and going to the dining room to get some breakfast with my future family.

Because I was wearing jeans and a polo shirt, Yagi raised more than an eyebrow when she informed me that I'd better be wearing, as she put it, something more elegant and military. I was going to respond but a quick glance in her direction told me that she was nervous about today as, after all, all of Arka would be told that her husband, King Herc, was murdered and not as previously thought that he died in a flyer accident. Instead I smiled at her and told her that my uniform was already prepared and that I would dazzle everyone in the courtroom so, 'Don't worry, Mummy dearest.'

She looked up at me and said, 'Mummy? Yes, I suppose I will be your mummy soon and I am very dear.'

Beautiful and Vianna burst into intense laughter at her remark. I suppose it was a way to prepare for both Vianna and Yagi for what would be announced in court in just over an hour.

But now I knew enough about the both of them to know that they were very nervous and needed time to prepare, so I told them to just relax and get ready while I took Beautiful to school. Both of them were very grateful for this, but not as grateful as Beautiful as she loved it every time I took her to school. She always made sure that everyone knew that I was her real dad. I turned to Beautiful and told her to go and get ready while I said goodbye to her mum. She sprinted off towards her room leaving her mum, Queen Yagi, the servants and I behind in the dining room. Vianna embraced me and whispered a quick, 'I love you' into my ear, but her mother immediately exclaimed, 'Yes, we all know that you love him, now come and get ready!'

As I was walking out of the dining room towards Beautiful's room, I had to sneak in a quick remark to Yagi, 'See you later, Mummy!'

All in all, she seemed to like it, so why not? After all, in few weeks I will be her son-in-law. Heck, that thought still made me nervous.

What are the Chances?

Beautiful was in her school uniform and already waiting for me outside her room, so I asked her if she really was that keen on me taking her to school, to which she responded that it really made her so happy when I took her to school. She grabbed my hand and off we went out of the palace and towards her school.

On the way to school, she told me that although that day when we first met was the best thing that ever happened to her, she was still missing her classmates and the two teachers who died that day. Then, as an afterthought, she told me that the school director is still upset about that day, and that she was adamant that the overseer's office had cleared that area as safe. She also told me that what she learned in her class about sarks was that they don't wander out of their territory without a very good reason. Those sarks were so far out of their territory that the school director even mentioned to other teachers that it was as if someone had lured them there.

I squatted down looked her straight in the eyes and asked her how she knew what the school director had said. She became all shy and cute and told me in her loveable voice that she was eavesdropping again. I kissed her on her forehead and told her that it was a very bad habit of hers and she should find a new hobby. She angrily but cutely pouted but slowly nodded and began smiling after. Then we slowly walked towards the school and mingled with the other parents and kids on the way.

When we got to the school gates I gave a her a hug and a kiss on the cheek and told her that, if possible, I will meet her after school, but also told her not to be upset if I don't as I didn't know what would come up in court or how long it would take.

What are the Chances?

By the time I got back to the palace, Vianna and Yagi had already left for court and Chamberlain Vern informed me that transport will pick me up in half an hour to take me to court.

Panic began to arise as half an hour just wasn't enough for me to get ready. When I was notified that the transport is awaiting me, I was still half dressed. Eventually I was ten minutes late, but as far as I was concerned, it is not as long as waiting for me to be called to give evidence, since Vianna made me aware that I might be the very long time.

When I got to the courts, I was quickly ushered into a waiting area where I was asked to wait until I got called by the high prefect to give my expert evidence.

After four hours of waiting I was ready to storm into the courtroom and tell them to go and play with the traffic on one of their highways.

CHAPTER 17

I was thirsty and bored, so I stuck my head outside the door from the room I was in and I saw two court attendants. One of them who spotted me was just about to ask me to go back in when I told him that if I didn't get some sort of refreshment very soon, then I was going to walk out. Without hesitation, several drinks were provided for me and an apology with them. I was also informed that right now cadet Matt is giving her evidence in court.

Sipping my ice cold drink I suddenly burst out in a fit of laughter. I was glad that I was alone at this moment. The sudden realisation that I was supposed to be going back to the past, over hundreds of years, and for some unknown reason I packed my Number Twos sent me bursting out in laughter. What was I expecting? A parade or something? But if I had to praise something, it would be my preparation for all eventualities, no matter what they were. Although my joy was short-lived, as the boredom and fatigue began kicking in again.

How long would I have to wait? I was getting frustrated and fed up. They could have at least allowed Jihon in here so I could have some sort of conversation.

Finally, after almost six hours of boredom, I was called to give my evidence. When I walked into the room where I was to give my evidence, I was taken aback by my surroundings. It was nothing like any courts I had ever seen back on my planet. There were rows after rows of people and all of them were wearing very official attire. The rows only split in the middle where Queen Yagi and Vianna sat with palace guards around them. On a slightly raised tier, from where I was going to give evidence, were the suspects. Kran, and his friend Brud, gave me a very hateful look when I walked in.

As I was wearing my uniform with all the trimmings, everyone present was dazzled. When I was introduced, everyone was very quiet. I wasn't sure if they were impressed or whether they were just puzzled by this white guy standing there looking like an idiot. Once I was introduced, I was just about to start giving my evidence when High Prefect Baka interrupted me by informing everyone present that I would be the future king of Arka soon. As strange as that sounded, perhaps it would make my presence feel more reputable in the court room.

It took about an hour to give my evidence: how I obtained it and how DNA worked. Then it took another twenty minutes when the Kran and Brud's defence team tried very hard to discredit my findings. Nevertheless I gave my testimony and almost everyone but the defence team were happy with it. When I finished my part I was just about to step down, from where I was giving my evidence, when I spotted something very familiar on the evidence table where the team of prosecutors where located. I raised my voice and asked High Prefect Baka if I could ask a question of the prosecutors. He told me to ask away, as something new could come of this. So I came up to the evidence table pointed to this round spiky thing with little holes and asked what this was. As there was about twenty of those things, naturally I had to ask since they seemed important. One of the prosecutors informed me that they were sarks lures. So I asked them what are these lures were doing here, to which he replied to me that they were found in the Krans residence.

And then it clicked! Sarks lures!

I still remember tripping over one of them that first day I met Beautiful and I distinctly remember that I saw at least one or two more of them as I was sneaking off back to my place.

Once I put it all together, I definitely did not like the conclusion I just came to. But I still needed proof, so I raised my voice and informed High Prefect Baka that I had just put something together after it was bothering me for a long time. I asked him to give me some time to look into this as this may be very relevant to traitor Krans' deeds. One look at me and Baka knew that I was very serious about something, so he adjourn the court proceedings until tomorrow.

As I was ready to leave, I looked at Kran and told him that if I found evidence to what I think he's done, then I will drag him from his seat and beat the crap out of him. Then I quickly left the court and contacted Jihon to meet me at the flyer in the palace. I also contacted Sergeant Tus and told him to get his friends ready as I needed their help and told him to make sure that they were all under arms.

When I got to the flyer Jihon, was already waiting for me, but unfortunately he was not dressed for our excursion, so I was glad that many months ago he made himself at home in my place and moved a lot of his gear into one of the many empty rooms. I told him that first we were to pick up Tus and his boys, secondly we were going back to my place to change and then we are going to the place where I saved Beautiful from the sarks. He didn't ask why but told me that I must have a very good reason to go back there. I told him that once we picked up the boys, and are ready to go there, then I will inform everyone on what we are doing and why.

When we picked up Sergeant Tus and two other sergeants, Jihon immediately knew that we were for a serious excursion. I notified Tus and his pals that we will make a quick stop at my place and then we would get going. I could see that all of them had this 'what-are-we-in-for' look, but I wanted to tell them once we got to the area.

It didn't take us long to get changed and kitted out for what we needed to do and all of us were on the way to the place where I first met Beautiful.

As we were leaving the flyer, one of the sergeants made a comment that last time he had seen me this heavily armed was when I was waiting to destroy the four towers of the Zolg fortress.

From this, I could tell his observation had showed him the severity of the situation despite not knowing the circumstances. I smiled and told them all to be on their guards as the sarks could still be around here. When we got to the clearing in the middle of the reeds, it was time to tell them what we were doing here and why.

'Right, gentleman, it is time for you to know what we are doing here, so each of you take five of these plastic bags and all of you take these latex gloves and put them on as I definitely don't need any DNA contamination. We are looking for sark lures. When you find them make sure you put the plastic bag over them before you pull them out of the ground. As for why we are doing, this is because I suspect that Kran had placed those sarks lures to kill Princess Olnia; the other children and the teachers were collateral damage, that's all.'

Once I let the cat out of the bag, I think that I had just learned all the Arkan cuss words there were in just few seconds. Sergeant Midko was particularly upset at what I said as he was an uncle to one of the children that died that day. I can't imagine how all those families felt losing their children – even the poor teachers' families.

As we all knew what sarks lures looked like, all of us went into the high and razor sharp reeds to look for them. I already had a good idea where one of them was as I distinctly remember stubbing my toe on one as I was sneaking away that day. Still, it took me around twenty minutes to find it, since I'd not been here for a while, so I tried to retrace my steps on that day as I clearly remembered that I saw one more of those lures. I eventually found it but by now it was getting dark and we still couldn't be sure if the sarks were still around. Momentarily, I used my radio to tell them all to head towards the flyer.

Jihon and I were the first ones back and I was happy to see that he had found two lures as well. Then the sergeants came back and between the three of them, they had found eight lures. Looks like I am going to be busy when we get back to the palace. I got Jihon to fly us back and after tagging Tus and the other two sergeants, so they could go through the protective barrier into the palace, all five of us went inside.

When we got back Jihon immediately initiated the sergeants into watching movies from my planet, which I was fine with it as I wanted to cook something tasty for the boys and the movie kept them all entertained and busy while I cooked.

I quickly washed up and start preparing a hearty good meal for a soldier – or soldiers in this case.

When the food was ready I called all of them into the dining room and we all got stuck into the food. One thing about solders is that they never give you the third degree about what you give them to eat. In this case, I made sure that I made more than normal as soldiers get hungry and if they enjoy the food they always want seconds. As a matter of fact they enjoyed the food from my planet so much that they had thirds and fours. Boy those three could eat.

I got Jihon to put another movie on as I started to collect the DNA from the twelve sarks lures that we had found. By the time I collected the entire DNA from all twelve lures, it was way past midnight, so I asked Jihon to show the boys to the many spare bedrooms I had while I finished soaking all the DNA in the solution overnight. I was tired too and I wanted a clear my head before I start entering the DNA samples in the briefcase. This was way too exhausting to do in one day. One thing is for sure, I could never be a scientist.

I was so tired that I couldn't even remember how I got to my bedroom or how I even got undressed. The second my head touched the pillow I was out for the count.

WHAT ARE THE CHANCES?

When I got up I was refreshed and ready for another day. But before I got going, I took a very long shower to energise me for the rest of the day.

When I got downstairs Jihon and the boys were already up and Jihon was trying very hard to make them all hot chocolate, but as all the instructions on the replicator were in English, he didn't have any luck. Maybe one day I will teach my baby brother my language. Maybe …

I came up to Jihon and asked him if he needed any help. The cheeky thing told me that he can't get the hot chocolate as all the writing was just a scribble. Scribble! I have seen the Arkan writing and a chicken can create better letters than them.

Oops that was bit patriotic. Or is planetrotic?

I smiled at him and told him to let me do it, that way we will get hot chocolate sooner.

After I made everyone a cup of hot chocolate, I went to the kitchen to make everyone some good old-fashioned bacon and eggs for breakfast. Jihon already knew what they were but when the boys tried it, I thought that I would have to work the replicator in overtime as boy all four of them could eat. Especially when they liked something.

Once we all filled up on bacon and eggs and tidied up, I told them to follow me. It was time to find out if Kran had anything to do with the children's deaths.

Swiftly, I explained to the boys how the DNA briefcase worked. Now, it was time to find out the truth by entering each of the twelve samples separately.

What are the Chances?

The first two samples I entered only showed a ninety-four percent match for Kran, but it didn't matter as he used to have a son who could have helped him set the sarks lures. The next three were ninety-nine percent matches for Kran. By the time I finished entering all twelve samples, seven were a ninety-nine percent match for Kran and the other five only ninety-four percent, which could only belong to Kran's son. Once I explained to the boys what this meant, Sergeant Midko, the uncle of one of the poor dead kids, was ready to storm into the court and remove Kran's head from his shoulders. I told him to leave it to me. Understandably, he was reluctant to leave it up to me but good old Tus reminded him that soon I will be a king and I can get away with things that he could not. Eventually Midko relented and agreed to let me deal with Kran. I just have to make sure that the beating I will give him will not result in Kran's death. Not a good start to being a king.

I asked Jihon what time it was and when he told me how late it was, I immediately got everyone to get ready and as we did not have the time to change, we all went in our battle uniforms. That should stir up some fuss in court. I grabbed the DNA briefcase and the boys grabbed all twelve of the sarks lures and all ran for the flyer as it will still be at least an hour and a half before we returned to the capital. After arriving, we would proceed straight to the court.

Jihon knew we were running very late, so he told me that he would take care of things. I wonder if my baby brother can stop the time because at the moment, it looked like we will arrive just in time for High Prefect Baka pronouncing the sentence.

What are the Chances?

True to his word my baby brother landed our flyer right outside the front doors of the court. That stirred some trouble as the commander of the Prefect Corps came storming out of his office and headed straight for us. What didn't help was when we all stepped out of the flyer in battle dress. He ran up to us, just about to say something, when Jihon opened his hand suggesting he should stop and then in a loud voice declared, 'Under Royal Command. Please let us do our job, Commander.'

Wow! He backed off immediately and let us all proceed to the court. When we got inside the court, we definitely got some alarming looks from almost everyone. But my luck was in as we were marching towards the doors of the courtroom where Kran and Brud's case was being heard, and we had run into the case clerk who looked like he was awaiting us. I came up to him and told him that we have urgent additional proof in the Krans case and that we must present it immediately. He asked us to wait outside while he slipped back in to inform Baka. When he came back he told us to go straight in and present our findings. The people in attendance were definitely taken aback by all five of us walking in battle dress. I stopped in the middle and asked Sgt Midko to hand the twelve lures to the prosecution. While he was doing this I turned to Vianna and Queen Yagi and asked them to forgive me for what was about to happened in her royal court. Both Vianna and Yagi nodded their head in understanding – I hope it was their understanding – and then I turned to High Prefect Baka on the high row and asked him in all the time that he knew me, had he ever seen me not keep my promise?

What are the Chances?

His reply was never.

So I told him to please excuse me for a while then I came to the row where Kran was sitting, reaching out to grab him by the scruff of the neck and drag him across the bar. Then, I threw him onto the floor and started beating him. I was so mad for how low he had stooped that I just kept hitting him and hitting him and I did not stop until his nose was broken and some of his teeth were knocked out and until he was badly bleeding. He was still alive but not by much. When I stood up I could see that Jihon and the three sergeants kept everyone at bay while I was executing some justice on Kran's face. There were some shouts from many people in the rows but that quietened them down when I shouted at the top of my voice to be quiet.

Once everyone went silent, I inclined my head in a way of an apology and then I informed everyone why Kran got a beating of his life. When I informed them that Kran and his son were responsible for the massacre of the school kids and the two teachers, the people in the rows exploded too. Even they wanted to get hold of Kran and do some very unpleasant things to him. Vianna and Yagi were amongst them. Many of the people in court were related to those poor kids that were mauled that day and all because Kran wanted to kill Beautiful. I glanced at Baka, even he was furious that Kran did this. But as he was the high prefect, he ordered everyone to be quiet and then asked me for what proof I had. Momentarily, I informed everyone that yesterday, after seeing all those sarks lures on the table in court, I remembered tripping over one that fateful day and Jihon, the sergeants and I went looking for the lures where the massacre happened and we had found twelve of them. I then explained how I recovered the DNA from the lures and the results showed that seven were a ninety- nine percent match for Kran and five of them were only a ninety-four percent match for Kran, which meant that the other DNA had to belong to Kran's son. His damn son helped him plant the sarks lures all over the area where the school trip would take place that fateful day. To my and everyone's surprise, Krans wife screamed at Kran and told everyone that she remembered her husband and son taking the lures and leaving to plant them. She did not know that they would be planting them in the area of the school field trip as her husband told her that they were planted on the land not far from theirs as he want to expand their lands. She then looked at the bleeding Kran and screamed, 'MONSTER!'

Even his own wife had turned on him. I supposed she'd had enough of his, as she called, monstrous dealing and she even added that she wanted him dead for getting her son involved in his schemes.

I turned to look at the sergeants and remarked that is one way of getting a divorce.

When the ruckus died down, Jihon quickly added that after contacting the school, he was informed by the director that Kran indeed enquired where the school trip would be taking place. So, after this bombshell, Jihon, the sergeants and I were making our way out of the courtroom when High Prefect Baka announced in a clear voice that both Kran and Brud should suffer death by Lugii. Meanwhile, his wife was sentence to twenty years of hard labour in the mines. Jihon even remarked that she would be able to dig and lift with the Zolg general, who was already there serving the rest of his life for the invasion of Arka.

As we were leaving the prefect building, I was stopped by Vianna and Yagi and asked to accompany them to the palace. I bid farewell to Jihon and the sergeants and went with them back to the palace. As we were travelling back, Yagi looked straight at me and told me that Vianna had definitely found the right husband who even her dad, Herc, would have wholesomely approved of. Then she smiled at me and told me to enjoy my last week of freedom as, after the wedding, I will be a king and no longer can run around righting wrongs. And then she added that is Baka's job! Poor Baka.

When we got to the palace, both of them immediately ganged up on me and wanted to know everything about the fateful day that Beautiful nearly died.

Bleeding heck! I am not kidding, Yagi's word 'freedom' had a totally different meaning to what it meant back on Earth. My last week I was so busy that I didn't even have a single moment to myself. I was being groomed in palace etiquette and when I wasn't, Beautiful and Vianna kept me very, very busy. Actually, I take that back – they kept me extremely busy. A hectic plethora of things were rushing by and piling on but before I knew it, it was finally the day before my wedding and after hours and hours of insisting that I could pack my stuff in my place on my own, all three of them left me alone.

I was just about to contact Jihon to come and pick me up when I ran into Sania, so I asked her to tell Jihon to come and pick me up. This way, I knew for sure he'd drop whatever he was doing and come here quickly. My baby brother has such a soft spot for Sania, it's very endearing. I can't wait for those two to get married.

Within an hour, my baby brother arrived and then the both of us were on our way to my place. While we were travelling we were reminiscing when Jihon asked me if, as from tomorrow, things would change between him and I since I will be a king. This meant that he would not be able to call me his big brother anymore. I looked at him and asked him, 'Whatever gave you the idea that things will change between us?'

We might not be blood-related, but we are brothers. He will always be my baby brother. If anyone ever tried to cause trouble between us, then I will stamp on them. But I did reiterate that if he ever called me a king or anything like that, then I was going to take him hiking through that dense jungle on Arka. Naked. Without any weapons.

He threw me a sour look, identical to that of a baby sucking a lemon, and laughed, 'You know, I bet the palace won't allow to you go trekking aimlessly in any deadly jungles anymore.'

Chuckling back I told him that I take that as a bet. After all I will be the king and if I want to have some exciting fun with my baby brother, like hiking through a dangerous jungle, then I gosh darn will! Besides, he should know and always remember this saying, 'It's goood to be a king!'

We both joked and laughed with each other until we were landing outside of my place. As we were walking towards the barrier that I activated to keep unwanted people out, Jihon asked me if I was also going to take that monster tank with me. After a light snicker I said, 'As much as I'd love to, I better not as the palace guard would have a fit if they saw that looming in at the palace front gate every day.'

When we went inside I told Jihon to start packing up the front room while I went to pack my clothes and other stuff that I wanted kept private from my baby brother. It took me over an hour to pack up my bedroom and when I went downstairs to where Jihon supposed to be packing, he was sitting comfortably sipping a beer and watching a children's film. I was just about to shout at him but realised quickly that this is probably the last time he will get a chance to watch any of the films from my planet, as I was well aware of Beautiful's intentions for the movies.

I opened a beer and sat next to Jihon and we watched the cartoon he was enjoying. I still couldn't believe that somehow I ended up on a distant planet, and as from tomorrow I was going to be a husband – something I never thought I would be. I almost chocked on that.

Me.

A husband.

When I scoffed at the thought, Jihon asked what was on my mind. Since I knew he'd probably understand, I told him. He added that I would also be a king. That twit really had to remind me about that. I really did not want to be reminded about that so I told him to shut up and watch his movie.

But if I did not get back to the palace tonight, Vianna and Yagi would send out regiments of search parties looking for me.

What are the Chances?

To take my mind off things, because Jihon was very much addicted to hot chocolate, so it was not a surprise when I suggested that we could disconnect the replicator carefully and pack it up first that he shot straight up to do that. I think that he was not the only one that wanted to make sure that the replicator, or replicators, as I brought more than one with me, would be coming back first with us as everyone that tried the hot chocolate and other goodies wanted more afterwards. After the replicators, I quickly disconnected the television and the box that had all my movies on it before Jihon suggested we watch another movie.

However, as much as a movie did sound good, I wanted to get on with it since I was very nervous about tomorrow. To be honest, I just wanted all of that over with as quickly as possible, but that will not be the case as Yagi was going all out to make Vianna's and my day very special. Two days ago, Yagi informed me that Arka's good friends and allies, the Morrins and Alphians, will be present at our wedding and later that day, I met the rulers of Alphia and Morrin.

When Jihon told me that the Alphian skin colour was red, I for some reason accepted that without a second thought – I am the real alien after all. When I met the Alphian king and queen, they were a nice shade of red, but when Jihon told me that the Morrins were yellow, for some reason I took that as slightly yellowish skin colour. This was a mistake. When I was introduced to the youthful King and Queen of Morrin, I was a little taken aback as they were not just yellow skinned, but rather a shiny yellow skin colour, something like a highlighter pen would be. For a few moments there, I almost whipped out my sunglasses and put them on.

WHAT ARE THE CHANCES?

Now, because I'm a curious idiot, I started imagining what kind of baby an Arkan with blue skin and a Morrin with shiny yellow skin would have. Would it be green? Or would the babies have blue skin with highlighter yellow stripes all over the body. I hope the latter.

Sometimes my imagination can just run wild.

Although yesterday, I heard one of the palace toadies call me the 'White Arkan King'. Oh well, maybe Vianna and my children will have blue and white-striped skin …

As I resumed packing, I realised that since I –gently – bullied Jihon, the packing was already almost done. Alas, all I really had left to do was to secure all of my weapons that I brought from my planet. Meanwhile, Jihon was taking all my bags with my clothes to the flyer. I strongly suspect that Jihon would love to take the TV and the box with all the movies back to his place, but Beautiful already informed me that she would like them, so unfortunately Jihon will miss out.

After securing all my weapons and ammunition and taking it to the flyer, Jihon reminded me about the top drawer in the visitors room where I placed my inactive traveller. I smiled at him and told him that I really forgot about that thing, but I suppose it will make a good paperweight or something. Gradually, I walked back into my palace, really taking in my surroundings and the air. I'm going to miss this place. More importantly, I'm going to miss the person I was while I stayed here. Even though things will change, it makes me happy deep down.

Momentarily, I made my way to grab the last thing from my previous life. The traveller. Entering the visitor's room made my chest feel a little heavy, just as if something strange was going to happen. After an attempt to shake this feeling, I came up to the drawer where the traveller was stored, hoping to take it and leave swiftly. But the second I opened the drawer, a vibrant, sky blue light lit up the area I was standing in.

I was shocked beyond belief. Mia ... she never died. No one died. Does this mean we won, Andy? In my life as a soldier, it became easier the longer I served to detach myself from any scenario. But I fear this was the instance I cracked. An ensemble of emotions jerked me back, a queasiness in my stomach arising and a pressure on my chest emerging as if my heart were clenching. Even if all of these feelings encumbered my mind now, you could never tell by my physical reaction. Outside I was stone-cold. For the first time in a while, I had asked myself the golden question.

What do I really want?

Do I want things to return to normal, but to a life in which I am dead to anyone on the surface? Honestly, a little. But after staring at the pulsating light for what felt like years, I picked it up, familiarising my hands with the feel of Mia's design once again. As I turned around, I met eyes with Jihon staring at me.

Without a doubt, Jihon knew what this meant. I had told him what it was and how it worked countless times. The expressive he gave me, a concoction of disbelief, worry and ... sadness. He knew that all I have to do is lift the little cover over the button on top of the traveller. Quite frankly, I was one press away and anything I would had brought with me would be gone. I'd be back on my planet, with my normal life again. Just how things should be. I like things being how they should be.

WHAT ARE THE CHANCES?

The thumb of my left hand strayed towards the cap. With my nail I lifted it up and hovered my thumb over the button. In a flash, I made my mind up and all was well. This is what I've wanted.

The end.

WHAT ARE THE CHANCES?

PTO

EPILOGUE

Or is it?

This button on the traveller could help me stay single. This button can get me home. Jihon eyes showed sadness, and he really embraced me as his big brother. We had some great adventures in all my time on Arka.

As I made my mind up, I deeply exhaled and gripped the traveller with both hands. I looked up at my baby brother and said, 'My life is here now!'

Breaking the traveller in two, we both watched the sky blue light extinguish instantly.

I walked onto the terrace in the garden, overlooking a great body of water, and threw the now inactive traveller as far as I could into the dark blue sea.

When I turned around, Jihon was behind me. When I tried to say something, he just embraced me. 'I will always be loyal to you, James, I'll always be a good baby brother to you.' I could hear his voice shake a little with emotion.

I told him, 'I feel at home here and I really feel like I belong on Arka.' He glanced up at me, his eyes telling me he was appreciative and thankful. And of course, Jihon had to remind me that tomorrow I will be a husband and a king. I almost turned round and jumped into the dark blue waters to go and retrieve the traveller. He just had to remind me about my sentence! After that, we locked all the doors and I made sure that all the sonic pulsars were still working as I did not want the Kani to reclaim this place.

As we were flying towards my doom tomorrow, sorry I meant to say towards my future, I decided to get totally smashed tonight because as from tomorrow, I would have to be sensible and upright. Well, sort of …

I had quick smirk as I remembered that my mother always said that I will never find anyone to marry on Earth. Well I did find someone amazing and she is from Arka. My mother was right I suppose.

When we landed in the Royal Gardens, Chamberlain Vern was waiting with a host of servants and busybodies to help us unload all my stuff. As we were finishing unloading the flyer Queen Yagi and all her splendour appeared trying to tell me what was in store for me later that night, but I held up my open palm and told her to cancel everything she had planned for tonight as instead: Jihon, Vern, Baka, Rak, Tus and I will be getting very drunk and I will see you and Vianna at the sentencing, sorry I mean wedding, tomorrow.

Immediately, Yagi asked, 'What about tonight's dinner with Vianna?'

I told her, 'On my planet, it is very bad luck to see the bride the night before, so I have no intention of seeing Vianna tonight.' Then I added that tonight is for the boys to get sloshed.

As expected, she didn't understand the sloshed bit so I had to explain that it meant to get very, very, very drunk. Then as I was walking off, I threw a quick remark acknowledging my farewell to Yagi, 'I'll see you tomorrow, Mummy.'

*   *   *

Last night was a total blur. It was clear as day that all of us got totally hammered. As I held my head in my hands in attempt to tame my headache, I suddenly spotted General Mass snoring his head off on the floor of the bar we all went to. How the heck was he even here? Looks like he invited himself in but for all I know, I was so smashed that I had probably dragged him in here myself. I tried and tried to recall even just a minute detail of last night, but goodness my head was not having it.

'Oh my head ... never again!'

After saying that, I laughed as I must have said the exact same thing for many years and never learned my lesson. What can I say, I'm a delinquent.

The proprietor, smiling and holding a glass with some liquid in them, came up to me and told me to drink this. I didn't question what this mixture was as in two hours the wedding ceremony would start. There was no time for hesitation. And if this will sort out my head and stomach, I'll chug it. So I pinched my nose and gulped.

After squirming from the taste, I woke everybody up and told them to drink this as well. I stood there, expecting to be surrounded by a bunch of squirming men, but instead, they all gulped it down like it was water. At times like these, I really do feel like a foreigner.

What are the Chances?

But instead of wallowing in the despair of my exclusion, I decided to enlighten everyone with the announcement of breakfast on me. After all, we all really needed a filling meal to soak up the underlying regret.

By the time we had finished breakfast, it was an hour before the wedding ceremony started and Queen Yagi was waiting for me at the front doors of the palace. I noticed that Uncle Vern suddenly made himself scarce so I was left alone to face Yagi – Lord please save me.

She had this disapproving look on her face, but I was still recovering from all that drinking so I couldn't really care. She asked me whether I actually tried my wedding attire on but I stopped her and informed her that I was a Highlander, thus I will be getting married in my kilt!

It had a note of finality in it so Yagi dropped the subject and asked me if I needed anything before the ceremony started. I thanked her and told her that I needed some water, as I was dehydrated from all that alcohol – except I did make a point to not mention that last part, I like being after alive after all. So immediately she got the servants to run for the water while she walked me to my room.

As we were walking into my room, Yagi told me that Vianna and Olnia had missed me last night, but she didn't make an issue of this thankfully. But honestly, as cold as it sounded, I couldn't say I remembered missing them since I was drunk out of my head. I'm sure I would've had I not been so far gone.

I went into my room and headed straight for the shower as I really needed a good soaking. Shortly after the shower, I shaved and brushed my teeth; as I was just about to start getting dressed, when Beautiful came into my room and gave me a great big hug. I must be honest, I was feeling a bit uncomfortable with this as I only had a towel wrapped around my waist and underneath it, I was completely naked. So I gave her a kiss on her forehead and told her to go and tell her mum that I love her. To my delight, she did that immediately.

Finally, I was left alone to get dressed.

But even after getting dressed, I was still feeling rather dehydrated. Darn alcohol. I drank two more bottles of water at, honestly, an impressively swift rate. I really hoped that I wouldn't need to rush off to the toilet for a pee when the Faith priest would ask me if I'd take Vianna to be my lawfully-wedded wife. That would definitely be a bad start to our marriage.

As I stepped out of my room, Jihon, in full dress code, with a palace guard wearing the ceremonial uniform reserved for special occasion, was waiting for me to escort me to the Faith building where the wedding was going to take place. And my coronation. I really didn't want to be a king at first and, guess what? I still don't. But as I am marrying a queen, that's sort of expected of me. And for Vianna, I think I can make the sacrifice. I smirked as I remembered Yagi's expression when I asked her that instead of being anointed as the king of Arka, could I substitute the title 'husband of' instead. She almost had babies when I said that.

During my escort to the Faith building, Jihon was very impressed by my kilt and even dared to ask me if I had anything under my kilt.

WHAT ARE THE CHANCES?

'Now, that would be telling, wouldn't it?' I chuckled and flung my index finger across my nose.

Firstly he frowned in confusion, before his eyes widened in shock and slight fluster. And this, my friend, is why I love Jihon.

When we arrived at the Faith building, my baby brother's mum and dad were waiting for me outside as it was customary for parents to escort their son or daughter to the alter to be sacrificed – I mean married! The altar was adorned with the finest bouquets of flowers, the bridesmaids all wore the prettiest embroidered dresses, but no one looked better in it than my Beautiful. The flag of Ark hung in the back, catching my eye. In my head, I could not stop repeating the words, 'Oh no, I'm going to be a king.'

As I neared the altar, my legs turned to jelly – as in legs, literal gelatine. I'd like to think I've dealt through many hardships in my life, so why now? Why is my body giving up on me now? Of all times! My dad instantly helped me up and whispered to me that the same thing happened to him the day he was getting married to Mima. I smiled at him and thanked him.

While my nerves still prevailed, knowing this happened to him did help my legs solidify.

It wasn't long before Queen Vianna, with an escort comprising of her mum, Beautiful, Baka and his wife, Seline, arrived. Vianna was wearing the most beautiful ivory-coloured dress I had ever seen. She really was a stunner. I'd never thought aliens could be this attractive – or maybe that's just her. As much as I adored her long hair, seeing it tied back with a small Arkan head ornament let me see her face perfectly. My goodness did the light catch her beauty well. The sight of my future wife was utterly breathtaking.

Unfortunately, my love-saturated thoughts were overridden by an intrusive thought.

She smiled at me when I caught her eye. Then our escorts stepped back and only Vianna and I were left at the altar. The Faith priest waffled for a while and while he was entertaining himself, all I could do was keep thinking to myself, 'I don't need to pee, I don't need to pee!'

Once he finished his bit, he turned to me and asked me if I would take Queen Vianna to be my lawful wedded wife. I was not kidding when I said I really needed the toilet after drinking all that water, so, smiling, I swiftly said, 'I do!'

Clearly, my undertone of urgency didn't alarm anyone as Vianna was very happy with my response and mistook it for enthusiasm. But at least I was safe from Yagi's wrath. Once the priest asked Vianna if she would take me as her husband and king, she instantly said she would and before the priest could even say we could kiss, she launched herself at me and kissed me passionately. I had to admit, the moment was pretty magical.

But the ceremony was not over for me because now, I had to be anointed as king and a joint ruler of all Arka. He asked me to kneel, to which hesitantly I did, and he started the anointment. I thought the wedding was overwhelming, but this … this was a one-of-a-kind feeling. Once I get up I will no longer be Sir Commander James Duncan, but rather King James of Arka.

The White King of Arka.

Now what are the chances of that?!